My Fair Bluestocking Paperback Edition

Published by Rogue Press.
Editing by Katie Jackson

For more information, contact author Nina Jarrett. www.ninajarrett.com

MY FAIR BLUESTOCKING

INCONVENIENT BRIDES

BOOK THREE

NINA JARRETT

To the quiet heroes I have met who provide mentorship to those who need it most. And to the many amazing people I have met who incorporate charitable endeavors and love of our fellow man into their daily routine.

You inspire me.

PROLOGUE

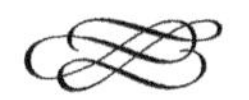

June 20, 1820, Balfour Terrace in Mayfair, London

A SMALL HAND pressed against his forehead, startling him from his sleep. Richard Balfour's eyes shot open, and he suppressed a groan. "Ethan?"

"Papa, I can't sleep."

"Is something wrong, son?"

"I miss Emma."

The Earl of Saunton sighed heavily as he sat up. "Let's go to the kitchen and see what we can find so we do not wake Mama."

Standing up, he scooped his little boy into his arms. Another night of coaxing his four-year-old son to go to sleep loomed ahead, and Sophia was expecting, so she needed to get her rest. Thankfully, Richard could sleep late as he had no early morning plans, but he missed his dawn rides. They were becoming a distant memory because of Ethan's eccentric sleeping habits.

Ethan rode atop his shoulders all the way to the kitchen, where they enjoyed biscuits and milk while Richard mused over how to help the boy.

To his eternal mortification, Richard had been unaware of his son's existence until two months earlier. Having recently reconsidered his roguish ways, Richard had set his man of business to investigating his immoral behavior's unknown effects on the women of his past. He learned of his son the same week of his unexpected marriage in late April. Ethan was an unexpected consequence of dallying with a maid during a summer house party five years before. Unbeknownst to Richard, the maid had retreated to her aunt's family in Derby, where she had died in childbirth, leaving her aunt, uncle, and six cousins to raise Ethan.

Unfamiliar with children and their needs, Richard had swiftly arranged to have Ethan brought to him in London in a misguided effort to do right by the boy. He had not considered the potential consequences of removing his young son from a loving family home in the country to live in a huge, empty townhouse in London with only Richard, his bride, and his brother to replace the eight members of the only family Ethan had ever known.

It was Richard's intent to be a father who took part in his son's life in order to make up for his own contemptible history. The governess he had hired with the hopes she could fill this Emma's shoes was a wonderful woman, but not as wonderful as the much pined-for Emma, it would seem.

It was much later that morning when Richard eventually rose from bed. His first thought on awakening was that he needed to seek a resolution to the nocturnal visits. Sitting down beside his wife to eat his breakfast, he broached the subject, gesturing to the footmen to leave the room.

"Sophia, I must do something about Ethan's sleep. Since

he has come to live with us, I think I have had about three nights of unbroken sleep in total."

Lady Sophia Balfour quirked a red-blonde eyebrow. "He woke you again last night? How did I not know this?"

"He did. Actually, he has woken me every night this week, but now that you have a babe on the way, I have been taking him downstairs so we would not wake you. This lack of sleep is inadvisable for him and it is definitely inadvisable for me. It is as if I am out all night carousing, but with none of the merrymaking. And even I could not rout every night, not even in my heyday!"

Sophia grimaced in sympathy, sipping on her tea while she contemplated the problem. "I appreciate your discretion in leaving me undisturbed. However, it has become obvious that you snatched Ethan from the Davis family too abruptly, despite our efforts to address it."

"When I made the decision, I did not realize I was dealing with a small child with close connections. My father forbade emotions when I was a boy, so how was I to know that such sentiment existed? You must help me think of a solution."

Sophia sighed. "I think you made a mistake when you had your man of business make the arrangements to bring Ethan to you. If you had gone to meet his relations and spoken with them, the change would not have been so drastic for him. It is possible he is worried about this Emma whom he keeps mentioning, or that there is some bedtime ritual we are unaware of because we never spoke with her. It was too hasty, the changes you brought to his young life."

Richard sighed. "I know I caused this problem. My old ways were dishonorable, and my attempts to repair my mistakes have been clumsy. If you are accusing me of being insensitive or inconsiderate, I will not argue."

The countess grinned. "We agree, then. It was not well-done of you."

Richard sighed again, dramatically. "I will be the first to admit that this whole caring about other people bit is new to me and that there was a clever method of going about this that would have eased the transition and been more considerate of all the parties involved. But I cannot change my past mistakes, bride, so I beg you to tell me how to fix it?"

Sophia giggled as Richard grabbed her and tickled her neck with kisses.

"Stop or I will not tell you how!"

The earl growled into her neck before giving her a playful nip. "Never. Tell me how to fix this, or I will smother you with adoration!"

She gasped. "I think—stop, I cannot breathe—we must invite this Emma Davis to join us in London. Perhaps we can offer her a Season."

"Spend more coin? It is not enough I gifted a healthy estate to the Davis family for their benevolence in raising the boy after his mother died. Now I must pay for a London wardrobe for their daughter?"

"This Emma raised your son. She taught him to read and how to play chess like a little champion. She nurtured his genius that you are so proud of. And what price would you like to place on your sleep?"

Richard groaned. "Any price. I will have my man of business arrange it."

"Nay, husband. That is how you arrived in this predicament. It is you who should fetch her."

"I cannot. Ethan needs me here, and I have several parliamentary commitments over the next few weeks, which cannot be avoided. It is imperative we take action now. The boy has dark rings under his eyes, which he did not have when he first arrived."

"Then you will write to them yourself and we will send your brother to collect her. The Davises are related to you through Ethan, and your autocratic conduct is the reason for your current lack of sleep. Besides, Peregrine needs a project. I am disappointed that he has returned to his clubs and wicked widows."

"Damn, woman! I hate writing long letters."

"Husband, it will help you learn your lesson. Arrogance bears consequences, my love. Writing out long letters and paying for a new wardrobe are your penalty."

CHAPTER 1

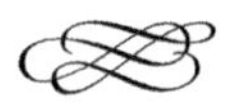

"A real gentleman is always perfectly presented. Dirt on the collar is a sign of low breeding and will repel the ladies."

July 1801, the late Earl of Saunton to his son, Peregrine, on his sixth birthday after finding him playing with his tin soldiers in the gardens of Saunton Park.

* * *

"Emma, Emma! We have news from London. It's about Ethan!"

Emma tipped back her head in dismay, her hand balancing the back of her bonnet. Her bonnet ribbons were twisted—again—and she was doing her best not to throttle herself by accident.

"News of Ethan?" she called out to her sister across the garden. Jane swung her head to find her, squinting at the sun which was behind Emma's back.

Jane hurried over, her face pulled into a perplexed expression. "What on earth are you doing?"

"I'm trying to trim *those* roses without hanging myself on *these* ribbons." She pointed with the shears, causing her sister to wince in alarm as she waved the sharp tip close to her face.

"I see. Perhaps I should take those from you before you put an eye out."

Emma handed over the pruning shears. She was not known for her grace, but she had yet to do herself a bodily injury, and she would prefer to keep it that way. Once her hand was free, she was able to straighten her ribbons and retie them. Bonnet nestled comfortably, she looked back to her younger sister.

"What is this about Ethan? Is he well?" she demanded.

"Our little cousin is now the son of an earl, living in London in a grand townhouse! Of course he is all right!"

"Our little cousin is the illegitimate son of an earl we have never met. There is no *of course*. The arrogant jackanapes did not have the grace to meet us before he snatched Ethan from our home!"

"By jackanapes, you are referring to the father and not the son?" Jane teased.

"Ha ha! Yes, the father."

"The father who gave *our* father this fine estate in Somerset, that elevated our income and our status, in gratitude for raising his son?"

"Who forced us from our very nice Derbyshire farm to this strange county with none of our friends and neighbors!"

"And gifted us a fine library, generously filled with books, that has kept you too occupied to miss your friends and neighbors?"

Emma huffed in disgust, yet conceded. "It is a very fine library," she mumbled.

"Yes, it is. If you were honest, you would admit you care for our new library far more than for any of your long-forgotten friends and neighbors. You love your family best, and we are all here with you!" Her sister swung her arms up to present their home and gardens.

"Except for Ethan!"

Jane cocked her head before admitting the truth of it. "Except for Ethan. But Ethan is with his father, where he belongs. The earl will provide him with the education and opportunities befitting a young gentleman of his birthright."

Emma did not venerate this unknown Lord Saunton, but even she had to admit she had lost no relationships that could rival the library he had gifted their family as part of their new estate. She simply resented the man for stealing Ethan away from her and missed the little boy. His abrupt departure had pierced a hole through her soul. If Emma was being honest, she would admit that her little cousin now had opportunities to learn and nurture his genius far beyond their limited means.

But she did not want to be honest. She wanted to be resentful. Lord Saunton had not even bothered to fetch his own child, sending a carriage and a man of business in his stead. *Arrogant arse!*

"Now come inside and hear the news! It is quite exciting," Jane effused, grabbing hold of Emma to pull her along.

Once inside, Emma made to go and wash herself up, but Jane mercilessly tugged her into the drawing room in her excitement.

"What have you dragged me into the drawing room for? Could you not impart the news of Ethan and Lord Arrogant, who stole him from us, while I cleaned up?" Emma demanded, before noticing that her sister had turned to her with an alarmed expression.

Then she noticed her mother sitting on the settee with the best tea service on the table in front of her, and just in view beyond the generously stuffed wing chair facing the settee, there was a pair of expensive black riding boots.

Emma's stomach dropped when a tall gentleman unfolded from the armchair to turn and face her. She noted the silky, sable curls framing a strong, handsome face, and the forest green cutaway coat that perfectly reflected his emerald green eyes. The gentleman was a perfect adult version of Ethan. One day her cousin would likely share the same broad shoulders, narrow hips, and chiseled jawline that made her heart quiver in her chest. But hopefully her cousin would not inherit the indolent, sulky airs.

Wincing, Emma sank into a curtsy. "My lord … um … welcome to our home."

The man's gaze traveled down her length to peer at her feet. Darting a glance down to where he stared, Emma discovered to her horror that the hem of her muslin dress was coated in mud and grass stains from the gardening she had been engaged in. Tilting her head back up, she caught a fleeting sneer of disdain.

Belatedly, he gave a brief bow before responding in a polite voice, "Not Lord Arrogant, I am afraid. Just a mere spare. Mr. Peregrine Balfour at your service. And you must be the famous Emma?"

* * *

EMMA WAS NOT what Perry had expected. He knew from meeting with Richard and their man of business, Johnson, that the Davis family were descended from Welsh roots, which explained the mass of black hair escaping from her enormous straw bonnet trimmed with a plethora of tangled ribbons. Dark, almost black eyes stared up at him in consternation from under the brim of the ridiculous headpiece.

While the younger sister who had gone out to collect this flibbertigibbet from the gardens was tall and graceful, this girl was shorter with a boyish, slender frame. She appeared to have a rather pert set of breasts which had drawn his eyes down before he could stop himself, but the state of her attire had quickly distracted him. He had never met a female who looked so horrifyingly disheveled.

Miss Emma Davis had the appearance of a wild thing living off the land, albeit a bit too pale to truly be a creature of the outdoors. He resisted the urge to shake his head in astonishment and wondered what was so special about this tart little piece that his young nephew stayed awake every night to worry over her.

Blazes! I could kill Richard for sending me out to rural Somerset on this inane errand. He suspected Sophia's hand in this. She was always encouraging him to 'find a project', whatever that meant, but Perry was uncomfortable with this jaunt to the country. It was bringing up terrible memories of his father and … the woman from the village, whom he preferred to not recall.

He would happily have turned back in Wiltshire and returned to London, but Richard was adamant that he needed Perry to succeed, and he found, to his dismay, that he wanted his older brother to be pleased with his results. Which was why he now stood in the arse-end of Somerset, mocking this little hoyden … with an intriguing bosom he resolutely avoided staring at despite his baser instincts. If not for the impressive bosom, she would appear to be a young boy by her frame, hidden though it was beneath the hideously ill-fitting gown, but there was nothing childlike about her chest.

His thoughts returning to the moment, he noted the young woman was looking at him expectantly. He guessed she had said something, and he failed to answer because of his wayward musings.

"I apologize. I missed what you said because I was distracted by my handsome surroundings." With a pointed look at her hem, he delivered a facetious smile that only she could see now that the willowy sister and mother were behind him.

As expected, her eyes narrowed at his mocking. The other inhabitants of the room would perceive nothing amiss by what he had said, but Emma had clearly recognized the slight to her appearance by the flicker of his gaze.

"Well, if you will excuse me, I shall just go freshen up."

"Not necessary, please, let us enjoy an invigorating cup of tea together now that I have come all this way to visit." Perry was uncertain why he was baiting the girl, but he enjoyed observing the flare of her nostrils as she attempted to squash her ire.

"I must look a fright. I can return for tea in ten minutes."

"Not at all. The pleasure of your company will be much more desirable than your departure. Please ..." Perry held up his arm to escort her to a seat. A low growl emitted from her throat as she complied, causing Perry's lips to quirk in amusement. The girl was trapped by the presence of her mother and her sister into being polite. He was quite certain that if they had been alone, she would send him to the devil. She vibrated with fiercely repressed energy, which he felt compelled to stoke. How far could he push her before she exploded?

This afternoon's visit to Rose Ash Manor was turning out to be more entertaining than he had expected.

Emma settled into her chair, which was diagonally across from him. She removed her gardening gloves before lifting her hands to release the enormous bonnet and, after setting it down on an end table, attempting to tidy her pinned-up hair. She failed abysmally, and Perry repressed a grin at the strands that stuck straight up in defiance of her futile attempts. He wished he could be present when Emma finally found herself in front of a mirror and discovered how silly she had looked while she had sipped tea with the brother of Lord Arrogant.

Tea with mere Mr. Arrogant, if you will.

Mrs. Davis poured a cup of tea and handed it to her eldest daughter. Perry sipped his tea, withholding a grimace. Ever since his brother had wed a couple of months ago, he found himself drinking tea and nibbling dainty biscuits far too frequently. Just more evidence that marriage wrecked a gentleman.

Emma was looking at him suspiciously from the corner of her eye. It would seem she did not favor the aristocracy, but he had to admit he had goaded her. She flung an accusing look at her younger sister across the table, and in his peripheral vision he could make out the sister mouthing something as he smiled at Mrs. Davis. "I am sorry" was his guess as to the covert communication between the two sisters. Emma relaxed perceptibly into her chair. Interesting. He filed it away while he considered how to move forward with his news now that he knew the object of his mission was likely to be unreceptive to his invitation.

"I was explaining to your hospitable mother that Ethan has been settling into his new life at Balfour Terrace like a champion. The earl has hired a governess to help him continue the education that you began, and my nephew has convinced every member of our household to play a daily game of chess." He coughed into his hand. "At least, in my case, the days I am in residence."

He could perceive the grimace Emma was restraining at his last remark. He could practically hear the tirade in her head about idle gentlemen and their useless days spent in the pursuit of pleasure.

"A governess?"

"Yes, Lord Saunton hired a governess rather than the conventional tutor. The theory was that it would assist

Ethan's transition if we emulated your presence as closely as possible."

Mrs. Davis appeared impressed with the strategy. "That was thoughtful of the earl. Ethan spent most of his day with the women of the household."

Perry smiled, then broached the reason for his visit. "There has been one … minor issue since he joined us."

All three women straightened in alarm at the announcement. What was it about his young nephew that elicited so much single-minded concern from not only all the members of his own household, but this one, too? When he himself had been a boy, barely anyone had noticed him except for when his father 'tutored' him, which had always been an excruciating time wherein Perry wished he could be anywhere but near the late earl.

"It is nothing serious," he assured the ladies. "It is just that he has trouble sleeping. He prowls the halls at night and wakes my brother every night."

Emma frowned. "Why? He has never done that before," she demanded with a heavy tone of censure. Her mother, a cheerful blonde woman he guessed to be about forty years of age, shot a reproving glance at her daughter. "I mean … What is keeping him up? Ethan always slept very well at our home in Derby."

"I am afraid it is all your fault, Miss Davis. The boy misses you and worries after you."

Emma deflated in her chair. "I … see. We were very close. I have raised him since the day of his birth. His mother … my cousin … she did not survive."

"Most commendable, and the earl is very grateful that you have taken care of his boy for these past years. He is impressed with the lad's manners and intelligence."

A pleased smile crossed her face before settling back into its previously rigid lines. The young woman was clearly unhappy about his presence and resented the method in which his brother had taken Ethan from her life.

"Which is why the earl would like you to visit."

* * *

SHE FROZE with her cup halfway to her lips. Carefully, Emma placed the cup back on its saucer, which she placed down on the table, attempting to hide the tremble of her fingers. She missed Ethan terribly. They had spent their days together for his entire life, and his departure to London to live with his newly discovered father had left her bereft.

It was no secret the boy was a by-blow, but it had startled her entire family to learn he was the natural born son of a powerful earl. In his gratitude, the earl had gifted them their new estate, Rose Ash Manor, and the Davis family had entered the gentry as new landowners. A generous gesture, to be sure, but the arrogant lord had not deigned to visit and meet their family. His man of business had negotiated with her parents and collected the boy.

Now he sent his younger brother as an errand boy to collect her.

I would love to see Ethan. Her hand stole into the small pocket of her muslin dress to stroke the miniature tin monkey that Ethan had loved to play with. He had thrust it into her hand in the last moment before he had boarded the earl's carriage, insisting she take it. Emma had been struggling to hold back a storm of tears and been unable to insist it was his favorite toy, so he must keep it. Then he had been gone, a cloud of pebbles and dust kicked up by the carriage wheels marking his departure while he waved from the back window.

Now she carried it with her as a reminder of the boy she had raised.

But life moves on.

Ethan had a new life, and she had no wish to visit London. Truth be told, she was enjoying their new home and assisting her papa to transition from tenant farmer to estate owner. There were so many new skills they were learning, and she was needed here. She would see Ethan when he visited the Davises over the holidays.

"That sounds lovely, but I am afraid I must decline, Lord Ar—Mr. Balfour." She took pleasure in thwarting the gentleman. He might be as handsome as a Greek god, with his broad shoulders, riveting eyes, and powerful thighs encased in form-fitting buckskins, but he was even more arrogant than she had envisioned the earl to be. Perhaps being the spare gave him a chip on his shoulder that added to his general air of entitlement.

"Miss Davis, I do not think you understand. The earl is offering to sponsor you for a London Season. He will purchase you a new wardrobe and provide a dowry of one thousand pounds."

Emma heard her mother and Jane gasp at the news. It was profoundly generous, but Emma did not much care for society. Wealth was important, but she was satisfied with their current circumstances. She would eventually meet an honorable young man who wished to marry her here in Rose Ash. Perhaps a young man in trade, because she had no love of all the new requirements for her behavior now that she was a young lady of the gentry class.

"I am afraid I must decline. Please enjoy your journey back to London." With that, she made to stand.

"Mr. Balfour, how remiss I have been!" Mrs. Davis interjected. "You were on the road for days, and all we offered you was tea and biscuits. I shall have the housekeeper arrange sandwiches immediately. Emma, do you care to attend me?"

Emma's heart sank. She could hear the forced tone of her

mother's customary good cheer, which was not a good sign. A lecture out in the hall was definitely forthcoming. She pasted on a smile and rose along with her mother, following her out of the drawing room. The moment they reached the hall, her mother spun to face her, grabbing hold of her hands.

"Emma, it is a generous offer, and I implore you to consider it."

"I do not wish to go to London. It is dirty and sure to be noisy. I have no wish to marry a gentleman of the *ton,* nor even the gentry!"

Her mother's pleasant round face reflected her concern. She tucked an errant blonde curl behind her ear and gazed at Emma with serious ice-blue eyes. "I shall not force you to do so, but you burn your bridges every time you open your mouth. It would not hurt to learn a little diplomacy, Emma. The world is a lonely, brutal place, and we are fortunate to have such a large, loving family. Look what happened to my niece. She worked in respectable service until the earl ruined her and left her with child." Her mother paused, a flash of grief evident at the memory of her late niece who had left Ethan an orphan in their care. "Kitty was fortunate that your father agreed to provide her with a home despite the disgrace. Many husbands would not have been so accommodating, but your father is a good man and, for my sake, he agreed to weather the scandal of it all. He deserved to receive this estate as a gift after the hard choices he made. Even now, Ethan could be in a foundling home being raised by impersonal strangers."

"I am sorry, Mama, but I do not wish to have a Season. It would be a disaster. I cannot dance, despite Jane's best efforts, and we both know that I am woefully unskilled at polite conversation. It would all be a horrendous failure. I wish to stay at home."

"Emma, I just want you to find a young gentleman of

your own. So that you may know the joy of having your own children one day. Watching you with Ethan … You would make such a wonderful mother, my dear."

Emma stared down at her shoes. It was her deepest desire to raise her own children. She had so much love in her heart, and children were so much easier to communicate with. Her time with Ethan had been pure joy, and she wished for her own child—one who could not be removed when his unknown parent suddenly surfaced.

Her eyes focused on the muddy hem of her skirt, as if to mock her. "I cannot go … I would be an utter disaster in high society."

Her mother stared at her in contemplation for several long moments. "I will not force you to accept the invitation. Although I am disappointed you are allowing fear of failure to drive your decision. You are usually so courageous, Emma."

Emma resolutely stared down at the evidence of her gauche manners, noting how the mud had dried and the fabric would likely be permanently stained.

Mrs. Davis sighed, reaching out to tuck a curl behind Emma's ear. "As you like, but do not be rude to the earl's emissary. The earl has been exceedingly generous to the Davis family, and we have secured a brighter future for your brothers and sisters through his benevolence. I expect you to scrape together some deportment and address the earl's brother with respect, young lady."

Emma nodded. She knew she had a tendency to be too straightforward, too brutal in her candor, which is why she had not yet been courted in Derby or in their new Somerset town. Nor had she made many friends outside of her family circle.

Quelling her tongue for the duration of the spare's visit was not too much to ask of her.

* * *

PERRY SIPPED on his tea and smiled at the younger sister while the mother took Emma to task in the hall. Jane Davis was quite a stunning girl, but Perry avoided innocent young ladies. He had no interest in being caught by the parson's noose. Strangely, it was simple to steer his attention off the graceful creature seated near him. Her viper of an older sister was the one he was struggling to keep his eyes off of, for some inexplicable reason.

The little shrew excited his blood, and the impulse to provoke her was almost overwhelming in its intensity. Emma was so distractingly disheveled—a wild thing. His thoughts drifted to what it would be like to bed such a rumbustious creature.

Good Lord, how long had it been since he had taken a woman to bed that he was entertaining such whimsical thoughts? *Ten days is not an interminable time.* He should be able to manage his lustful inclinations.

Perry picked up a dainty biscuit and swallowed it in two bites. *Perhaps I am merely tired and hungry from traveling?*

Mrs. Davis and Emma reentered the room and walked over to resume their places around the table that held the china tea service. Emma sat perched on the edge of her seat as if she was moments from running off, while Mrs. Davis took a seat on the sky-blue sofa. Despite his dislike of the country, Perry had to admit that the Davis drawing room was attractive and cozy. It felt like a home, with the piles of books teetering on end tables, the inexpensive but tasteful *bric à brac* adorning the shelves, and the cheerful landscape paintings on the walls. From all appearances, the Davis family maintained a comfortable and close-knit home—something that Perry had yet to experience in his life.

Richard had charged him with this mission, and he

intended to succeed at it. When he had responded with expletives and denied his willingness to undertake the trip to Somerset, his brother had appealed to him. *"I need your assistance, Perry. You are a man accustomed to getting what you want. I need you to turn that charm on to the Davis family and obtain their agreement to escort their eldest daughter to London. I will send you along with Sophia's lady's maid for propriety's sake on the return journey. This is an important family matter, and I must send a relation whom I trust to handle the affair."*

Why pleasing his brother made him feel uplifted, he did not know, but when he had assisted Richard with his troubles back in May, after his unexpected wedding, Perry had found himself unexpectedly elated to contribute meaningfully. He would never dare inform the new countess that, indeed, he might need a project to fend off the persistent ennui that was plaguing him these past months, but in the privacy of his own thoughts, he admitted she might have a valid point.

Which was why succeeding was imperative. His brother needed him, and he would not fail. As his brother had pointed out, Perry always achieved what he wanted, so he was scrutinizing the young woman and noting her reactions and expressions. He had formed a conclusion about what motivated her, which was not personal gain or status within society. Now that she had returned to her seat, Perry would make an offer that the little termagant could not refuse.

CHAPTER 2

"Females are purely ornamental. When you forget this truth, you will uncover the need to drown your sorrows in drink. Here, take a sip of my brandy. It will help you forget the silly chit."

July 1802, the late Earl of Saunton to his son, Peregrine, on his seventh birthday after finding him climbing the trees of Saunton Park with the daughter of the stable master.

* * *

"Before I forget, my brother wrote you a letter, Mrs. Davis." Perry drew the missive from his breast pocket and handed over the folded pages to Emma's mother. From the corner of his eye, he saw Emma fidget in her chair, visibly agitated. The little minx was clearly angry with the earl, which seemed churlish considering that he had gifted her family an entire estate, including the comfortable drawing room in which they currently sat. *Ungrateful chit!*

Mrs. Davis unfolded the letter and read it carefully, giving a small smile of assent when she reached the end.

"Well … what does it say?" Emma's caustic tone drew a sharp look from her parent.

"The earl extends his apologies for how he handled the matter of retrieving Ethan. He states that he is not well-versed in family matters and that his new countess has pointed out his error in not handling such a delicate family matter in a more sensitive manner. He realizes his actions have created some distress for Ethan, whom he is very fond of and impressed with, and he would like our help to ease the transition."

Perry pointedly ignored it when Emma growled out a response below her breath. It sounded like something to do with Lord Arrogant. Richard would be most amused at the sobriquet when Perry informed him of it. Perhaps he would call Richard that from now on. *Yes, I shall fulfill your bidding, Lord Arrogant.*

Mrs. Davis turned back to address Perry. "I appreciate the thought his lordship put into the matter. However, I am afraid Emma has decided to remain here at Rose Ash. Perhaps she can compose a letter of advice for the earl, along with a letter for Ethan to ease his concerns regarding her?"

Perry had expected the resistance from the moment he had laid eyes on the girl. Which was why he had been gathering his observations in the manner of a man preparing for a seduction. But it was not seduction that Emma required, it was underhanded manipulation. She might not care for pretty dresses and the promise of wealth and status, but he knew what would change her mind, and he anticipated her forthcoming resentment when he neatly won this tense negotiation.

"That is a pity, Mrs. Davis. I would have enjoyed escorting your daughters to see the sights of our great city.

And the modiste our family uses, her creations are sublime. Every young woman dreams of owning such gowns to attend balls and dance the evening away in the arms of charming gentlemen. My brother is very protective of his family, and only the very best of gentlemen would be introduced to two such important ladies."

As predicted, the younger sister leaned forward in excitement. "Daughters?"

Perry feigned an expression of innocent surprise as he turned to look at Jane Davis. "Did I fail to mention the invitation was for both of you?"

Jane inhaled in elation, her face lighting up as she looked at Emma. "Emma, this is so exciting! A Season in London! I have always dreamed of dancing the waltz in a grand ballroom. Please, we must go!"

There was no mistaking the accusatory glare emanating from his right. His prey could feel his trap tightening. His assessment of her character would prove out over the next few minutes when she finally admitted defeat and accepted that she would leave Somerset in the morning. The strong-willed young woman valued her family, and her sister would be the one to secure her cooperation.

"Jane, I am sure we can request the waltz be included at the next local assembly!" Emma's face displayed desperation, but the sister was not listening.

Perry decided it was time to further tighten the noose. "Not to mention how disappointed the Duchess of Halmesbury will be when she learns she will not be sponsoring you. She was quite looking forward to it." *Or she will be as soon as she is told about it.*

"A duchess! Mama, where did we put the trunks? Perhaps I can start packing before dinner!" Jane was up on her feet, clapping her hands together exuberantly. She was brimming with such enthusiasm that she did not hear Emma's protests as she rushed from the room. "Should I take my fashion plates? No! They will have far newer designs than the ones I have collected!"

Emma threw a murderous scowl at Perry, clearly ready to leap out of her chair and do him an injury. Swallowing a smile, Perry ignored her, looking over at the mother, who seemed to be holding back her own smile of amusement.

"Well-played, Mr. Balfour. It would seem my eldest daughters will leave with you in the morning, if my husband agrees. Would you care to stay for dinner?"

A moan of protest emitted from his right. "Mama!"

Mrs. Davis turned to her eldest daughter with a placatory expression. "Admit when you have been outwitted, Emma. My advice is … do not play chess with this gentleman. His talent for strategy surpasses your own, young lady. Or would you like to stand in the way of your sister—your closest friend in the entire world—embarking on the adventure of her dreams?"

Emma turned to Perry, fire in her black eyes. "Jane was not included in the invitation—admit it!"

His lips drew into a condescending grin. "I do not know of what you speak. Lord Saunton was quite explicit that your sister should accompany you under the same terms I put forward."

Her head swung back to her mother. "Mama, I do not wish to go. Speak to Jane. Make her see reason!"

Her mother frowned politely. "Attempt to get between Jane and a new wardrobe fit for the peerage? I would not dare. It is out of my hands, I am afraid."

"Then she can go alone!"

The cheery mother suddenly grew stern. "Absolutely not. You are to ensure nothing happens to Jane. You are the responsible one, Emma. I expect you to take care of your sister and ensure no harm befalls her. She has just turned eighteen, and she does not understand the ways of the world like you do."

"But ... but ... I am not that much older than her!"

"You are more—" Mrs. Davis paused, looking for the right word while Perry watched on. "—mistrustful. Besides, this visit will be good for you. You spend far too much time in your books and gardening. It is time to experience the world."

Emma looked like she had more to say, her thoughts playing across her face until she suddenly slumped in defeat, gnashing her teeth in frustration. "Yes, Mama."

Personally, Perry could not be enjoying himself more. He had succeeded in his mission, and the fact that he had just neatly doubled the planned expenses on behalf of his soon-to-be-very-vexed brother only sweetened the feeling of victory. *Richard said success was imperative, after all.*

Timing it perfectly, he leaned forward to gaze triumphantly into Emma's angry eyes before turning to smile at the mother. "And I would love to stay for dinner, Mrs. Davis."

* * *

PERRY BROWSED the books in the manor library while he awaited the descent of the large Davis family for dinner. In keeping with the style of the drawing room, the room was attractively furnished. The family had good taste ... except for the girl he had come to collect. Emma wore the most unflattering colors and styles, looking more like a dowdy than a new member of the gentry.

It did not appear to be for lack of funds or resources. The younger sister was well turned out in dresses that were only a few months out of style, likely based on fashion plates that had taken time to reach them in the country. Perhaps the younger one was adept with needlework?

Nevertheless, he still had trouble shaking the memory of the impressive bosom from his thoughts. It was most inconvenient to be experiencing lustful musings over the little hoyden. Clearly, he needed to get back to London and find one of his willing widows to slake his excess primal urges.

Behind him, he heard light footsteps seconds before the library door thumped closed behind him. His lips quirked as he realized he was about to be confronted and the young *lady* did not want her family to overhear her tirade.

Taking his time to grate on her nerves, he slowly turned around with a sardonic smile painted across his face.

"Miss Davis, what a pleasure to see you."

"Why are you doing this?"

"Doing what, exactly?"

"I made it clear I did not wish to journey to London with you, and you deliberately maneuvered me into it."

Emma had cleaned up and donned a fresh gown. Her hair was vaguely styled, and she appeared fractionally less wild than their first encounter. However, it also proved she needed a decent modiste and a lady's maid if she were to enter society. The dress appeared to be about fifteen years out of date, billowing like a tent around her slight frame, and buttoned up to her chin. Her hair was a cloud of untamed curls. It made him wince to think of all that weight stacked on her delicate head.

Mentally, he sighed. Richard had better not develop any notions about him preparing the little hoyden beyond delivering her to Balfour Terrace. Polishing the young woman into a lady fit for society was going to be a herculean task.

"Miss Davis, your mother believes this trip will be good for you. Do you not wish to meet eligible young men?"

"What is the point?"

Perry frowned in confusion. "All young women wish to marry, do they not?"

Emma snorted. "Let us be honest, none of the young gentlemen of London will be interested in courting me!"

His brow furrowed from the startling realization that the obstinate young woman lacked confidence. To his disgust, concern wormed its way into his heart. "Emma, the earl will ensure you are ready. He will purchase you the very best clothing, provide you with a lady's maid, and ensure you receive tutoring on any subject you need to master. My brother will take care of you."

"Do you not understand? It will not be enough. I am happy with my life. When I step into society, I feel unkempt, ridiculous. People view me as a child. A poorly dressed one. Then I open my mouth, and I can see their need to get away from me. Then there is you"—Emma flapped her hand in his general direction—"the very pink of the *beau monde*. Flawless in your attire and perfect etiquette. You and your priggish friends are just going to make sport at my expense, the silly country mouse who does not know a pleat from a … a …" The errant hand now waved over her own form while she struggled to find a comparable word. It was obvious she was wholly illiterate on the subject of fashion.

"*Gros de Naples?*"

Emma stopped to stare at him with her mouth agape. "Is that a real thing?"

He shrugged. "I guess you will find out when you visit my brother's favorite modiste."

Her expression turned black. "Do not mock me. I asked you a direct question! And why would your brother have a favorite *modiste?*"

Perry felt a momentary wash of shame. This was not an appropriate subject for an innocent young miss, even if she was a little wild. Clearing his throat, he drew a deep breath.

"I misspoke. It was formerly his favorite modiste, but now it is frequented by the new countess and her cousin."

Emma looked him over. "I see. So it is true the earl has reformed?"

"He has."

"It is most indiscreet to inform me of such matters."

Perry stretched his neck unobtrusively to relieve his discomfort. "My brother's … affairs … are well-known, as well as his recent marriage and reformation. His regard for the countess is infamo—I mean … famous." He corrected himself at the last moment, recalling with whom he spoke.

Emma mused over this. "He married her for love?"

Perry had to quell the urge to roll his eyes. "He did."

"He must have changed drastically since the time that our cousin, Kitty, knew him, then." It was rhetorical, so Perry did not acknowledge her.

"As to my friends, I shall allow no one to snub you, Miss Davis. This truly is about assisting Ethan to adjust to his new home. My brother and the countess are earnest about taking care of your young cousin."

Emma stared up into his eyes, setting his nerves on edge when he peered into her coal-black abyss and sensed a profound perceptiveness. She was gazing into the very depths of his soul, but he had no wish for her to see the darkness that resided there.

"So, we shall call a truce, then?" she offered.

"Hmmm … I do not know about that, Miss Davis. You are such a delight to tease, and it is a long journey back to London."

Her eyes narrowed in animosity. "Pretentious buck!"

"Now, now. Name-calling will not get you far in the drawing rooms of the *ton*. You will need to learn subtler methods to put your foe down if you wish to succeed."

A ghastly smile of restrained hatred crossed her face as

she dipped into a deep curtsy. "Mr. Balfour, you are an astute man. I am sure you know what you can do with your *subtler methods*." With that, she strode past him to exit the room.

"Much better, Miss Davis. Much better," he responded in an encouraging tone, as if teaching a young child. The only sign that she heard him was the guttural sound of frustration before she slammed the library door in her wake.

* * *

EMMA STOOD in the stable yard of Rose Ash Manor, thankful for her thick carriage dress in the chilly morning as the soft pink and gray of first light dappled the sky. Breathing into her freezing hands to warm them up, she watched while her and Jane's trunks were tied down to the roofs of the two carriages belonging to the earl. *Two! What extravagance!*

She had met the countess's French lady's maid and Mr. Balfour's valet—*I cannot believe he has brought an actual valet along to collect some country lasses from Somerset*—and fumed that the presence of the maid confirmed what she had suspected. Jane was not part of the earl's original plans, and Mr. Arrogant had extended the invitation to maneuver Emma into accepting against her will. Why else would a female servant have been sent, other than to act as a companion on the return journey?

She turned to find Mr. Arro—Balfour, staring at her attire with an appalled expression.

"What?" She scowled her botheration.

"I have never seen anyone dress in that particular shade of … mud?"

Emma gritted her teeth in annoyance. "It is very serviceable, and nothing spoils one's clothing like a long, dusty trip in a carriage."

"Serviceable?" He repeated the word back as if it was the first time he was hearing it.

"It is rude to comment on my attire in a derogatory manner."

He shrugged nonchalantly. "It is rude to comment on rude behavior."

Her blood rose. *Please, Lord, bless us with excellent weather so we may reach London as quickly as humanly possible!*

She knew it was going to be a long journey either way. If the weather held, it would take as much as two days to reach their destination, and if it did not ... heaven help her, it could be as much as a week if it rained. In that much time, she would either kill him or fling herself under the carriage wheels to get away from the irritating man forever.

"It is just that your sister is so fetching in that blue velvet, and with your coloring so similar, you are sure to—"

"Mr. Balfour! Is this how society behaves? Comparing one sister to another, to her face?"

He rolled his eyes. "As you wish. Clearly, the choice to wear a gown the color of mud is your prerogative. Far be it from me to interfere with such a *brave* choice."

She could hear the sneer behind his innocent smile. Jane looked lovely, it was true. Jane always looked lovely. Did the idle dandy think Emma did not know? She had tried to wear what Jane wore, and it did not look right. Her sister was tall and elegant, while Emma was realistic about her short, boyish frame. There were no illusions that she would attract a gentleman of the *ton*. Since Ethan had departed, she had wistfully imagined having her own child, but to do that, she would need to attract a mate.

Clumsy, small, inelegant Emma attracting a man? It was laughable! And vulgar for Mr. Balfour to discuss her failings openly. Emma's only hope was to marry an equal, or perhaps someone down by society's standards, who would appreciate marrying into the gentry. A successful tradesman, she had reasoned many a midnight hour when her desire for a babe of her own had plagued her so she might awaken with dark circles under her eyes.

Eventually, all the trunks were loaded and tied down. She watched the servants embark on the second carriage. Then one of the footmen helped Jane up the first carriage's steps, where she disappeared into the luxurious interior with a flash of blue skirts. The footman turned to hold out his hand to Emma, who took it gratefully to navigate the steep stairs, holding her … mud … skirts in her other hand. Once inside, she peered at the rich, butter-soft leather squabs and thick pile of the rug on the floor before taking her seat next to her sister.

When she had settled down into the comfortable seating, she looked up to discover Mr. Arro—Balfour—ascending. She squeaked in alarm. "Are you traveling with us? I thought you would ride back or … or …"

"Or travel with the servants?" he queried sardonically while settling into the seat directly across from her. "Nay, Miss Davis. As I stated, the journey is long and you are entertaining, so I shall sit here and watch you."

"Mock me, you mean?"

He shrugged. "We shall see where the day takes us, shall we?"

Emma scowled at him before pointedly turning to watch out the window. She raised her hand to wave at her family gathered outside to bid their goodbyes. Her round, pretty blonde mother, her swarthy father, and her three brothers, along with little Maddie, the youngest. They waved their goodbyes and within moments were out of sight when the carriage took a turn in the winding drive of Rose Ash Manor. The sun was barely risen, and they were now on their way to London for a Season.

Emma could scarcely believe it. She had tossed and turned the entire night in trepidation. She knew she would be a colossal failure, but if Jane found her young gentleman and Emma spent some time with Ethan, it would all be worth it. At least that is what she kept telling herself repeatedly whenever the feeling of dread crept into her chest, a dark shadow of gloom as she considered the embarrassment sure to find her.

The carriage turned onto a main road, a turnpike that would lead them out of the town of Rose Ash. Emma's heart sank into her shoes as she contemplated her arrival at the grand townhouse of the Earl of Saunton. Sighing, she reached up to untie her bonnet at the same time as Jane. They looked at each other, giggling at the synchronistic movements, before removing their bonnets to place them on the bench next to Mr. Arro—Balfour. *Zooks, Emma, you must learn to call him by his name before you slip up and call the earl, himself, Lord Arrogant to his face.*

Jane lifted up the basket she had brought with her, searching through her things to pull out an embroidery frame. On the fabric fastened to it, Emma could see the beginning of a perfect rose and thorns, along with a tree in the background. Her talented sister was commemorating their new home at Rose Ash, it would appear. Emma sighed. She wished she possessed anything approaching such a skill. Instead, she leaned down and drew a book from her own basket, settling back into the puffy squabs to find her page.

Across from her, she heard a groan of disapproval. Glancing up, she found Mr. Arrogant staring at the cover of her volume. "You cannot be serious? A text on animal husbandry while we drive to London to sample the sights? What opportunity will exist in Town to participate in the pursuit of animal husbandry?"

Emma scoffed in rebuke. "We both know that Jane is the

one who will find a wonderful gentleman, at which time I will return to Rose Ash and resume my familial duties. Running an estate requires a vast store of knowledge on all things, and when we lived in Derby, we possessed little cattle. Now we have more, so I plan to ensure the prosperous future of the estate through a wide range of income sources, including breeding more sheep. There is a fortune to be made in supplying the local wool industry."

Mr. Arrogant swiped a hand over his face in dismay before rubbing the back of his neck. "Have you ever thought that your troubles with men might stem from your unladylike pursuits?"

Emma stiffened in anger. From the corner of her eye, she could see Jane tense up, before she carefully put her embroidery away. Pulling a shawl from her basket, her sister rolled it into a pillow and lay back into the corner, with the shawl propping her head. Within moments, she emitted a low, bleating snore. She was asleep.

Emma had always envied Jane's ability to sleep whenever and wherever she wished. Apparently, her sister did not desire to take part in the conversation, nor overhear it, so she had swiftly exited the conversation and left them to their sniping.

Lifting her hand to straighten her hair, she saw the look of disdain that flashed over his features. She guessed her hair was frowsy, as usual. She could not help it. Jane had beautiful, silky locks of ebony, while Emma had somehow inherited a mess of tight curls. Her own locks could be called ebony too, she supposed, but it seemed insolent to draw a comparison to the lush head of hair that framed her sister's perfectly proportioned features and high cheekbones.

Egads! The differences between her elegant sister and herself rarely bothered her, but since meeting Peregrine Balfour the day before, she was experiencing the most inconvenient self-consciousness. Perceiving herself through the eyes of the sartorial buck, one of many she would encounter on this trip, was giving her a taste of what it would be like to make the rounds in London. She hoped Jane appreciated what she was doing in the name of family because this entire *adventure* would be excruciating for her. Every single minute of it.

Shaking her head in disbelief, Emma looked back at her book, determined to ignore the obnoxious nobleman for the rest of the morning until they reached an inn for lunch and a change of horses.

No man had ever infuriated her as much as Mr. Peregrine Balfour, and before this journey was over, she might truly do him an injury.

CHAPTER 3

"No young woman of any value will ever consent to wed a worthless spare. However, the consolation is that wicked widows will welcome you into their beds with open arms."

July 1803, the late Earl of Saunton to his son, Peregrine, on his eighth birthday after observing his son's fascination with the local squire's daughter.

* * *

Perry did not understand his desire to be close to the ridiculous, yet fascinating, Emma Davis. Something about the young woman fired his blood and made him feel invigorated. He had planned to ride his own mount as they made their leisurely way home, but he had been drawn into the carriage where he had watched her read for the past two hours, breathing in her unique scent of chamomile and wildflowers.

There was no arguing that he was behaving like an untried youth battling his first infatuation. She had delicate features, a sweet heart-shaped face, and those large black eyes were haunting in the way they peered directly into his soul. He should know. They had been the subject of his troubled sleep the night before. Emma also possessed exquisite skin, glowing and smooth, just like her sister. But it was not her little sister who had captured his imagination.

He could only be grateful Emma was so incompetent with her attire and dressing her hair, or he would be in serious jeopardy. Fortunately, her mud carriage dress dampened any possibility of ardor. That awful hue washed out her lovely skin tones to make her look sickly in the shadowed interior of the carriage.

Nevertheless, there was something endearing about the earnest expression on her face as she licked a finger to turn the page. All signs showed her to be riveted by the dry text she had brought along. Perry was almost envious of her single-minded focus.

He contemplated napping similarly to the sister who had fallen asleep at the beginning of their journey and who had yet to rouse herself. His sleep the night before had been outright challenging. The loud noises of the busy coaching inn barely muffled by the time they crept through the cracks in his room to pester him in his bed.

Not to mention that each time he fell asleep, he had found his trembling fingers unbuttoning a disheveled muslin dress, covered in mud and grass, which he would peel back to reveal a luscious set of perfect breasts. Each time, he would startle awake to find himself in the uncomfortable bed, his gaze fixed on the ceiling while sweat soaked the bedding. Which was not quite as regretful as the raging erection that had made him leave his bed several times to douse himself in the cold water provided in a jug by the washstand.

He must be in dire need of a woman if a silly country shrew was causing such lustful dreams.

Come morning, he had been relieved to find Emma dressed in the mud-colored carriage dress, which effectively hid her bountiful breasts under the thick fabric and copious nips and tucks of the bodice. There was nothing ornamental about her appearance, but then, she was not like any of the females of his acquaintance.

Across from him, Emma stirred, as if reading his mind. She raised her hand to unbutton the outer carriage dress, likely intending to continue her travel in the muslin gown peeking from below the hem. The last thing he needed was for her to reveal her pert bosom and stimulate his senses once more. Within such close quarters, the consequences could be embarrassing.

"Keep it on!"

She glanced over at him in consternation. "Why? The morning has been warming up, and I wish to be comfortable."

Perry searched for a reason, realizing his tone had been unnecessarily sharp. Curling his lips into a persuasive smile, he ventured an explanation.

"We shall turn in to an inn for lunch soon, at which time you can stretch your legs. As you pointed out, there is much dust, and I am sure you would like to keep your day gown from being stained."

Emma appeared to be preparing a retort before she sighed and relented. "You are correct. It would be pleasant to wash up and keep the gown pristine. You finally concede that the carriage dress is serviceable?"

Perry's heart was in his mouth at the memory of the bosom that plagued his dreams. He nodded, uncertain what he had just agreed to, but immensely relieved she had remained buttoned up. Emma was the least ornamental female he had ever met. These lustful thoughts were unseemly. As soon as he reached London, he would make himself scarce and find his way into the warm bed of an inviting widow.

Perhaps remaining in the carriage was not the best plan. On the other hand, he planned to leave the chit behind the moment they reached Town, so perhaps he should soak in the pleasant sensation of contentment he enjoyed in her presence as long as he could. Perry scowled. Where had this vacillation arisen from? *You are buffle-headed.*

Before he knew what he was doing, he barked at Emma, "You really should find better reading material!"

He groaned mentally. *Good Lord, Perry, leave the girl alone.*

A large pair of black eyes glowered over the edge of the book. "What, pray tell, did you do to keep yourself amused on the way to Rose Ash?"

"I rode my mount and enjoyed the country air."

A triumphant look settled on her face. "I knew it! You are in the carriage to be close to me."

"No—I—" Perry scrambled for an explanation as to why he was in the carriage. Other than the truth, which was, he wanted to be close to her.

"Admit it, Mr. Balfour. You have made it a sport to irritate me."

Relaxing back, he grabbed her explanation with profound relief. "Irritating you is considerably more entertaining than riding."

Emma rolled her eyes. "Would you care for a book to read, Mr. Balfour? It would appear you are in want of something to do?"

Perry drew a deep breath, suppressing his aggravation while he contemplated the notion of reading. He admitted to himself it would be a better choice than being lost in his thoughts, so he gave a brief nod. Emma marked her page with a ribbon and closed the text she was reading. When she leaned forward to grab her basket, Perry helplessly observed how the position pushed her breasts up prominently, despite the ugly carriage dress. A fresh twinge of desire in his groin was his punishment for looking. He closed his eyes while Emma rummaged through her basket.

"Here you go."

He opened his eyes to find a green volume with gold lettering being thrust into his hand. "*Pride and Prejudice, Volume One*?"

"I have the other two volumes when you are ready. It is a delightful book about *etiquette*." The last was said with deliberate emphasis.

"You have read a book on etiquette?" The disbelief in his voice was plain. "And you expect me to read a romantic novel?"

Emma clenched her jaw. "As you wish, Mr. Balfour. It will be a romantic novel or a book on animal husbandry. The choice is yours." Perry eyed the thick tome she was currently reading.

He sighed. "I shall read the novel."

Taking up her text on animal husbandry, Emma settled back into her seat to ignore him.

Perry opened the book and read the first line.

JANE DAVIS WAS at that age when she was a strange mix of giddy girl and astute young woman. Emma could not figure out which version of Jane had just spoken to her, as she stared at her younger sister with her mouth agape.

"Have you gone mad?"

Jane shrugged as she plaited her hair to prepare for bed.

They had stopped for the night at a comfortable coaching inn. Once again, it was clear that Jane had not been expected on the return to London because they were sharing a room that had been reserved for Emma when Peregrine Balfour had passed through on his way to Rose Ash.

The weather had been mild and the drive easy. Apparently, Mr. Balfour had planned a leisurely pace to London, which was appreciated. They had stopped for a meal at a pleasant inn earlier that day, and the one they were staying in that evening was the best she had ever seen. A cheerful rug on the floor, a large bed for her and Jane to share, and one of their trunks had been brought in for their convenience.

"Jane!"

"I stand by what I said. Mr. Balfour continues to tease you because he is smitten."

Emma shook her head in disbelief. "But … but … he is … *him*, and I am … *me*." Emma waved her hand back and forth in a manner that did little to make up for her lack of words.

"Emma, you are a unique woman. Despite your lack of attention to your appearance, you are quite comely, and Mr. Balfour cannot stop looking at you. Is it mad to remark that I think he is taken with you for some reason? I think he is like one of those little boys who runs around the village terrorizing the girls they admire in a bid for their attention. Perhaps he does not know how to behave because his emotions are not matured. Perhaps he has never met a woman like you before."

She scoffed. "That is patently ridiculous. Mr. Balfour is a handsome second son of an earl with a healthy annuity, I am sure. Any young lady he wanted could be his. He teases me because it is sport to him. He as much as said so."

"I do not believe that is what I am witnessing."

"Jane, he is clearly experienced with women! I am nobody!"

"Women, perhaps. Ladies, not so much. And definitely not intelligent young ladies of honor. More like harlots, if I were to hazard my guess."

Emma stood staring at her younger sister in amazement. Jane truly believed her words. Not just that, the subject of her conversation suggested she was not the naïve young miss as Mama had intimated the previous afternoon. A flash of pride filled her at the beautiful young woman of grace and wit who stood before her. Jane was going to excel at her Season. The next moment, Emma recalled the lunatic proposal that Peregrine Balfour was infatuated with her and stamped her foot in outrage.

"This conversation is absurd! Mr. Balfour—nay, any gentlemen of the *ton*—will not give me a second glance. And if he were enamored with intelligent young ladies of honor, it would be you he was mooning over, not me!"

"Emma, we are two very different personalities. There is something about you specifically that calls to the gentleman. I know when a man has his eyes on me, and trust me when I tell you that Mr. Balfour is not mooning over me. It is you who has captured his attention."

Emma cocked her head. Jane had gone mad. There could be no other explanation. The stress of an unexpected Season among the elite had gone to her head and driven the reason from her mind.

Jane continued as she tied her plait off with a ribbon. "If you yourself were not so infatuated in return, you would notice the signals."

"WHAT?" Emma clapped a hand over her mouth. Had she just howled? In a public inn? What was the matter with her? Nay! What was the matter with her sister?

Her concern over Jane's state of mind grew. Perhaps Emma should insist they return home. She did not know how to take care of Jane if something had gone awry. This conversation was so far outside of her experience, Emma briefly considered that she, too, had been driven mad by this ill-advised trip.

"Usually, if you think a man is of inferior intellect, you would simply politely rebuke him and walk away. But Mr. Balfour is an intelligent and worthy adversary, so you are engaging in debate with him. Clearly, his skill has attracted your admiration. The more he bests you in conversation, the more fascinated you become. It does not hurt that he is one of the most attractive men you or I have ever laid eyes on. I think you will be married long before I, Emma." Jane stated it so calmly, as if she had not just delivered a statement of such profound insanity that her family would need to lock her in her room lest the neighbors try to send her off to Bedlam.

"MARRIED?" Emma struggled for breath, Jane's pronouncement having knocked the very air out of her lungs. Fisting her hands, she drew a fortifying breath. "Jane, are you all right? Did you eat something that disagreed with you, or are you feeling pressure about this trip? We will finish the journey, and I will ask the earl to send us home with an agreement to return later. We can prepare at home, find a tutor to assist us, and then return when you are ready."

Jane gave a soft laugh. Walking over to Emma to take up her hands, she looked into Emma's eyes. "He is not what I would have predicted for you, but he is a very interesting gentleman and I am positive you will work out your differences."

Emma felt her eyebrows draw together. "Jane, Mr. Balfour is not the marrying kind. He is a man who engages in scandalous pursuits. You have seen the gossip columns about him and the earl. He will never settle down."

"The earl did."

"The earl has a title, and he needs an heir. Once he has an heir, all pressure is off his brother to procreate. Hence, Mr. Balfour will probably never marry. There is nothing about his conduct that suggests that he is in want of a wife. Consider

Pride and Prejudice. 'It is a truth universally acknowledged, that a single man in possession of a good fortune, must be in want of a wife.' Do you see there is no personal wealth for the young man to pass on? He is the earl's dependent."

Jane smiled. "Indeed, consider *Pride and Prejudice*." With that cryptic remark, she dropped Emma's hands. "Time for bed, I think."

"You napped all morning!"

"And embroidered all afternoon. All that fine needlework and travel has quite taken it out of me. Which side would you like to sleep on?" Jane climbed into the bed. Within seconds of her head hitting the pillow, she emitted a low, huffing snore.

Damn Jane and her uncanny ability to sleep like a carefree babe! How dare she fling such outrageous accusations and then simply fall asleep? Emma paced the room, her ire at full staff, as she muttered under her breath at the surreal conversation they had just had.

Yes, Mr. Balfour was the most handsome man she had ever laid eyes on, but that did not mean she admired him! And what rot about his intellect impressing her. The man was a buffoon. Yes, his emerald eyes made her want to drown in his gaze, but that was just a customary response to an attractive male. His words made her palm itch to slap his face. He fired her blood and made her want to grab him by his pompous shoulders and shake him until … until … until …

"Oh, God!" Emma dropped into the armchair in the corner and lowered her head into her hands in misery. *Until he kisses me like he means it.*

What a horrifying discovery to make of oneself. She was merely a shallow young woman whose head had been turned by a tall, perfect specimen of a man with no thought of the obnoxious personality housed within. She was going to hell. *Nay, I am already there.*

Jane's proposition that he felt the same yearning to embrace her in return was beyond comprehension. Physically he was perfect, a Greek god, and she was … a country mouse with the hair of a bird's nest and the fashion sense of a … a … a country mouse. Emma snorted into her cupped hands. Developing an infatuation was robbing her of her intellect. Her analogies were evidence of the spreading weakness of her mind.

This would lead to heartbreak. Hers, not his. She could never allow Mr. Arrogant to know she had developed an infatuation. How mortifying! If his mockery was aggravating now, it would be intolerable if he discovered she desired him. Emma groaned.

What was she to do? She had read enough books to know this could not end well for her, and she did not want to become a young woman who attempted to step so far above herself to be painfully snubbed for reaching so high. She would not be an Icarus who tumbled to her death by developing lofty notions that she could ever hope to attract such a beautiful specimen of manhood.

This requires a healthy dose of realism, Emma Davis!

She would just have to focus on preparing for the Season and doing well enough to not be considered a fool. She would help Jane find a young man and then immediately return to Rose Ash. There was no doubt that Jane would have men flocking to meet her. Her sister was very popular, both in Derby and Somerset, but had yet to exhibit any interest in the gentlemen who attempted to court her.

In the meantime, Emma would studiously avoid developing any romantic notions about the rogue who served as their escort. Once they reached London, he was certain to disappear into his clubs and scandalous pursuits, at which time Emma would return to her normal state of mind. All she needed to do was avoid engaging with Peregrine Balfour until her return to Rose Ash.

* * *

THE NEXT MORNING, close to midday, Mr. Balfour laid the last volume down on his lap with a contented sigh.

Emma looked up from her reading.

"Did you enjoy the novel, after all, Mr. Balfour?" *Great, Emma. What happened to your determination to not engage?*

"It was excellent. Truly a masterpiece."

Emma tilted her head in astonishment. "Truly?" It was her favorite work of fiction, one that made her feel better when she was most gloomy about her marital prospects. To hear him echo her thoughts was most unexpected.

"Mr. Darcy was most astute about the troubles of a gentleman."

Emma frowned in suspicion. "What do you mean?"

"This Bennet flibbertigibbet was most unsuitable for him. A gentleman of such class and distinction. Quite lowering to be caught in her snare."

Emma leaned forward. "I am not sure you understood—"

"—the troubles of dealing with country mice? I am quite familiar, thank you. The story is quite tragic, a true romantic piece."

"Tragic?"

"That he was brought down in station by such a lowly family."

Emma shook her head in disbelief. "Mr. Bal—"

"He should have escaped when he had the chance. When he learned about the sister's elopement, he had his opportunity to escape, and he blew it."

Emma, to her dismay, squeaked in distress. "That was not—"

"And what a prideful and ill-mannered young woman this Elizabeth Bennet was."

Jane carefully hooked her embroidery needle through the fabric and put the embroidery frame down on her lap. She reached out to place a soothing hand on her sister's clasped fist. "Each reader takes away their own interpretation of the story, Emma."

"But—"

Mr. Balfour frowned in confusion. "I do not understand. Have I said something you disagree with?"

"Mr. Darcy was insufferable!" Emma exploded.

"I do not understand."

"The man was arrogant and pompous. He did not politely dance with young ladies at the Meryton assembly, which is the duty of every gentleman of character. And his first proposal was disrespectful of Miss Bennet!"

"Mr. Darcy could not encourage any belief that he would marry a silly chit from the country when he was a man of such import. And I would say it was highly respectful for him to offer for her rather than arrange for her to be his mistress, a role she was eminently more qualified for!"

"It is a comedy and a beautiful love story!"

"It is a tragic drama where a man is brought to his knees because of his failure to delegate women to their proper role!"

"What role is that?"

"Women are purely ornamental. When a man forgets that, he will discover the need to drown himself in drink! In fact, I could do with a drink right now!"

"ORNAMENTAL!" There was no denying that last was a shriek. Emma was so furious, she wanted to fling herself across the carriage to pummel the arrogant idiot with her fists.

A strange expression passed over Mr. Balfour's face. The man looked utterly shocked, subduing Emma's fury. Her behavior had been untoward, but he—

"I apologize."

Her mouth fell open. She had thought her behavior shocked him, but it appeared Mr. Balfour had been inspecting his own and found it wanting for some reason.

"That is something my fa—someone once said to me when I was a young boy. I did not know that it infected my thoughts until I said it out loud. I apologize for such inconsiderate opinions. Miss Davis, Miss Jane, please accept my apology. You are both lovely young ladies, but, more than that, it has been a pleasure to drive with you. You have been wonderful company."

Mr. Balfour reached up and knocked on the roof of the carriage. It gradually drew to a halt. The moment it stopped, he opened the door and hurriedly pushed down the steps to disembark. "If you will excuse me, I believe I shall ride my mount for a few miles."

Leaving the carriage, he bowed politely before shutting the door gently and disappearing from their view.

Emma and Jane turned to stare at each other.

"I think the gentleman hides a dark youth."

Emma groaned at hearing the words. The last thing she needed was to empathize with the devil, who taunted and tempted her so. "Please do not tell me I have to care about his point of view. I … I thought about what you said, and I admit I have grown attracted to him. But, Jane, it is a disaster! The first man to attract my admiration is wholly unattainable. And, worse, we do not even like each other. Now I witness him having a grand revelation about his erroneous thinking. This is already such a pickle!"

Jane broke into a wide grin. "What an adventure this is turning out to be!"

"Jane!"

"Well, I am highly entertained. There is a gentleman who needs a woman's influence in his life. Did we not read in Debrett's that his mother passed away when he was only four or five years old? That is Ethan's age, poor man. What if he did not have an Emma to fill his mother's shoes?"

"Please do not make me sympathize with the impudent man! His ghastly teasing has made me quite nervous about appearing in London society." Now, besides being attracted to the rogue, she was beginning to feel concern over his well-being. Next, she would imagine she was in love with him, that she could save him from his troubles, and her torture would be complete.

Zooks, Jane's sentimental whimsy is going to get me into trouble!

Jane ignored her. "I think I understand why he is so intrigued. There is no more womanly influence anywhere in England than you, Emma! Look at the way you took care of Ethan when Kitty passed away, and you were just a girl. Younger than me at the time!"

"Thank you, but—"

"Though, even I have to admit your conduct these past two days is most unbecoming, so I am not sure how he would know that. Quite unlike your usual even temperament. When will you allow Mr. Balfour to meet the real you?"

Emma shook her head in disbelief. "Never, Jane. There is no future for the two of us. I have admitted my attraction, but if Mr. Balfour is harboring any interest in me, which I very much question, I would merely be a novelty. Even if your observation is correct, the moment a more alluring woman showed up, he would immediately lose interest in the strange little rabbit he had to fetch from Somerset. He is an elegant member of the *beau monde*. A fashionable buck of the great city of London, while I am just an inelegant bluestocking from the country."

"It all sounds so eerily familiar," Jane mused. "Almost as if it were the plot of a grand romance." She glanced pointedly at the book Mr. Balfour had left lying on the opposite bench.

Emma followed her eyes. Picking up the third volume of *Pride and Prejudice*, she humphed in rejection. "Our Season in London is not a work of fiction, Jane. In the real world, such an ill-matched couple could never find their way to a fortunate marriage, you sentimental goose."

CHAPTER 4

"Always maintain a good relationship with a talented modiste. Purchasing fine gowns for a reticent paramour will make her grateful in bed."

July 1804, the late Earl of Saunton to his son, Peregrine, on his ninth birthday after his son came downstairs to discover him engaging in a night of debauchery with the neighbor's wife.

* * *

Under any circumstances, Perry hated to be reminded of his father. The late Earl of Satan had been the very worst roué imaginable. The orgies held at Saunton Park and Balfour Terrace alike … There had been a serious cleaning project when his brother had inherited the title.

Perry had borne witness to every interminable year, month, week, day, and hour of the old man's slow descent into madness because of the pox he had contracted from his indiscriminate sexual relations. His lone parent's eventual death in the year of Perry's seventeenth birthday had been a sweet mercy.

The moment Richard inherited, he had asked Perry what he would like to do now that Richard was the head of the household. Perry had never experienced such utter joy. His tyrannical father had kept him imprisoned in the Saunton —*Satan*—household his entire youth. When most boys went off to Eton or Harrow, including his older brother, their father had confined Perry at home with stern tutors, forcing him to spend far too much time in his parent's depraved company at his constant whim. The old man had found some sort of diabolical entertainment in apprenticing his younger son in his twisted ideal of a proper gentleman, especially when drinking, which was frequent. It had been pure hell.

So when Richard had given him a choice, Perry immediately opted to apply for Oxford, where Richard himself was attending classes. It had been such unprecedented freedom to attend university. He had made friends for the first time, chosen his own activities, acted as the master of his own life rather than the unloved son of a cruel and lascivious nobleman who deserved to be jailed. Perry would always be grateful to Richard for discerning his needs at that time.

Hence, Perry avoided all memories of his father as if the hounds of hell dogged his heels.

The worst part about what had just occurred in the carriage was that it was he who had brought his father into the conversation. The moment those vile thoughts on women left his lips, Perry had realized who was doing his talking for him. It had been shocking. *Was this how Richard felt when he asked me if he was becoming our father?*

Perry shuddered, resolutely staring at the roadway as he guided his gelding ahead of the carriages. He might be a worthless spare with no purpose other than to exist, in the unlikely event that something happened to his older brother, but he hoped he was more of a genuine gentleman than the repellant lord who had sired him.

In the distance, Perry could see the blackish-brown haze that hovered over the city of London, a stark contrast to the lush country and fresh air he currently rode through. Soon they would enter its foul air, much worse because it was late June. A new king sat on the throne, and it was rumored that Queen Caroline might be publicly tried for adultery, so the peerage was trapped in London for the summer.

No human should be forced to be in London when the heat rose and the noxious, soupy air rose with it. Perry would return to the carriage before they reached the city limits, at which time he would offer some explanation for his uncouth behavior. The low opinion of women that he had stated … He shook his head. He knew he needed to make it clear that he did not perceive the young ladies in the despicable manner he had inadvertently voiced. Hearing those words come from his mouth had been thoroughly mortifying. It did not help his shame when he thought about how his late father would have been proud to hear him echo his demeaning opinions.

First, Perry would clear his thoughts, then he would repair the damage.

* * *

THE CARRIAGE CAME to a stop once more. Mr. Balfour reappeared and opened the door to lower the steps and rejoin them. A footman prepared the carriage to continue, then disappeared.

The gentleman looked at Emma across the aisle, preparing to say something. Before he could start, she jumped in.

"Mr. Balfour, I wish to apologize."

His mouth closed in surprise, a slight frown marring his brow. After a few moments of silence, he ventured once more to speak. "I do not understand."

"I have been belligerent since the moment you arrived at Rose Ash Manor. I have had time to think on it, and I wish to apologize for my behavior. What the earl is doing for my sister"—*that sounded unappreciative*—"and me, too, is very generous. And you are quite kind to have delivered his message and to collect us …" Emma paused, then quickly continued. "And your travel plans have been very considerate. The inns you chose have served fine food, and our room last night was most comfortable. I apologize for my rudeness and lack of acknowledgment regarding the trouble you have taken to make our journey a pleasure."

Mr. Balfour stared at her, nonplussed. In fact, her words seemed to be unwelcome. Eventually, he gave a deep sigh.

"It is I who should apologize. I manipulated the situation to coerce your cooperation. And my words earlier were unforgivable, for which I again beg forgiveness. Both you, Miss Davis, and you, Miss Jane, are fine young ladies of quality and intelligence."

Emma bit her lip, uncertain of what to say next. This was deuced awkward.

Jane leaned forward to respond, much to Emma's relief, who was positively tongue-tied at that moment. "Mr. Balfour, we are practically family through our connections to Ethan, and it is my understanding that we will all be residing at Balfour Terrace together. Could we please do away with the formalities? Please call me Jane. Emma?" Jane glanced over at her for her agreement.

Emma nodded. "Please, it will be much easier for us to get to know one another if we relax the formalities. You may call me Emma."

He contemplated their request before answering. "My close family call me Perry."

"Well, Perry, we will forget about your earlier remarks. There has been no disrespect in your conduct, and I believe we can all agree that the discussion grew too heated. People have a tendency to say things they do not truly believe in the heat of anger, and my sister regrets becoming so reactive. It is not her usual manner." Emma frowned in mild confusion at Jane's proclamation. Her young sister was indeed maturing before her very eyes into a peacemaker, and an adept one at that.

Perry leaned forward to take up Jane's hand. Dropping a brief kiss on her fingers, he smiled and sat back in his seat.

"Then a truce has been called?" Emma wanted to be sure she understood this new arrangement.

Perry turned his gaze to hers, a devilish twinkle in his eyes that made her breath catch in her chest. The man was unbearably handsome.

"I would not say that. It will take up to two hours to reach our destination and, as we are all family now, I must communicate how deplorable that shade of mud is for your appearance, Emma."

Emma groaned. "Not this again."

Jane made a humming sound until Emma looked her way. "Perry is correct, Emma. That shade is most unbecoming for a woman of your complexion and coloring. When we reach Balfour Terrace, you must take it off before you disembark so you might meet the earl and his countess in the day dress, which is fractionally more appealing than the carriage dress."

"Not you, too!"

Jane clapped her hands in excitement. "What fun we will have at the modiste! I cannot thank you enough for looking after Ethan so well that the earl has invited us! I am ever so grateful for your maternal skills, Emma."

Perry bit back a laugh. "Three cheers for Emma!"

Emma sank back into the luxurious squabs, folding her arms in resentment. Worse than a condescending Mr. Arrogant was pseudo-family member Perry banding together with her sister to tease Emma about her attire. *Zounds! This is going to be a very long summer!*

* * *

EMMA COWERED in the corner of the carriage, watching out the window in horrified dismay. London was so … huge! There was building after building, streets leading in every direction, and people. So many people. People on horseback, in wagons, on foot. Not to mention liveried servants on elegant carriages and scruffy drivers on dilapidated hackneys.

And then there was the smell. It was wholly indescribable. A combination of rotting river debris, coal smoke, body odor, and urine all combined into a thick soup.

Which did not even begin to describe the noise. Hawkers bellowing, and hooves and wheels hitting the hard cobblestones, blended into a constant cacophony of sound. She wanted to jump from the carriage and run all the way back to Somerset.

Emma's fingers crept into her pocket to finger the tin monkey. It reminded her that at the end of this unexpected journey, she would be reunited with little Ethan, which would make this all worthwhile. She could see for herself how he was faring in his new home and ensure he was not disregarded by Lord Arrogant, parental neglect being customary in the peerage, from her limited knowledge.

"Look at all those shops!" Jane squealed in delight. Emma flinched as a hired hackney careened far too close for comfort.

"Are we observing the same view?" Her sister seemed genuinely delighted, while Emma had never felt as terrified as she did in that moment. "Zooks! Can we go back home?"

Perry cleared his throat to get her attention, while Jane continued to chatter obliviously about the displays in the shop windows. Emma peered at him, her heart beating rapidly from fright. "You will get used to it, Emma."

"Never!"

He contemplated her for a moment. "We will always be in a carriage, and that coat of arms gilded on the side makes people wary of interfering with us. Most of the time, you will be in residence at Balfour Terrace, which is a large town-house in a clean neighborhood. In fact, you will barely leave Mayfair. It will be much better once we pass through to where we are headed."

"Are you comforting me?"

"I am."

"But I thought teasing me was the entertainment."

"We are nearly home. Not much need for entertainment at this moment." Perry grinned, flashing pearly white teeth. He looked positively boyish, and she wanted to leap into his arms and press her lips to his before burying her face into his silky hair to find out what he smelled of. Clean linen, leather, and fresh country air was her guess.

Emma chided her heart into resuming its rhythm. *Think of him as family, you silly chit!*

Without thinking, she reacted how she would if one of her younger brothers was tormenting her. She stuck out her tongue. Perry froze, his gaze riveted to her mouth while he slowly turned a ruddy hue. Even his breathing seemed to be affected.

Emma swiftly drew her tongue back into her mouth and clamped her lips shut. Perry continued to stare while his hand came up to fiddle with his snowy cravat. She felt herself blushing in turn. *What an incredibly childish gesture. He must think I am certifiably insane!*

Suddenly, he turned to look out the window. "See, we are entering Mayfair."

Emma swallowed and followed his gaze. As promised, the buildings were more elegant, the streets appeared cleaner, and the quality of the vehicles noticeably improved. Soon they turned in to a quiet street before coming to a stop in front of a massive townhouse, several bays wide.

Jane, who sat on the side closest to the grand home, giggled into her hands as she craned her neck to look up at its edifice. "My word, it is magnificent. Is this Balfour Terrace?"

"It is." Perry's reply was a little terse. Emma surreptitiously glanced his way. He still appeared very uncomfortable.

Have I gone too far? Likely, no other lady of his acquaintance had ever stuck their tongue out at him.

He must think me the very worst of uncouth women.

Emma discovered she was genuinely upset that he might be repelled by her impropriety. A heavy weight settled on her chest when she observed how he studiously avoided looking in her direction while the footman opened the door and lowered the steps.

Perry disembarked first, holding out a hand to assist Jane down. Emma composed herself, feeling ill at the possibility that she had disgusted the gentleman. She had clearly misjudged their burgeoning relationship.

Instead of turning back to help Emma from the carriage, Perry moved toward the steps with Jane's arm tucked in his. Emma was bereft as a footman held out his hand to assist her. Her eyes prickled from the idea that she might have lost his esteem, albeit a strange esteem. Lud! She found herself completely forlorn at the loss of his playful regard.

Emma fought to regain her composure as she quickly removed the carriage dress and folded it over her arm. Shaking out her skirts, she followed the retreating pair up the steps as the great doors of the townhouse opened.

Agitated, she checked her bonnet that she had donned while they traversed London. Her hands were trembling with anxiety. She was about to meet Lord Arrogant himself, and Perry and her sister had left her behind after poking fun at her apparel.

And Perry is appalled by my conduct! Emma did not think it possible to feel more self-conscious than she did at that moment.

She followed them into the house, finding it difficult to see in the interior as her eyes adjusted from the bright sunlight.

Inside, she saw a gentleman who looked very much like Perry giving a large, friendly smile as he bowed over Jane's hand. "Miss Emma Davis, such a privilege!"

Jane giggled in delight as she curtsied. "I am not Emma, my lord. I am her sister, Jane Davis. Emma is behind me."

His lordship straightened, his face briefly somber as he turned to find Emma. He looked perplexed as his eyes ran over her.

The earl was disappointed! Emma closed her eyes for a second, swallowing the lump in her throat.

She had repelled Perry with her immaturity, and now the earl was disappointed in her appearance. She clasped her hands to disguise their trembling.

"My lord" was all she could get out of her mouth as she sank into a curtsy. She had only just arrived, and she was already a failure. *Do not cry, Emma! Do not cry!*

* * *

After they completed introductions, with Emma being uncharacteristically reserved, Richard turned a questioning glare to his brother. Perry tilted his head to acknowledge they would discuss the matter momentarily. First, he needed to ensure the young ladies were shown to their rooms so they might bathe and change into clean clothes.

Speaking to the family butler, Perry made arrangements, ensuring he kept his eyes averted from Emma lest he leap on her like a primitive barbarian to rip the clothes off her body before feasting on her soft skin. He had been struggling to breathe since the moment she had stuck out her tongue, rampant lust surging through him in the manner of an invading army overpowering and laying waste to his defenses. Her unexpected appearance sans mud-colored armor had further intensified his craving. There was no evidence that he was any sort of gentleman, and he was desperate to quell his desire. It was a life-and-death struggle to maintain a polite calm. Gravitating to the affable Jane had been his feeble attempt to center his world, which had just turned upside down.

Perry had never experienced such an unmanageable urge in his nearly twenty-five years on this earth.

The Davises were dispatched to their rooms, and with great relief, Perry made for Richard's study where he poured himself a strong drink before settling into one of the plump armchairs covered in a cheerful ivory fabric embroidered with red, gold, and green floral designs that perfectly complemented the bottle-green silk wall coverings.

Look at me, cataloging the decor! My unmanning is complete!

Richard entered the study and shut the door behind him before crossing to his desk to take a seat. "Why are there two Davis girls?"

"Emma did not want to come. I had to manipulate her

agreement by stating you had extended the invitation to both of them."

Richard sighed, sinking his head into his hands. "Let me guess. Two wardrobes, two dowries."

"You make it sound like you are on the road to debtors' prison."

"Of course not! But one of the tricks to building up wealth is to not squander it."

"Stuff and nonsense! It is a pittance for you."

"You may recall with all the recent amends I have made to the young women I wronged in my depraved past that there have been quite a few pittances being handed out."

"Are you in financial straits, then?"

Richard chuckled. "No, the finances are fine. Fortunately, I am saving a fortune on gifts and modiste bills now that I am enamored with only one woman."

"There you go. You are practically saving money by getting married and doing your little crusade of amends."

"I would ask why you did not send me a message ahead of your arrival to inform me of the change? Radcliffe must prepare a second room for the young woman. He is most put out, I can tell."

"What? Spoil the fun of seeing your face when the additional expense was revealed? You should know me better than that, brother. And you cannot tell if Radcliffe is put out. He is the most unflappable butler in Mayfair."

Richard shook his head. "You are such an arse, Perry."

Perry looked down into the amber of his drink, considering his subsiding primal urges to devour the peculiar Emma whom everyone had been talking about these past two months. "I am what I am."

Perhaps he should discuss his crisis of lust with Richard? No, he was not accustomed to sharing things, and it was too shameful.

"Do we know what the young ladies need to prepare for the Season? My man of business can organize tutors, and the sooner we set him to the task, the better."

Perry mused, feeling regretful that his time with Emma had ended. She made him feel things he had never felt before. The darkness of his soul felt just a little less heavy in her presence. He had been smiling more—a genuine smile, not the glib curvature of his lips that he had mastered for his friends and paramours. A few times he had even felt, dare he say, cheerful? When he walked out of the townhouse to seek his fellow spares and heirs this afternoon, it might be days before he saw her again. Why did that prospect make him feel so depressed?

"I can save you the funds, now that you have two young ladies to provide for. I shall tutor them." Perry's eyes widened as he stared into his drink. What the blazes had he just said? He had already calculated a retreat from the young woman. Now he was offering his services as a tutor?

Looking up, intending to retract his offer, he found Richard staring at him in astonishment. "I am sorry. Did you just offer to tutor two young women with dancing and finishing lessons?"

Perry frowned, preparing to deny his earlier statement.

"Perry, this is wonderful! You are finally taking Sophia's advice to involve yourself in a project! And no one is more astute at navigating the *ton* than you. The young ladies are most fortunate."

Shaking his head, Perry rose to his feet. "No, I did not think it through. I am far too busy to undertake such a responsibility. Set Johnson to hiring the tutors you mentioned!"

Richard walked over to grab him by the shoulders. "Nonsense, this is inspired! You studied all those etiquette books while you were at university, so you are an expert."

"I did that to perfect the art of seduction. You would not want a rogue around the young ladies, would you?"

Richard pulled a face of dissent. "We both know you have no interest in innocent young misses. Not with the parson's noose an ever-present threat. I have no concerns."

Perry scrambled for a counterargument. Richard did not know what a threat he posed for one particular innocent miss. He must stay away from Emma, or he could not predict what might transpire if he found himself alone with the disheveled temptress.

CHAPTER 5

"You are a mere spare! Why would I waste coin on Eton for you?"

July 1805, the late Earl of Saunton to his son, Peregrine, on his tenth birthday after his son requested to join his older brother away at school.

* * *

Emma had composed herself by the time the hawkish butler showed them into a grand bedchamber where servants scurried back and forth with hot water.

"This is your room, Miss Davis. We are preparing the one next door for your sister, but we thought you would like to refresh after your long journey, so I trust you are willing to share this room for an hour or two?"

She inclined her head. "Of course. Thank you, Mr. Radcliffe."

The butler smiled infinitesimally, his eyes crinkling slightly. "You are welcome, Miss Davis. I do not wish to be presumptuous, but Lord Saunton mentioned I should assist with preparing you for high society when possible. It is customary to call a butler by just his last name."

"Oh! Is that not what I did?"

"Just Radcliffe, no mister."

Emma was nonplussed. "Truly? Why?"

"I could not say. Tradition, I suppose."

"I see. Thank you … Radcliffe."

"My pleasure, Miss Davis. We are all very pleased to host you. Master Ethan will be most excited when he learns you are here."

"Is he expecting me?"

"No, his lordship wanted to surprise him. Once you are ready, I will show you and Miss Jane to his lordship's study so Master Ethan can be brought down."

Emma cheered up at the thought of seeing her little cousin.

"If that is all, I shall leave you to it. We placed tea and light refreshment on the table over there. Once again, I apologize for the inconvenience that you must share the room briefly." Radcliffe pointed out a silver service before bowing to leave. He stood at the door awaiting the servants' exit and then departed the room to leave the two girls alone with a maid who was to assist them.

Emma walked farther into the bedroom, which was as large as the drawing room of Rose Ash Manor.

"This is rather stately, is it not, Jane?"

Jane ignored her. She was standing in front of a large carved wardrobe with her mouth hanging open. "This is as large as our gardening shed! His lordship must have given you one of his most luxurious guest rooms!"

The maid coughed into her hand discreetly. "It is a family room, miss."

Jane turned to Emma with raised eyebrows. "A family room! We are in the family wing in the townhouse of the

Earl of Saunton. He has practically declared us to be his relations, Emma! What an honor!"

"Miss, can I help you undress? While the water is still warm?" The maid waved her hand toward the two copper tubs in front of the fireplace.

It was about thirty minutes later that both sisters stood bathed and dressed in their chemises when there was a knock on the door. A moment later, the door opened and an elegant noblewoman entered along with the lady's maid who had accompanied them on their journey behind her.

"Emma, Jane, I am so pleased to finally meet you. I am Sophia, the earl's wife."

Both Emma and Jane sank into a curtsy, Emma feeling silly doing so only half dressed. "My lady," they intoned politely.

"Nonsense! You are to call me Sophia. We are practically family. I am ever so grateful that you are here to assist us with Ethan, so there will be no ceremony within the walls of our home."

Emma hesitated, then nodded her head. The countess was charming, with her red-blonde hair artfully coifed and her blue eyes sparkling. She was only two or three years older than Emma, and she possessed a warm smile that she was flashing at that moment.

"We appreciate the offer of sponsorship … Sophia."

"I have brought Miss Adèle Toussaint to assist you to dress, so we may go downstairs to meet with the earl." The countess gestured to the lady's maid. "Miss Toussaint is the very best lady's maid in London. We will provide you with your own abigail to assist you for the remainder of the Season. Now, which one of you is Emma?"

* * *

EMMA AND JANE followed the countess down the main staircase and into the entry hall. They each wore their best gown, and Emma was astonished how Miss Toussaint had tamed her curls using some sort of French hair tonic. Bouncy and light, her curls were perfectly formed, which delighted her because she needed a confidence boost after her nerve-racking arrival when the earl had appeared to be displeased with her, and Perry had avoided all contact. She had just arrived in London, and already she was failing at this visit to high society.

Feeling happy that her hair was not the customary mess, even if her gown was not the most elegant, she paused in the hall to look about in amazement. It was a revelation, with its shining black-and-white checkered marble floor, elegant antique furniture carved from dark hardwood, and Italian frescos on the ceiling of Greek gods cavorting on Mount Olympus. She had been too distracted to notice the grandeur when she had first entered, but now she was awed. The contents of the room were worth more than Rose Ash Manor and the entirety of its estate. Biting her lip, she acknowledged her doubts had returned. How could she ever possibly fit in to this magnificent life? Jane was beauty and grace, while she was … Emma. Down-to-earth, loyal, and undeniably clumsy.

She had already alienated Perry. How long could it possibly take to upset the earl or Sophia? Her heart sank. Stepping lively to catch up to the countess and Jane, who were entering a corridor across the hall, she chased after them, cursing her shorter legs as the taller women easily ate up the distance of the passage beyond.

The countess came to a stop in front of a door, rapping her knuckles on it. Emma came huffing up behind them, taking a moment to ease her breathing and steady her nerves while from inside the earl called for them to enter.

Sophia opened the door and entered, along with Jane. Drawing a calming breath, Emma followed them in, then halted when she saw Perry sitting in an armchair near the fireplace. He immediately averted his face, rising to leave the room while the earl came forward to greet them. Emma's breath caught painfully in her chest.

He is still offended by my crass behavior in the carriage! The tears that had threatened earlier rose back up to prickle her eyes while a heat rose over her cheeks to leave her feeling steamy and gauche as her eyes followed his exit.

"Perry, wait a moment, please!" the earl commanded. Perry stopped at the door, clearly reluctant.

"Miss Jane, would you accompany Perry to the drawing room where Ethan will come down to meet with us? I wish to have a word with Miss Davis."

Jane tilted her head graciously. "With pleasure, my lord."

"My wife has recommended we do away with the formalities. Ethan is my son, and you are Ethan's kin. For all intents and purposes, we are extended family, so please call me Richard."

Jane curtsied. "Please do me the same honor. Jane is much simpler, I think?"

The earl smiled, his emerald eyes warmed with pleasure. "It will be my honor, Jane." He gave a brief bow, and Emma watched as Perry and Jane left the room. The earl led Emma to the seating area, and all three of them took a seat on the grouped armchairs. Sophia was the height of sophistication, sitting primly in her indigo day gown. It prompted Emma to take note of how she herself was sitting. She fidgeted into an awkward position, doing her best to look ladylike as she folded her hands into her lap to emulate the countess.

"I am ever so grateful that you have come, Emma."

Emma realized the earl was addressing her. She turned her gaze to where he sat, firmly setting her thoughts aside.

Perry's sudden disaffection was inconsequential, and she needed to put it from her mind.

"It is my pleasure to assist … Richard."

"Not Lord Arrogant, then?"

Emma choked. Searching her thoughts, she tried to recall what she had just said. Sophia bit back a laugh, raising her hand to her mouth as if to physically prevent it from escaping.

Richard grinned. "My brother has informed me you did not wish to visit. He mentioned your sobriquet for me, which I think my wife will tease me with later. The countess has already taken me to task for how I handled the matter with Ethan, so I am aware that the moniker is deserved."

Emma sought for words. Her embarrassment was complete. She had never felt so mortified. The interplay between her and Perry—she had thought it was a private interaction. Despite her pique at the time, she had grown to treasure their debates together, but Perry had apparently used it as anecdotal amusement to inform his brother of her conduct.

"… we shall cooperate to make Ethan settle in better here in our home. I know we may not have much time because such lovely ladies as yourself and your sister will be snapped up by the discerning gentlemen of London in no time."

Her eyes widened in disbelief as she listened to the earl mock her. Lovely lady? Snapped up by discerning gentlemen? The earl thought she was a fool to be coddled! The lump in her throat grew, and then, to her great shame, Emma reached her limit. She burst into tears.

* * *

Perry came back down the hall to find Richard leaning against the closed door of his study. His brother had his arms folded and was staring at the floor in scowling bemusement.

"What is this? I thought you were consulting with Emma about how to deal with Ethan so we could inform him she was here?"

"I made her cry!"

Perry stiffened in alarm. "What did you do?"

Richard looked at him in consternation, making Perry realize he had barked the last, which was quite out of character. But if his brother had insulted Emma, he would happily set him straight—with his fists.

"I honestly do not know. One moment, I was welcoming her to our home, and the next, she burst into tears! Sophia shooed me out so she might address the situation. So, I have been booted from my own study to stand by like a damn footman. Just further evidence that I have no skills when it comes to dealing with family matters."

Perry took a deep breath, stretching his neck to ease the tension that had hit him at the news that Emma was distressed. "You did fine by me when I needed you. It has been a long journey, and the young lady was adamant that she did not belong in London. Tell me what you said, exactly?"

"I was telling her how grateful we were that she had come to assist us with Ethan. Then I mentioned we would work together to help him settle in ..." Richard looked pensive.

"And what else?"

"Then I think I mentioned she would likely not be with us long because a lovely lady such as herself would be married off before long."

Perry slumped against the wall next to his brother. "Emma suffers from the delusion that she is unattractive. A long journey coupled with my teasing over the last couple of days, she likely thought you were condescending to her about her appearance."

Richard frowned. He opened his mouth to say something and then closed it again, clearly trying to work through many thoughts. Eventually, he tried again. "I have so many questions."

"As do I. I expect you to straighten this out and make the young lady feel welcome."

"How can she think she is not comely? With that ebony hair and the flawless skin?"

"Not to mention those fierce black eyes," Perry agreed.

Richard shot him a look. Perry averted his gaze. His equilibrium had not quite returned to its normal state. When Emma had entered the study earlier, he had not sufficiently recovered from his earlier flare of lust to acknowledge her entry, and now he realized how he had deserted her when they had arrived at Balfour Terrace. Did that play a role in her current flusteration? He had promised she would be well taken care of and then left her standing on the roadway to make her own way inside because of his own discomposure.

After a pause, Richard continued. "You have known the young lady for two nights and two days, by my count. How do you know what is going through her mind?"

Perry straightened up. "I left Jane unaccompanied. I should return."

"Perry?"

He sighed, relenting. "She is not difficult to read. She is quite a straightforward young woman. Emma is … direct. Simple. Intelligent, but … candid." Perry stopped. He was unsure how to explain. Emma was … Emma. And he would knock down his own brother if he hurt the girl in any way. Nothing must ruin her pure, simple perfection. However, the ridiculous clothing definitely needed to go.

* * *

Sophia was seated on the low table between the armchairs, her hand covering Emma's as she struggled to regain her equanimity.

"I assure you that the earl was not condescending your appearance, Emma. You are utterly lovely! The issues you mention are easily fixed with the right modiste and a good abigail to dress your hair. You cannot possibly think my appearance is easy? Without Adèle to dress my hair, I would be a mess myself. In fact, while she was away, I barely left the townhouse. I do not know how to style my hair in the latest fashions. I simply point at a fashion plate, and she does her magic."

"I have no knack for this. I would not even know which fashion plate to point at. Jane is artful with such things, but not I."

"Emma, it is all a matter of practice. I am certain that Jane has been reading fashion publications and practicing styling herself in that manner. While you were teaching our dear little boy how to read and play chess! Now that you have time to practice, you will attain skill in these endeavors."

"You really think so?"

"I do."

Emma hiccupped as her tears dried. "I was sure the earl was mocking me like Perry used to do."

Sophie cocked her head, a question written on her delicate features when she arched a red-blonde eyebrow. "Used to?"

"Until I upset him. Now he will no longer look at me."

Sophia was thoughtful for a moment. "This has been a sudden and drastic change in circumstances, has it not?"

Emma nodded. "I am quite out of sorts. I do not belong here. Embarking on a Season is laughable. My sister is elegance and grace. I know she will find an eligible young man. I agreed to come for her sake. But there will be no eligible men for me."

"Why do you say that?"

"I have not been courted as the daughter of a tenant farmer in Derby. Nor has any young man expressed interest in me as the daughter of a landowner in Somerset after the earl's generous gift of the estate. If I have failed there, there is no reason to believe I will turn any heads here in London, where my lack of sophistication will be more obvious."

Sophia glanced down to pick at her gown with fidgety fingers, her cheeks pink with a slight blush. "Emma, I must confess that I partook in three Seasons without being courted. I even began my fourth before the earl staked his claim two months ago and married me. I was destined to be a spinster. I reveled in that fact. It is not about turning the heads of hordes of gentlemen. It is about finding the right partner to complete your life. Richard is"—the countess sought for the right word—"perfection. But only for me. He was exactly what I needed at the very moment I needed it. My advice is not to worry about what other people think and to search for the right partner who fulfills your unique needs."

Emma stared at her hands clasped in her lap. "You were on your fourth Season?"

Sophia made a sound of assent.

"And the earl was the very first man to court you?"

"Correct."

Emma drew a deep breath and looked up into Sophia's stormy blue eyes. "I would like to find the right gentleman."

Sophia smiled gently, squeezing Emma's hand beneath her own. "And so you shall."

Emma gave a tremulous smile. She felt like a right ninny for her emotional outburst, but she was glad they had talked.

The countess was not what she had expected, and she liked the young woman very much. "I am quite embarrassed."

Sophia shook her head in dismissal. "Pish! We are all family here, and it is our fault you are so out of sorts."

Emma blew a sigh of relief. The countess squeezed her hand again in encouragement as they sat in companionable silence and Emma relaxed.

"Emma, if I may ask a question?" Sophia waited for her agreement. "You said Perry used to mock you. What did you mean?"

Blushing, Emma once again dropped her gaze.

"We were sparring for the last couple of days, and we had just agreed that, for all intents and purposes, we are all family, so we should relax the proprieties. Then he teased me about something and … I stuck my tongue out at him. It was deplorable behavior on my part."

Sophia cleared her throat. "I beg your pardon, but I do not understand what the problem is?"

Emma lifted her hand to rub her face in distress. "Well, he must have been offended by my conduct because he is quite unfriendly now."

"Emma?"

She looked up at Sophia.

"Perry may possess the glib manners of the *ton*, but he only behaves that way for his own benefit. It is a masquerade. He does not care a whit about proper behavior, from my experience. He is merely cautious about how he is perceived by others, but etiquette is not personally important to him. Further, I find he is quite playful with his family, so I do not see him being repelled by some lively horseplay. Could you explain what you mean? What happened, exactly?"

"I stuck my tongue out at him. He stared at me most oddly, turned beet red, and seemed to have a mild apoplexy, in that he could not breathe properly. Since then, he has avoided looking at me in the most obvious manner …" The threat of tears returned, as Emma's voice grew thick with repressed emotion. "I regret what I did because … I thought we had a rapport of sorts, and now he knows I am the most uncouth of women."

The countess twisted her lips. It looked like she was repressing a smile, which Emma thought was a peculiar reaction to her troubles. She waited for the other woman to say something, but it took several moments for the countess to eventually speak. "My dear Emma, I assure you that Perry is not offended. In fact, I am quite certain he will be returning to your side soon and you will find the matter has been forgotten, and the teasing has fully resumed."

Sophia stood up in a swoosh of skirts, mumbling as if talking out loud to herself while she moved to let the earl back into his study. It sounded like she said, "And if he does not do so on his own determinism, I will be meddling because Perry has finally found himself an interest, it would seem."

When the door opened, the earl stumbled back into the room before righting himself. He looked about before posing a question. "Are we all right, then? Everything sorted? Why does Emma appear to still be upset?"

"It is nothing that a few moments to orient herself will not mend. Come and finish saying your piece to Emma so we can let Ethan know she is here."

The earl closed the door, and the couple returned to their seats.

"I apologize for any insensitivity on my part, Emma." The earl uncomfortably fiddled with his cravat. "My brother explained what I did, and I think I understand now. Please be assured that I truly believe you are a lovely young woman and that we have several gentlemen in mind to introduce you to once you are feeling adequately prepared."

The countess beamed. "There is no rush. Take all the time you need to prepare. In fact, I insist that Perry himself assist the young ladies, Richard."

Richard glanced at his wife with a perplexed expression in his emerald eyes, a familial trait in that Ethan, Perry, and the earl all possessed the same riveting shade. Although it was only Perry who made her want to grab him by the lapels to press her face to his and breathe deeply to discover his scent.

"That is what he said. Before he retracted his offer. Perry seems quite invested in what happens with Emma, for some reason I cannot fathom."

Sophia turned to her. "You see, Emma. Perry is quite satisfied to spend time in your company. Everything will be as usual momentarily, dear."

Emma could not deny that she sincerely hoped that the countess was correct. She suspected this feeling of loss would only dissipate after Perry made some jest about her attire or teased her about her etiquette. How humbling to discover she had been enjoying his attentions, as infuriating as his barbs could be.

CHAPTER 6

"Stewards exist to take care of the estates. Bankers exist to provide an estate owner with concerns. Drink exists to make us forget our concerns. But none of this signifies to you because you are my spare, so you exist to entertain me. Drink up."

July 1806, the late Earl of Saunton to his son, Peregrine, on his eleventh birthday after his son posed a question about the tenants of Saunton Park.

* * *

The entire family, Emma and Jane included, gathered in a large, tasteful drawing room decorated in hues of burgundy and navy. An intricate Persian rug graced the floor, surrounded by an eclectic mix of armchairs, while what appeared to be gas lights cast their glow into the shadows of the cozy room. Through the paned glass of the sash windows, Emma could see a summer garden that she was eager to visit.

As Sophia had predicted, Perry had been quite attentive

since she had entered the room. His face had reflected concern as she had taken her seat, and he had leaned over to question her in a solicitous voice.

"Have you been taken care of, Emma? Do you need anything?"

It was not quite his sardonic demeanor, but at least he was no longer avoiding her. In fact, he had thrown her several glances since her arrival, which had cheered her up immensely.

Feeling more her usual self, she looked around the room and straightened in pleasure to see a table with a fine chess set laid out near the fireplace, set up and ready for a match. Perry followed her gaze. "It is for Ethan, who will come down expecting to play with each one of us in turn. Hopefully, the surprise of your visit will get me out of this evening's game."

"You truly play with him?"

"Did you think I was making sport? The little tyrant will release none of us without a match for the day. I take it you are the one who taught him to love it so?"

Emma bobbed her head. "I love playing chess. I have studied many texts on the subject, but Ethan's skills were still rudimentary when he left us in Derby."

"His skills are advancing quickly with all the time he has spent playing. You will be most impressed when he convinces you to play before the end of the night."

"I am so pleased. I must say, he appears to be receiving more attention than I expected in a noble household. It is quite a relief."

Perry snorted. "The entire household revolves around Master Ethan. Even with a second child on the way, I think Ethan will always take first place."

Emma and Jane both clapped their hands over their mouths in joy. "The countess is with child?"

"Good heavens! Ladies and their fascination with babies! Yes, there is a babe on the way. Sophia and Ethan discuss baby names after they play for the evening. He is excited to be getting a younger brother or sister. I have to hear all about it during our own match."

Emma dropped her hands back into her lap to smile at Perry. "You are a good uncle, Perry."

He straightened in his chair, a nonplussed air about him, as he turned his gaze from the chess set back to Emma. "Why do you say that?"

"You spend time with him. In between your pursuits. That is what a good uncle does."

"How do you know that is a good thing? What if I am a bad influence on the boy?"

Emma shrugged. "That seems unlikely. You are intelligent and well-versed in etiquette. I am sure you are patient and playful with him. That is what a good uncle is."

He seemed embarrassed but pleased at her proclamation, relaxing back into his chair to await Ethan's arrival.

At that moment, the door opened and all heads turned to watch as a young nursemaid walked in holding the hand of the adorable little boy. Dressed in short breeches and a coat, it startled Emma to see him looking so dapper. The sable waves framing his face shone in the light, and his green eyes widened to find so many people awaiting him, but Emma noted the deep shadows under his eyes. His recent nocturnal habits were clearly wearing him down.

Looking around, Ethan inventoried the inhabitants of the room before finding Emma in her chair near the window. His face lit up.

"Emma!" He pulled his hand from that of his nursemaid and came flying across the room. Emma dropped onto her knees to catch him in her arms in a close embrace, her eyes moistening with tears to feel his little form pressed against her once more.

"Ethan, you look so handsome!"

"What are you doing here?" He pulled back to look at her in awe.

"Your papa said that you needed me, so I came to visit."

Ethan buried his face in her shoulder, his little arms around her neck. "I am so happy you are here! I missed you so much!"

"I missed you, too." Letting him go, she brushed the tears from her eyes and raised herself to reseat on the chair. Then she leaned down to scoop him up to place him on her knee. "Now explain why you have been so desperate to see me? You have all these new relations to play chess with, a nursemaid to care for you, and a governess teaching you lessons. It does not sound like you have any time to miss me?"

Ethan looked around at the others in the room before leaning forward to whisper in her ear, "They all get up so late. It is not like the country. I miss feeding the animals with you in the mornings."

Emma gave him a quick embrace before whispering back, "What about your governess and your nanny? Do they not wake with you early in the morning?"

"Yes, Daisy does, but we do not go feed the animals. There is so many people here. And I miss feeding the horses and playing with the dogs. It is different in *Lun-den*."

"Who is Daisy?"

Ethan pointed a little finger toward the nursemaid, who had brought him into the room. The young woman looked at them, a concerned expression on her wide, friendly face. Emma smiled briefly at her before turning back to Ethan. "Morning with you was an enjoyable time of the day. Now that I live in Somerset, I no longer feed the horses myself. Shall we go visit the stables now? Have you been there?"

He shook his head. "They are all so nice. I did not want to *com-puh-lain*."

"Silly goose! They are your family now, and your papa wants what is best for you. We will go to the stables now to explore, shall we?"

Ethan grinned. "I knew you could fix it."

Emma looked up to find the earl observing them, worry etched on his face. Raising her voice to normal volume, she addressed him directly. "I think a visit to the stables would be an excellent adventure. Will that be acceptable, Richard?"

He shot her a questioning look, but stood up. "I would love to visit the stables. Would everyone like to join us?"

The countess grinned. "I think we can all enjoy a walk around the gardens and a visit to the mews."

Rising, she walked over to the door in the corner that led out to the gardens. Soon, the room emptied, with the nursemaid bringing up the rear as Emma led Ethan after their party. The earl hung back, waiting for the two of them to reach him before falling in step with them. As they made their way across the lawn to the mews, he glanced down at his son. "Do you like the stables, Ethan?"

"I do, Papa. Emma promised me I could start riding just before I left the farm."

"Would you like me to teach you?"

Ethan straightened up, his little chest puffing out with pride. "You want to teach me?"

"It sounds very exciting." He winked at Emma before continuing. "The only problem is that we would have to get a good night's sleep in order to go out so early. I prefer to ride at dawn."

Ethan's face lit up like a candle. "At *sun-na-rise*? I would love that! I promise to stay in bed. Can we go tomorrow morning?"

"I will take you for a morning ride in the park, and then

we will see about teaching you to ride. But we can only go if you sleep tonight."

Ethan was ecstatic, pulling Emma's hand to catch up to the party that had entered the door into the mews. Soon they had oats in hand and Emma clutched the boy on her hip so that he might raise his hand to feed the first horse in the row. The earl refilled his little hand, and they approached the second horse while Ethan chattered about how large they were and how excited he was to ride with his papa.

PERRY WATCHED as Emma and his brother walked to each occupied stall and fed the mounts with his nephew. Observing the joy on her face while she chattered with the boy pulled at old forgotten memories he had long since buried.

Memories of soft embraces, the fragrance of gardenias, and his mother's calm presence as she held him to her in the manner Emma now held Ethan. How his mother used to talk to him about the flowers in the garden. How he would pick one in bloom which she would tuck into her blonde hair, bestowing a smile of gratitude. He had been a few months older than Ethan when those embraces ended and his mother abruptly disappeared. Many weeks later, his father had coldly informed him that his mother was dead. That devastated little boy still lingered in him. Those times in the garden were the last moments he had felt happy, had felt that life held joy and promise.

As always, the memory brought back his fifteenth year when he had found his vile father with the young maiden from the village, and any last vestiges of innocence he possessed had been destroyed. Perry pushed the memory back. The pain associated with it was still so fresh it could have happened yesterday.

Finally, they returned to the drawing room, and Richard sat down at the chess table for his daily chess game with his son. Emma and Perry were seated together once more across the room, observing them from afar.

"You are so patient with him," Perry murmured.

Emma was watching Ethan, her face lit with warm appreciation. "I could be nothing other than patient with the dear boy."

"Have you always spent so much time with him?"

Emma shrugged. After a moment, she spoke, peering into the fireplace as if perceiving the past in its swept hearth. "When Ethan was a babe, he did not speak. Not one word. My parents despaired he might be mute or impaired intellectually, but I knew better. He was watching and learning. Ethan likes to do things right, and I knew that when he was ready to speak, he would speak. So I spent time with him and played games with him whenever I could. And I spoke to him like he was a person. We had many one-sided conversations where I talked and he listened to me. One day, after his second birthday, he finally spoke. Not one word like Mama, or Emma, or anything else a babe would say. Nay, he spoke a full sentence to me. He asked me if he could have an apple. He had a little trouble enunciating the words, but he spoke the entire sentence. Yes, he is brilliant, but one has to be patient and tolerant with him or you miss all of his uniqueness."

Perry gave a heavy sigh. "I have not been very patient with you, have I, Emma?"

"No. You have not."

"Will you allow me to start afresh?"

She smiled gently as she turned her gaze back to Perry. "I believe I can be tolerant of your past behavior if you show a concerted effort to improve our relations. The countess informs me you are to tutor us. I hope you know how much of a challenge you are taking on with me. I am not skilled in social graces."

"It is not as difficult as all that. I would appreciate a fresh start, so I apologize for being sarcastic to you as you learn to navigate this new world you enter. I will endeavor to assist you in moving forward rather than be judgmental."

"That is all I can ask of you, Perry."

He smiled. For a moment, he contemplated a future with a woman like Emma at his side before he recalled that he—a worthless spare with nothing but time and an allowance provided at his brother's benevolence—had nothing to offer her. Emma could do much better than a reprobate like him.

He needed to return to his real life. A healthy dose of reality was in order before he imagined he could ever be worthy of this woman's esteem. He sat forward in his chair, forcing the words from his mouth before he wound up at dinner with the family and thinking he had a place in this world of shared appreciation.

"Well, I must be off. I am meeting my friends, so I will leave you to your time with Ethan."

Perry withdrew from the room, wondering if he had imagined the brief look of disappointment that flashed across her face. The truth was, he would much rather spend the evening with Emma, but he needed to get out of the way so that she could find an eligible young man worthy of her. *If only I had anything to offer her.* He could imagine it would be easy to commit to gazing on her pleasing countenance when he awoke every morn for the rest of his life, but that was not a future he could ever hope to achieve for himself.

* * *

EMMA WATCHED Perry leave with regret. For the first time since they met, they had fallen into companionable discussion, which she had enjoyed more than she cared to admit. Her fondness for him was growing despite her decision to avoid any attachment. The relief that the countess had been correct, that he had gravitated back to her side, was a pleasant surprise.

How had Sophia so accurately predicted what would happen? Emma turned to observe her watching the game between her husband and her adopted son. Sensing Emma's gaze, she looked up and winked before turning back to the game.

Emma smiled and sipped on the cup of tea that had been handed to her on their return to their drawing room. For the first time in two days, she relaxed while Jane chattered to her about how exciting it was to visit London. The countess seemed to think she could manage her change in circumstances, and Perry had reassured her that she would have the full support of the family. She was still astonished at what the earl had revealed. Perry had offered to tutor them! The earl said he had retracted the offer, but it did not signify in Emma's mind. He had volunteered his time, and that was what counted.

The evening progressed at a leisurely pace. They enjoyed a fine dinner, just the four of them—Emma and Jane, along with the earl and countess. After dinner, they had played cards and grown to know each other better. The young ladies had retired much later than they were accustomed to. Both had been yawning when they bade each other goodnight. Emma had tumbled into her bed as soon as the maid had assisted her out of her gown and into a night rail.

For once, she had fallen straight to sleep. Until she had woken up with a start. Somewhere in the distance, she could hear a clock declare midnight. Turning over, she attempted to resume the deep sleep she had been engaged in moments before.

When the clock announced half past the hour, she finally gave up. She briefly considered knocking on Jane's door to see if she was awake before scoffing. The Davis family were well aware that once Jane laid her head on a pillow, she would fall asleep for as long as she saw fit and then awaken cheery and bright-eyed, no matter what the circumstances.

Slipping out of bed, Emma lit an oil lamp in the low light of the banked fire. The night had turned chilly, with rain and gusting, and the maid had insisted it be lit before she had left for the night. Now Emma was grateful as it helped her to light the lamp. She pulled on her thick wrapper and a pair of slippers and set off to find a way to the lower level where the library was situated.

It took fifteen minutes to locate the lower floor and to try various doors. Finally, a footman had appeared, presumably to resume his duties as a sentry in the entry hall. The earl had mentioned that they were maintaining vigorous security due to some sort of incident a few weeks earlier, and Emma noted that the footman had a burly build and a slightly disheveled appearance which implied that he might not be a footman by calling. He had shown her to the library, where it was pure heaven to be surrounded by so many diverse books. Long and narrow, the room was filled with tables and seating, and it was well-lit with flickering wall sconces that had not yet been extinguished for the night.

Emma wandered around, orienting herself to how the shelves were organized. When she discovered a shelf of recent political speeches, she was ecstatic. Quickly leafing through them, she found precisely what she was looking for and took a book with her to the sofa by the fireplace. Settling down into a comfortable position, she kicked off her slippers and drew her feet under the edge of her wrapper, opening the book to the desired page and beginning to read.

A noise disturbed her, her eyes flying open as she looked round and tried to figure out where she was. It took a few blurry moments to realize that she had fallen asleep in the library while reading the book that was now closed and resting on her belly. Emma sat up and rubbed her eyes.

That was when she heard the sound again. Quickly standing up, she checked that her wrapper was securely tied just as three men stumbled into the room, shutting the door behind them with a clumsy bang.

She found Perry in the center, looking worse for wear. "Have you been drinking?"

Perry's gaze was unfocused when his eyes found hers across the room. "Emma."

"Indeed. A better question would be—have you been over-drinking?"

"Jiss a tipple or two," he responded.

"Your friend looks like he had more than two tipples." She jerked her head toward the tall companion with chestnut hair who was hugging the wall as if he was afraid he was going to topple off of it.

"This is Brendan Ridley, a friend of the earl and I from Richard'sssh Eton daysss." Perry waved in his general direction. "He is the shon of a baron from Shhhomerset, you know. You are practically neighborsss!"

Emma scowled. Was this what gentlemen did in London? Drink so much liquor, they could barely stand on their own two feet. Resentfully, she dipped into a curtsy. "Pleased to meet you, Mr. Ridley."

"Whazat? Whoz talking to me?" the young man responded, looking about as if to try to find the source.

Perry ignored all of it to wave at the other gentleman.

"And thississ Lord Julius Trafford, oldesht sson of Earl of Shhtirling up north."

Emma flicked her eyes in the direction of Trafford. A tall, wiry dandy with a tuft of wheat-colored hair at his crown, while the close-cropped hair on the sides was a darker shade of chocolate brown to create a startling contrast. He seemed less inebriated than the other two as he unashamedly stared at her bosom. Her hands raised to verify once again that the wrapper was properly tied. With the night rail and thickness of the wrapper, she was as good as dressed, she assured herself. Trafford could see nothing more than what she would reveal in a day gown and carriage dress.

Emma pointedly did not curtsy or greet the *gentleman*, who eyed her like she was a harlot from a street corner, but instead watched as Perry weaved toward the drink cabinet in the corner of the library. She supposed she should collect her lamp and leave. Turning to the end table to find the lamp, she reached out her hand before she sensed a presence at her side. Flinching, she glanced up to find Trafford had silently crossed the room to loom over her like a lumbering giant. Although, to be fair, at her height, everyone seemed a giant. *Just looming, then.*

Backing up several steps to avoid him, she watched in dismay as he leaned down to the sofa to grab her book.

TRAFFORD HAD WALKED over to the sofa and was holding Emma's book in his hand, squinting to read the title by the light of the fire banked behind him. Perry shook his head in bleary disbelief. *Idiot! Does Trafford not realize he could turn to the left to take advantage of the lamp on the table next to the sofa?*

His friend barked a laugh. It was uproariously loud, causing Perry to jump belatedly. "Look what this little bluestocking is reading! My word! *A Selection of Speeches Delivered at Several County Meetings in the Years 1818 & 1819!* Are you interested in politics, little mouse?"

"That is Miss Mouse to you, and no! I am interested in the future of agriculture and what changes we might expect from Parliament that could influence such matters … you insolent oaf!" Emma growled at Trafford.

"That is Lord Insolent Oaf to you, chit! And who gives a damn about agricultural changes? Should you not be trying on pretty gowns, or having your hair styled properly?" Trafford reached out to catch a lock of her hair between his forefinger and thumb. Perry shook his head belligerently and started across the room to remove his friend's digits or do him some other injury for daring to lay hands—fingers—on *his* Emma.

Before he reached them, Emma exploded. Thrusting a finger up in Trafford's face, she raged at him. "Land ownership is changing! One progresses with the times to take advantage of these changes or you will find yourself left behind in the past—extinct!"

Perry had halted his path to rescue her, fascinated by the fire in her black eyes and how she stood up to a man a foot taller than her with such eloquence and courage. Even through the haze of liquor clouding his brain, he could observe her sheer magnificence in that moment, the fire casting a halo around his angry little angel.

A rush of envy followed his esteem. Arguing was their thing that they did together! Did Trafford get her blood up in the same manner as he did? Shaking his head to clear his confusing array of reactions, Perry determined it was genuine anger she was exhibiting toward Trafford and not the seemingly flirtatious tension that they shared between them. At least, that is what he hoped.

"Why should a sweet young thing like you care about changes in land ownership?"

"You should care, too, Lord Oaf! One day you will inherit all those lands your father owns, and if you do not pay attention, you will fight bankruptcy as the income of your estates dwindles to pennies on the pound! The future is coming, and it does not care about your title or your indolent pursuits! It only cares about your ability to manage your accounts and make thoughtful plans for the future, you … you … you oversized twit!"

Trafford frowned down at her, at a loss for words as he attempted to understand what she had said. Perry realized this was a judiash … judicishish—*nay, judicious*—moment to intervene. Stumbling forward, he grabbed Trafford's arm and yanked him toward the door.

"My apologiessh, Emma, for inflicting my friendsss on you. If I had known yoowere in here, I would never have brought them inshhide."

Her black eyes were inscrutable in the low light when she turned her gaze to watch as he pulled Trafford with him. When he reached the door, he finally turned away from that penetrating stare.

"Ridley, 'tiss time to go." Brendan Ridley cocked his head. He was still leaning, bleary, against the door frame and disoriented. Giving a dazed bob of his head, he fell out of the room while Perry followed him, dragging Trafford along behind him.

"What was that chit on about? Agricultural speeches? Pennies on the pound …" Trafford's words devolved into mumbling, and Perry distantly realized that come morning he was going to feel very ashamed of this ill-advised carousing.

Thoughts of his father and the woman from the village

had been haunting him since he had left Balfour Terrace earlier in the evening to find his friends, at which time he had chased one drink with another, hoping to drown the images in his head. Instead, he had made an utter arse of himself in front of Emma. He knew he was going to pay for his error in the morning, and not just with a pounding headache.

CHAPTER 7

"I organized her for your birthday! After that fiasco with your brother, I thought it prudent to only gift you with one harlot for your first experience."

July 1807, the late Earl of Saunton to his son, Peregrine, on his twelfth birthday to explain the presence of the doxy in his bed.

* * *

"Well, well. If it isn't Sir Drinksalot!"

Perry groaned, clutching his head at Emma's loud outburst. "First, let me get some coffee in me, and then you can mock me."

Jane sat up in excitement, putting her fork down to take part in the conversation. "Coffee? I have seen advertisements for it, but I confess I am not familiar with it. We do not drink it in our household. I suppose we could now that we are landowners, but as tenant farmers, I never encountered any because of the steep prices."

Perry fell heavily into a spindly chair at the breakfast

table. The chair squeaked in protest, which made his head throb in response. "You will definitely encounter it shortly. Marcus? Can you bring me a pot? A very large pot."

The footman nodded and hurried to collect the silver coffeepot that was waiting on the sideboard along with the breakfast platters. Word of Perry's late-night antics must have reached belowstairs, because it looked like the servants had anticipated he would need coffee this morning. This afternoon? He did not know what damn time it was. He only knew he regretted the hard liquor from the night before. Since his brother had forsaken drink at Sophia's request, Perry had drunk wine for the most part. His body was protesting his abrupt return to the hard stuff.

The tall, tapered pot was placed before him, Marcus laying out a cup to pour the aromatic black brew.

"It is darker than tea!" Jane's shrill shriek pierced Perry's oversensitive ears. He had all but forgotten the women sitting at the table. Despite his perception, she had likely spoken in her usual exuberant tone.

"Yes."

"It smells heavenly."

"Yes." He raised the cup to his lips and drank with relief, only flinching mildly at the scalding heat. It was sheer heaven, given the pounding in his cranium.

"May I try a cup?"

Perry stilled, frowning. "It is more of a gentleman's drink."

"Why? Does it contain spirits or something?"

Emma snorted. "No, do not be silly, Jane. It is just one of those things that men claim for themselves to exclude women."

"Perry will let me try it. He is practically our family."

Perry listened with a scowl. He was too damned set upon to argue. If it would make her stop talking in that head-thudding voice, she could sip on brandy for all he cared. "Marcus, bring another cup, will you?"

The liveried footman obliged, a cup appearing on the table before Jane. He had brought a smaller, rotund pot of coffee with him, which he used to fill Jane's cup, carefully ensuring the end of the curving spout did not drip before placing it on the table.

Lifting the cup to her lips, Jane breathed in deeply. "My, it smells divine." She took a tentative sip, immediately pulling a face. "My word, it is very bitter." She placed the cup back down on its saucer.

Perry drank his own cup down and poured another. Slowly the room came into focus and, for the first time since rolling out of bed, he suspected he might survive the day.

"I wonder if it would taste better with cream and sugar?" Jane mused out loud. "I shall try it the way I drink my tea, I think." The footman promptly placed a little jug of cream and a sugar bowl in front of her. "Thank you, Marcus."

Perry shook his head. "One does not thank the servants, Jane. One does not even notice them."

Her face crinkled in confusion.

From the corner of his eye, he observed Emma's eyebrows draw together. "Why not?" asked his little hoyden. *Not mine*, he reminded himself, fighting the inconvenient urge to grab her and erase that frown with a gratuitous kiss on her pink lips.

"You will move amongst the *ton*. That is how things are done."

"Sir Drinksalot is giving us etiquette lessons over breakfast while he can barely hold himself up?"

Perry's lips quirked into a half-smile. "Indeed. As your tutor, it is my duty to inform you of your mistakes."

"And what of yours, Mister Carousing-After-Midnight?" Emma shot back.

"A lady does not remark on the activities of the gentlemen around her."

She sat back in her chair with belligerence etched in her posture. "Well, that is convenient. For the gentlemen."

"It is," Perry agreed with a deliberately sanguine expression. Emma huffed. Retrieving her fork, she stabbed at her eggs, likely imagining that she was stabbing him. Jane ignored both of them as she added her cream and sugar, stirring thoroughly before leaning back and lifting the cup once more.

"Zooks! That is delicious," Jane exclaimed, staring down at her cup in amazed delight. Lifting the cup again, she drank deeply before dabbing her mouth with a napkin.

Emma glanced over. "Just be sure not to drink any of it in front of company. Heaven forfend you sip on a gentleman's drink."

Perry grinned. "See! Already you are learning, Emma. Before long, you will be a well-behaved lady of the *beau monde*."

She growled and returned to her breakfast, pointedly ignoring his baiting. "I would like to point out that family, integrity, and upholding one's honor are far more important than which beverage one drinks and whether one is so crass as to note the servants to thank them for their service."

"You would think that was the case."

"Are you saying it is not?"

"I would say that etiquette is the grease of social interaction. Each level of society has rules of conduct to facilitate their endeavors. Ignoring those rules marks you as someone who does not belong."

"And why would I care if spoiled lords such as your friend Trafford believe I do not belong?"

"If you are living within this world, you need to solicit the cooperation of others. These are peers. They hold the very power of the realm in their hands, and ignoring that will put you in peril when you walk amongst them. You must learn the rules of the game so you may turn them to your advantage. Having said that, Trafford was unforgivably rude, and you were in your rights to defend yourself vigorously."

Emma looked pensive. "What about integrity and doing what is right?"

"What of it?"

Emma made a peeved sound. "How does one's honor fit into this world of rigid rules?"

Perry sighed into his coffee. It was too early, and he was too delicate after his night of hard drinking, to engage in a philosophical debate. "I suppose it might be possible to do both. How else would great statesmen make the progress that they do? They must envision the future and then employ etiquette and persuasion to achieve their results."

"You mean how you persuaded me to leave Somerset? By manipulating events and including Jane in the invitation?"

"Precisely."

Jane put her cup down with a clatter. "I was not included in the invitation?"

Perry pressed his eyelids shut for a moment to gather his wits. "Of course you were! Emma was posing a hypothetical situation. Not so, Emma?"

Emma set her jaw mutinously to glare at him over the table covered in snowy linen. "Yes."

Jane darted her eyes back and forth between them. "I do not understand. Was I invited or not?"

Emma pressed her lips together briefly while Perry cast her a challenging look. She finally relented. "Of course you were invited, Jane. I was merely doing what Perry suggested." She clarified, "Posing a hypothetical situation."

A look of relief crossed Jane's face. Turning her attention back to her cup, she poured another cup of coffee before adding her cream and sugar. Perry grimaced. The young woman was ruining a perfectly fine cup of coffee, but he had not the will to protest. The debate with Emma had drained him of any energy he had been painfully gathering together.

Then he recalled her utter magnificence when she had confronted Lord Oaf the night before. He straightened up in his chair, admitting to himself that he had only dragged his lifeless body from bed that morning because he had wanted to find Emma. To be near her fiery presence. It was invigorating to share time with her.

You have nothing to offer her, you worthless bounder!

The reminder to himself did little to abate his awareness of her proximity. He dropped his gaze to the plate in front of him and diverted his attention to forcing some food into his protesting stomach so he might shake off the ravages of the night before.

EMMA KNEW her brow was furrowed, but try as she might, she could not relax the muscles in her face. "But what if I do not want the soup?"

Perry rubbed his hands over his face, clearly still recovering from the night before. "You must accept the soup."

"What if I do not like the soup that is served?"

"It does not signify. One always accepts the soup."

Jane interjected, still babbling incessantly as she had been ever since breakfast. "I like soup. I like all kinds of soup. In fact, there are few soups that I would ever think to reject. I like brown soup. And white soup, especially with ground almonds, but I am not so fond of it when anchovies are added. It quite spoils the taste, in my opinion. Do you think soup will be served tonight for supper? What am I saying? Of course there will be soup …"

Emma shook her head in dismay. What had gotten into her? Jane was frequently exuberant, but this was an entirely new level of enthusiasm. "As I was saying"—she glared at her sister, who finally realized she was chattering and threw a hand over her mouth as if to hold the words inside—"why must I eat soup if I do not want it?"

Perry growled, then lifted his head to glare at her. "Emma, one must accept the soup. I do not know why this is the case, it just is. If you dislike the soup, or if it is soup in general that you so eloquently despise, then toy with your soup spoon and pretend to consume it until the fish course is served."

"I do not understand why it is poor manners to reject soup!" Emma brought her fist down on the table, causing the porcelain and silver to clink. They were seated in the formal dining room to practice table manners, and she did not feel cooperative. As a result, she was particularly feisty with their tutor, who looked drawn and gray from his excesses the night before.

Perry groaned at the cacophony of tableware landing back in place, clutching his head in agonized frustration. "Jane, could you leave us for a moment? I would like to converse with your sister."

Jane unclamped her hand from her mouth to push back her chair. "I think I shall locate some tea. I am quite parched for some reason."

With that, she stood and hurried from the room. Once they were alone, he turned to Emma. "I feel I owe you an apology for what transpired in the library. I did not know you were in there."

"Your *friend*, Trafford, was a complete boor. He ran his eyes down my form as if I was a street harlot!"

Perry frowned. "What do you mean?"

"His eyes ..." Emma waved at her bodice. Perry's gaze fell to where she indicated, lingering for several seconds before returning to her face. He appeared unfocused while Emma waited for his comprehension.

"I am sorry. I quite forgot what you said," he finally admitted.

Emma clenched her fists. "Trafford ... he was most unseemly with his gaze! Not to mention insufferably rude about my reading."

Emma was dismayed when Perry's face set into grim lines. *Is he angry with me or Trafford?*

"Trafford can be an arse—" He shook his head. "I mean, he can be a ..."

"I grew up in a house with rambunctious brothers. Arse is not the worst I have overheard."

"Then Trafford calling you a bluestocking was not that devastating?"

"No, I suppose not. I find it an honor to be associated with such intellectuals. Both Sarah Fielding and Samuel Johnson were members of The Blue Stockings Society. I do not care if it is now considered a derogatory term for intellectual women, since I would have proudly taken a seat at one of their meetings."

"Then why are you still angry with me? I swept them out of there the moment I realized it was ill-advised to inflict them on you. I am apologizing once more. What more do you need from me?"

Emma dropped her eyes, toying with the linen tablecloth. "I disliked seeing you in that state," she mumbled.

"Miss Mouse, are you concerned about my welfare?"

Her cheeks grew hot. "I am. You should not spend time with someone like Trafford. He is an ... arse."

Perry was silent for several seconds. "I think ... you might be saying ... that I am not?"

"No ... you are ... you. Not like Trafford." Emma glanced

up quickly to see how her words had been received. Perry appeared bemused, but pleased.

"That might be the nicest compliment anyone ever paid me."

"I barely said anything," she bemoaned in embarrassment.

"Nevertheless … thank you, Emma."

Hesitantly, she raised her head to return his gaze. "You are welcome, Mr. Arrogant."

Perry chuckled in reply, before nodding at the tableware. "May we continue this lesson, then?"

Emma rolled her eyes. "As you wish. Let the arbitrary rules of dinner time commence."

"We shall have to find Jane, then."

Within ten minutes, they had all resumed their places at the dining table.

"As I was saying, one always accepts the soup course …" Perry glanced at Emma expectantly.

"And if one does not wish to eat it, one toys with it until the fish course."

Perry grinned. "Precisely. Then one quietly sips it from the side of the spoon, never the tip. Now, you must eat the soup without making vulgar slurping noises—"

"Zounds! Perry, we have eaten soup before!" Emma protested.

"I felt I should be thorough, but I am glad to hear it. I shall watch this evening to ensure you both conduct yourselves correctly, so I expect you to be on your very best behavior."

"We shall see," Emma bit back pertly, secretly pleased that he planned to stay home that evening and unable to prevent a small smile at the news.

As their dinner lesson continued over the afternoon, Perry suggested dishes so that Jane and Emma might select the appropriate utensil. It turned out they were relatively well-versed, with the only exception that both sisters had selected a fork in response to Perry's query over tarts, rather than a spoon. By the time the lesson on table manners was completed, Emma felt relatively confident she could eat within high society without appearing to be a complete ninny.

Even the rules of precedence entering the dining room did not seem too complicated if they merely accepted that they were likely always the lowest ranking members at any such function, with Emma outranking Jane by a hair because of being older.

Now, if only she did not look like an unfashionable piece from a far-flung estate, then Emma might consider being seen in public to find out for herself if everyone was as rude as that Trafford fellow, or if there might be worthwhile personages of character to meet.

Climbing the steps to return to their rooms, Emma glanced down at her gown, and all her newfound confidence evaporated to leave a knot of anxiety in the region of her stomach. Raising her head to glance over at Jane, who was beside her on the stairs, did nothing to boost her self-esteem. Her sister looked delightful, dressed in a day gown of deep blue-green that she had sewn herself and which perfectly complemented her silky ebony locks, golden skin, and blue eyes. Emma blew a breath. Nothing about this trip was turning out to be simple for her, especially not her conflicting feelings about the handsome Mr. Arrogant, whom they had just left behind to change for dinner.

For some unfathomable reason, she felt drawn to the charming, indolent gentleman, which was problematic. She would be lucky to attract his attentions for a short while, never mind hold them for a lifetime. Which was academic because they had absolutely nothing in common. Nevertheless, Emma feared she was not guarding her heart or emotions in the manner she had previously calculated.

* * *

THE NEXT MORNING, Emma paced up and down in the hall leading to their bedchambers. Her stomach growled in hunger while she contemplated Jane's door. What was keeping her?

She waited several more minutes, but her sister did not appear. Finally, she walked up to Jane's door and knocked loudly. There was no reply. This was so strange. Jane was always awake first thing and ready to eat with a lively appetite. Had she left her rooms without Emma?

Shaking her head in bewilderment, Emma opened the door and walked in. The room was darkened, the drapes still drawn. Emma peered around the room before noticing the bed was occupied. *Jane is still sleeping?*

Padding over to the bed, she called gently, "Jane?"

There was no reply. Emma was utterly perplexed. Reaching out, she pulled the covers back to confirm Jane was in the bed, revealing the tousled locks of her younger sister. Who did not stir. Fear gripped Emma. Was something wrong with her? Reaching down, she shook her arm. Still no response, but at least she was warm. Grasping her arm, Emma shook her vigorously while raising her voice. "Jane!"

Her sister's eyes flew open in shock, and she yelped as Emma herself jumped in alarm. Jane was distinctly bleary as she slowly focused on her and they both caught their breath. "Emma?"

"You are still asleep?"

"What time is it?"

"Well, there is a little time left to eat breakfast before Perry accompanies us to the modiste."

Jane's face scrunched. "That late?"

"Why are you still sleeping?"

"I could not fall asleep. I was awake until sunrise."

Emma's jaw dropped. "But you never have trouble sleeping! You are the envy of the entire family."

"I do not know what happened. I was so restless, I simply could not relax. Look, I finished my entire design." Jane pointed at the side table where her embroidery frame displayed the completed stitching of the rose and ash she had begun in Somerset. "I must have finally passed out just after dawn."

Emma shook her head in amazement. "I never thought I would live to see the day, but you have had a few hours' sleep now, and we must keep the appointment Perry made for us to meet with the modiste. I think you will simply need to get dressed and eat so we are not too late."

Jane yawned widely, stretching her arms up before pushing the covers back and slowly rising to a seated position. "What an inconvenience! I was so looking forward to meeting with a London modiste to discuss fashion plates, but now I will prop myself up against a counter, doing my best to hold my eyes open."

"Perfect! It will mean I can speak to her without you monopolizing the conversation. I need help far more than you do because I do not know what to wear. You and I are entirely different heights, and our bodies are contoured differently. Besides, you already present as genteel in your attire."

"I tried to advise you on colors, but you never listen to me!"

"I am quite sure I will not look half as elegant as you do in those rich colors you wear."

"*Humph* … we shall see what the modiste has to say. I propose she will recommend the same colors that I have done and you will owe me an apology for ignoring me these many months!"

"Jane, stop quarreling with me and get dressed! I need to

meet this modiste urgently! I have nothing acceptable to wear, and I want something impressive."

Jane was struggling to her feet, but shot her a suspicious glance. "Why, is there someone you wish to impress? A certain Mr. Arrogant, perhaps?"

Emma dropped her gaze. "I do not know of what you speak, you silly girl! Just hurry and get dressed."

Soon they hurried downstairs to eat their eggs and ham in unseemly haste, fortunate that there was no one to witness it. Emma dabbed her mouth with a napkin, considering where they might meet Perry, while Jane sighed happily into the coffee which she had just poured herself. She drank deeply from the cup.

"Oh my, the whole day seems better now!" she exclaimed to Emma, who shook her head in absentminded amusement before rising from her chair. She needed to visit the modiste as soon as humanly possible. Even the servants at Balfour Terrace were better attired than she was.

CHAPTER 8

"Steer clear of intelligent women. They are dull company and difficult to seduce."

July 1808, the late Earl of Saunton to his son, Peregrine, on his thirteenth birthday.

* * *

It was with some trepidation that Emma ascended into the Saunton carriage after Jane. She was anticipating their arrival at the modiste while simultaneously dreading it. Emma was certain that nothing could be done about her appearance, while hoping that a magical transformation could take place so she might look as fine as her beautiful sister.

Distracted by her thoughts, she sat down firmly on the bench, only she miscalculated to find herself landed with a thump on the carpeting of the aisle between the seats instead. Her buttocks smarted while a fiery blush rose across her cheeks.

Perry coughed behind her from the open carriage door, completing her humiliation when she realized he had observed her graceless landing. He held out a gloved hand to assist her, which she reluctantly took to help raise herself onto her knees before fumbling to her feet, nearly flinching at the tingle his touch produced even through the gloves they both wore.

Once she was seated, he let her hand go and climbed in to sprawl on the opposite bench.

"Signora Ricci is very talented. She will make up a full wardrobe befitting a young lady of the gentry." Perry was clearly attempting to divert her attention and settle her nerves after the embarrassing drop, which Emma appreciated and resented. Why could she not be a charming young lady who might attract the attentions of a gentleman such as he? It was laughable to think she would ever entice a worldly man of such high standards with her gauche lack of polish.

"Oh, yes! A visit to the modiste will do wonders!" Jane's attempt to smooth over what had just happened was transparent. Emma felt her blush returning. Desperate to redirect the focus of the conversation, she sought for a change of subject that would not lead back to her ungainly spill. She could feel Perry's eyes on her as she stared down at her clenched fists. This was so mortifying.

"I am very pleased with the progress we made yesterday. Once your wardrobe is ready, we will invite our cousin and his wife to dinner, so you may practice with peerage."

Jane perked up. "Your cousin?"

"I forgot to inform you. The Duke of Halmesbury is our cousin. The duchess will sponsor you once you are ready to enter society."

"Oh! Her Grace is the duchess you mentioned in Rose Ash?"

Emma was thankful that Jane and Perry entered into a

discussion about family connections while she took a few minutes to compose herself. She might miss most of what they said, but Jane could inform her later.

"Yes, Halmesbury is very influential, and the duchess is an amiable young lady. I think you will find much in common because she grew up in the country and only recently came to London for the first time."

Emma drew calming breaths and gazed out the window as the carriage progressed several blocks before hitting traffic. Before long, the carriage drew to a stop in front of a narrow shop. The gold lettering above the entry proclaimed they had arrived at Signora Ricci, much to Emma's relief. She was long past due to tame her wild hair and wear something to complement her figure rather than merely cover it up, which she privately admitted was the general purpose of the clothes she usually selected for herself.

It was time to make a change and try something a little more daring and contemporary than her current collection of dowdy, muted gowns. Her eyes flickered to the source of her newfound interest in fashion. Despite herself, she wanted to attract a gaze of admiration from the handsome gentleman who glanced in her direction, a question in his emerald eyes when he found her eyes on him. If she could see his face suffused with admiration for her womanly form just once, she could then follow her pragmatic decision to steer her thoughts away from unattainable desires.

The fierce yearning that pierced her heart to be the object of his desire for even a few moments, instead of an awkward bluestocking from a small village, was bittersweet. The countess had assured Emma that she could attain a level of competence with her appearance. Emma was not entirely convinced, but it provided the hope that she might attract Perry's fleeting esteem.

Although she knew she could never hold the attentions of such a sophisticated rogue, she would be forever grateful if she could experience his regard and know what it was to be a beautiful and desirable young woman, such as her younger sister who never lacked admirers in Derby nor in Rose Ash.

She was determined to obtain at least one gown that elevated her appearance before she ruined it with a clumsy stumble or ill-advised commentary on the wrong topic, which perpetually made the young men in her company acquire a demeanor of desperate panic as they sought to extract themselves from her presence.

Lost in her thoughts, she failed to notice she was the only one remaining in the carriage. Perry stood, holding out his hand to assist her, a quizzical expression written across his features. Emma drew a shuddering breath, still fighting to recover her composure from the earlier mishap, then grasped his hand to disembark. She nearly wept at the inopportune heat that traveled up her arm at the contact. *Collect yourself, Emma! Perry is not and never will be your young gentleman!*

"Are you all right, Emma?"

She pressed her lips together, unable to complain about his solicitousness but shamed to be receiving it because of her tumble. That he was astute to her abashment only made it worse. "I shall never be ready to enter society."

Perry appeared concerned, contemplating her declaration. "I do not believe that is the case. I would never have manipulated the situation if I thought it would do you a disservice to be here, I swear it."

"We are both witness to the fact that I do not belong. I am not cultivated. Jane will do splendidly, while I will make a disgrace of myself."

Unlike Perry. He was perfection with his immaculate

clothing, his broad shoulders filling his forest green tailcoat, while cutting a dashing figure with his strong thighs, slim hips, and flat abdomen. He possessed the languid grace of a cat and the predatory gleam of a wolf.

Perry lifted a hand to tuck an unruly lock of hair behind her ear, the carriage door masking his inappropriate gesture from people walking by. "I think you belong wherever you wish to be. You are a determined young woman with strong opinions, and in certain circles, that will be welcome. I would change nothing about you."

Emma's heart melted. She stared into his fascinating eyes flecked with emerald and golds, knowing she must fight to hide the adoration his words inspired and even now must be plainly written on her face.

"Except, of course, for this unholy mess of a dress. This I would gladly burn on your behalf." His eyes had fallen to her mud-colored carriage dress, his distaste obvious. With that, Emma's feet landed back on the ground with a firm mental thump. She was almost grateful for the rude awakening, slapping his hand away to push past him and march through the shop door that Jane was holding open with a questioning eyebrow raised at the unseemly delay.

STARING down into Emma's coal-black eyes, Perry could see the warm affection his words had prompted. It had dismayed him to find himself swaying toward her, a second away from leaning down to claim her pink lips. But she was not one of his wicked widows and he had no right to her sweet fire, so he had sought desperately for something to put distance between them.

His eyes had, once again, found her pretty, rounded

breasts buried under that horrid mud gown which had provided him the inspiration to push their interaction into the abrasive once more.

Truly, that garment really needed to find its way into a fireplace. It was indescribably awful.

With their bristling animosity restored, he followed her into the shop to introduce her to Signora Ricci.

SIGNORA RICCI WAS an attractive Italian woman in her late thirties who liked to talk with her hands. It gratified Emma that the woman did not appear to be judgmental about her appearance, although the modiste had barely hidden her horror at the much-maligned carriage dress. She had quickly pulled it off Emma and sent it away with an attendant and an instruction to bring a pelisse from the back.

"We have a young woman who no longer needs *il pelisse*, and I think *il colore* is perfect for *la donna*!" she explained. "This color, it is *non bene*. Miss Davis, you need color!"

Emma was soon attired in a deep blue pelisse that was a little too long but well cut to enhance her shape. Looking in the mirror, she was astonished by how the shade made her hair shine in contrast and her skin glow. Perhaps Jane was accurate in her assessment that Emma had been wearing the wrong hues?

The garment was whisked away to be altered, Signora Ricci adamant that Emma must leave wearing it. She dared not ask about the mud dress because she suspected it was not in the shop any longer.

The modiste showed her fashion plates of gowns that she advised for Emma's contours, then showed them to Perry, who studied them carefully and nodded his agreement. After they had selected numerous styles, Signora Ricci draped richly colored fabrics over Emma's bodice so they could view the effect on her complexion. Emma's eyes widened in astonishment at how so very many of the silks and velvets enhanced her appearance in the mirror. Once, she caught the reflection of Perry's small smile as he reacted to her repeated amazement, and she could not help the flush of pleasure at his attention.

After a couple hours of browsing styles and fabrics, Perry placed the expedited order for Emma's and Jane's abundance of new gowns and scheduled an appointment for the fittings.

While they awaited the pelisse that Emma would need to leave the shop, the three of them wandered over to view a display of gloves near the front windows. Perry advised them to purchase a variety of colors to match their new wardrobe.

The front door opened, and two women in their late twenties walked into the shop. Emma's eyes widened at the attractive redhead dressed in a tight, low-cut gown which prominently highlighted her bountiful bosom. From the corner of her eye, she saw Perry stiffen.

The women caught sight of him and swayed over in a swirl of rustling silk skirts and a cloud of floral fragrance.

"Mr. Balfour! It has been too long!"

Emma noticed how he flicked a glance in her direction before taking up the lady's hand to bow politely. "Lady Slight, what a pleasure."

"Have you taken up with someone new, Perry?" Lady Slight purred, turning ice-blue eyes to inspect Emma and Jane with disdain.

"This is Miss Davis and Miss Jane. They are houseguests of the earl, distantly related to the Balfour family." Perry's explanation was diplomatic and his tone conciliatory. Emma wondered if the earl and he had discussed how introductions were to be made. She and Jane curtsied politely.

"Relatives!" The lady inhaled delicately, before both she and her companion giggled into their gloved hands. Emma narrowed her eyes. She knew when she was the object of mockery, and this was mean-spirited compared to the interactions between her and Perry.

Moving in front of Jane to assume a defensive position was pure instinct; Emma was prepared to battle with these harlots and their indiscreet bosoms. Their rank did not signify, and she would handle the matter so Jane could remain unaffected.

Emma only wished she was not wearing the ponderous frock that was so unflattering. It would have been nice to have been armored with the delightful pelisse that had increased her confidence earlier. However, notwithstanding her appearance, if they disparaged her sister, she would have no difficulty mounting an attack. She had trounced Lord Oaf of the inferior intellect; she would eviscerate this uppish—

"Surely, you jest! I cannot believe these girls are related to the preeminent Balfours! This young woman has hair as artless as the wilds of the Scottish Highlands. And a double dimity petticoat! Do they still make these? Confess, Perry! These are rural strumpets whom you are attiring!"

Emma was tempered that Lady Slight had focused on herself as the object of derision, leaving Jane out of it. She opened her mouth, ready to let her words fly, when Perry deftly stepped forward and ushered Emma back with a wave of his hand. She shut her mouth abruptly, curious to see how he handled this altercation and whom he sided with.

"Now, now, Harriet. There is no need to be jealous. You must know the earl has discovered a deep and abiding interest in familial matters. You would not want word to get back to him that you were rude to his houseguests. Saunton is an affable man, but he becomes quite incensed when he feels he must defend his family. I would not want you to be on the receiving end of his ire."

Hesitation flickered over Lady Slight's flawless face. After a few moments, she forced a chuckle. "Perry, you must know it was merely a jest! Miss Davis, you are aware I was just funning you?" The ice-blue eyes widened innocently to peer at Emma once more.

Emma inclined her head. "Of course, any friend of *Perry's* is a friend of *ours*." She had to admit she was impressed by the finesse with which Perry had smoothly dispatched the tension while clarifying that contempt would not be tolerated. He had even given the appearance that he was protecting the interests of the vicious viper. Comprehension wormed into the dark crevasses of her reticence—Perry knew they were likely to encounter these women at a social function and it would be less unpleasant if hostility and spitefulness had been mitigated rather than exacerbated.

Emma knew she had a habit of burning bridges with her incendiary tongue, while Perry's tactical manipulation allowed for polite discourse in the future. Maybe there was something to the art of etiquette and persuasion.

At that moment, the altered pelisse was brought out and the insolent woman and her companion wandered away. Emma was relieved to pull the garment on while Jane helped smooth it out. Feeling more confident than when she had arrived, they left the shop.

* * *

WHEN PERRY STEPPED out of the modiste's shop, still unsettled by the skirmish he had only just averted, a scene unfolding down the block immediately caught his attention. An older gentleman, accompanied by a footman, had just taken delivery of several bunches of moss roses from two young flower girls.

The girls appeared angry, while the overweight man, dressed in his vain finery and silver-buckled shoes unsuitable for street wear, smiled superciliously down at them. The old fop threw back his head in laughter before turning to walk away. His footman's face was pained as he hesitated, then followed his employer with his arms full of the moss roses.

Perry suspected that no coin had changed hands.

His suspicion was confirmed when the older of the flower girls wrapped her arm around the younger. From the way the smaller girl's shoulders shuddered, she was weeping.

Knowing the type of antics his own father would get up to during his reign as the earl, Perry hurried over to learn what had happened.

"Good afternoon, ladies. Do you require assistance?"

The older of the two flower girls looked up, clutching a large basket of flowers in one hand and still embracing the smaller girl with her other arm. Perry noted that the two girls wore aged, dark print frocks, which had been meticulously mended many times. They were both barefoot, but clean. The taller girl's ruddy face bore an expression of belligerence. "Tha' skinflint refused to pay us, and 'ee walked away with our profits for the day! We be orphans and we be needing tha' coin!"

Perry's ire increased. "Did he give you a reason?"

"We be privileged to serve an important gen'leman such as 'im. Those be our best flowers!" The girl's lip quivered despite her anger, and she appeared to be on the verge of crying. She could not have been more than fourteen years of age. Her little sister, perhaps nine years old, looked up, her face streaked with tears.

These two girls scratched out their survival, penny to penny, so Perry did not doubt that their profits had been deprived by the loss of several bunches of the popular moss roses.

"And 'ee called us hussies! Said we could make up our profits on our backs. But oi a good girl, oi am! Oi never go among boys!" This time, tears leaked from her affronted brown eyes, and Perry fought down a flare of anger. Turning, he looked down the busy street to find the prissy old man, but he had long since disappeared.

Somehow, even at the lowest rungs of society, these two children were keeping themselves from hitting the very bottom, but that day's loss could very well tilt that balance to send them hurtling into an abyss. Pasting a smile on his face, Perry turned back. "I shall pay for his flowers."

The flower girl stiffened, then straightened up in indignation fit for a duchess, letting go of her sister to place a fisted hand on her hip. "Oi do no' need your charity."

Perry withheld the wince that threatened to cross his face. He should have known better. Two young waifs eking out their livelihood on the streets, while avoiding the company of men, would be too proud for handouts. He calculated a response, seeking an excuse to give them the coins they sorely needed now that they had been robbed.

"I need your help." Perry sought for an explanation for his audacious statement, when he found Emma and Jane standing a few feet away observing the conversation. "These fine ladies are from Somerset." He gestured to the two women. "Miss Davis has been telling me how much she misses her gardens. Do you happen to have any flowers of fine quality for the young ladies?"

The flower girl's entire demeanor shifted, her sales prowess triggered by the question. "Oi sell flowers tha' be sweet. Oi have wallflowers, primrose, and green lavender. Bu' no roses ..." Her face fell slightly, but she held her large woven basket aloft to show her wares to Perry.

"Miss Davis, could you come inspect these flowers and tell me if they are … sweet?"

Emma stepped forward, leaning over to examine the flowers with solemn attention. "These are flowers of fine quality, Mr. Balfour."

"How much for all the bunches?" Perry asked. The younger one perked up, wiping her eyes with the back of her hand.

The oldest contemplated the flowers, her face screwed in concentration as she counted them out. "Tha' be one shilling." The girl's expression was hopeful when she looked up, but laced with worry. Perry guessed she was regretting the lost moss roses and the profits they represented.

"One shilling! For such fine flowers? I am not prepared to pay less than …" From the corner of his eye, he noticed Emma lift a hand to tuck a lock back under her bonnet, discreetly lifting three fingers as she swept the errant hairs back. "… three shillings!"

The little sister's mouth fell open at this news while the older flower girl beamed in delight. "Cor, tha' be righ' kind of you, sir!"

Perry pulled out a purse, careful to disguise with his hand that he pulled out three shillings, which he palmed over. The older sister smartly looked around for any observers before reaching up to clasp her hands around the coins so that the value could not be observed by any watchful eyes. She disappeared the coins onto her person while Perry reached down to lift several bunches of primrose and lavender, which he handed to Jane who wrapped her arms around them. Then he grabbed more bunches of paper-wrapped bouquets to pass to Emma before sweeping up the remaining wallflowers. Giving a brief bow, he addressed the girls once more, whose delight was palpable at their good fortune. "I thank you, young ladies, for your assistance. As you can see, Miss Davis is very pleased."

Emma beamed on cue, gazing adoringly down at the flowers in the crook of her arm.

"Ye be welcome, mister." They spun and scampered away, the empty basket bouncing in the wake of their flurrying skirts as they weaved through pedestrians to disappear down the street.

Perry breathed in relief that he had managed to discreetly assist them, then followed the women back to the carriage where the footman awaited them. Jane and Emma kept hold of the flowers as they entered and took their seats. Perry climbed up to join them, settling back into the squabs with an armful of flowers tickling his senses.

Once the door closed, the fragrance quickly permeated the compact space.

"It smells like a perfumery in here," commented Jane, her face buried in stems of green lavender as she breathed deeply.

Emma lifted her own face from sniffing primroses and met Perry's gaze. "You are a good man, Peregrine Balfour, to help those young girls while respecting their dignity."

Perry felt his cheeks grow hot, embarrassed and pleased by her quiet affirmation. "I despise it when members of the higher classes abuse their position to take advantage of the poor. They should act with the responsibility that their status infers."

Emma's lips quirked into a crooked grin, and she tipped her head in acknowledgment. "Very well-done of you, sir."

He shrugged. "Those girls deserved our support."

Emma tilted her head, appearing bemused as she gazed at him with obvious admiration for several moments before finally returning to fiddle with her blooms.

* * *

After dinner that evening, Perry sat in the study sipping on wine, unsure what to make of his day as he caught the scent of the green lavender that had been placed in vases about the room. The girl had been telling the truth about her blooms being sweet.

Richard dropped into the opposite armchair, lifting a cup of tea, which he scowled at. He was not yet accustomed to his new beverage of choice since Sophia had requested he leave off the liquor, but nevertheless, he was honoring the request.

"Will I ever grow accustomed to drinking tea?"

"There are other unspirited drinks you could consume instead."

Richard chuckled. "Unspirited! I like that. It perfectly describes this cup of tea. But, alas, no. Although it is an acquired taste, I find I feel more alert since I switched to drinking it. It clears my head agreeably, which is assisting my focus. I would like to further increase the production from our estates now that I have additional family to provide for. As my … by-blow … Ethan will need every advantage I can provide him. An inheritance of his own. Which means I need to expand my unentailed holdings. Not to mention the possibility of future daughters and whatnot."

Perry contemplated his older brother. The earl was known far and wide as a good-humored gentleman with an easy smile. But Richard had not grown up under their father's thumb. He had left for Eton when he was nine years old and spent most of his youth at school, and then university, only coming home for a few weeks a year.

In contrast, Perry knew he was far too serious. He could pretend otherwise with friends and loose women, but he seldom smiled with genuine sentiment and he never laughed.

Not until the last few days since he had met Emma. He

was surprised to chuckle or smile at the slightest provocation. In her presence, he was … almost lighthearted. However, this eccentricity did not bear inspection because she was unattainable to a worthless sot. He had nothing to offer, something that had become abundantly clear over the course of his life.

"What of you, Perry?"

Perry's brows drew together. "What about me?"

"Do you have any plans for the future?"

Aggravation tightened his chest. Big brother was going to attempt to steer him into a worthwhile pursuit again. Ever since Sophia had entered their lives, Richard had become quite maudlin company, spouting on about purpose and responsibility and attempting to get Perry to talk about his thoughts. His thoughts were far too dark to share with anyone, least of all his affable brother. Richard had proved himself a worthwhile lord and leader, but he had not lived in the shadow of their vicious father.

"Why do you ask? Are you planning on discontinuing my allowance?"

Richard straightened in his chair. "Of course not! It is your right to receive the benefit of the family fortune. It is merely fate that I was born two years before you."

Perry pasted the haughty smile on his face that usually extricated him from uncomfortable discussions. "Then, no. I plan to continue to fritter my coin on worthless pursuits suitable for a man of my standing."

Richard leaned forward, undeterred. The philanthropy bug—the same one that their cousin, the Duke of Halmesbury, suffered from—had recently bitten his brother, to Perry's great annoyance. *Did you not lately volunteer to accompany two country lasses around Town and tutor them to enter high society?* That was different, he assured himself.

"Perry, I feel I have been negligent. Only recently I was

reminded of how Lord Saunton—I mean, our father—placed two street doxies in my bed on my twelfth birthday. It was"—Richard searched for a word to fit the situation—"disturbing."

Yes, that sounds accurate.

"… I ran and hid in a guest room for several days and had to convince one of the maids to bring me food. Did … he try something like that with you?"

Perry's heart squeezed painfully in his chest while his head pounded so loudly, he could barely hear his own thoughts. He could not speak of it.

Change the subject!

"Our father was a hedonist who died of the pox. What more is there to say?"

His tone was light, but he was afraid of what Richard might read on his face. Quickly rising to his feet, Perry made for the door. "If you will excuse me, Trafford is expecting me." He was not, but Perry needed to avoid this dark *tête-à-tête*.

"Perry?"

He paused with his hand on the door handle, itching to run off but unwilling to manifest such a powerful reaction. He loved his brother, and he appreciated the effort, but there was no redemption to be found for his own tortured soul. No therapeutic discussion to heal such deep wounds. Perry had learned long ago to hide his thoughts in order to avoid humiliation, and tonight would be no exception.

"If you ever need to talk about it, I am here. I wish I could have done more to protect you, little brother."

"Protection? How maudlin you have become since you married, *Saunton*."

A contemptuous scoff, but in the privacy of his thoughts, Perry was trying to squash the torturous memories of his youth. Had he ever thanked his brother for offering him his first choices in his young life in the aftermath of their mad father's death?

He opened his mouth to say something, but snapped it shut when his courage failed him. Speaking on this would reveal too much. "Goodnight, Richard."

His hand trembled as it opened the door, and he left.

CHAPTER 9

"It is despicable how you treat the boy. Allow me to take him to my home and educate him properly."

July 1809, Peregrine's maternal grandfather to the late Earl of Saunton, on the boy's fourteenth birthday.

* * *

When Perry awoke, he found that the weather had turned gloomy overnight. A torrent of deafening rain roared against the roof and windows so one could barely hear one's own thoughts.

Perfectly fitting for his dark mood.

His valet cheerfully dressed him, chattering on about the heavy downfall and how it had prevented Cook from going to the market, despite Perry's best attempts to glower him into silence.

Perry finally went downstairs to the breakfast room, feeling worse for wear. He had drunk wine until the early hours with Trafford, who had waxed on about a widow he was bedding and read aloud some very poor poetry he had written for the—in Perry's opinion—inane woman.

It was all rather annoying, hence the need for wine. He had contemplated seeking out Lady Slight. Just two weeks earlier, he had enthusiastically bedded the woman at her townhouse in Grosvenor Square, but the thought of doing that now was singularly unappealing for some inexplicable reason. The widow had lost her allure for him.

So he had drunk and debated and smoked cigars until he was sure that everyone at Balfour Terrace would be in bed before returning home to stumble into his room in the family wing.

Now, near midday, he squinted at the bright light in the breakfast room, where every available lamp and candle had been lit. He was dismayed to find the entire family in attendance, including the Davis sisters. Both his brother and Jane sipped coffee, while the countess thrust a fork into an enormous pile of eggs and ham with a healthy appetite, probably because of her current condition. Emma sipped her tea while Ethan babbled ceaselessly to make his head ache.

Perry thought he would avoid them by coming downstairs so late in the morning, but they must have all risen late or waited for him to eat.

He walked past the chattering relatives without greeting, nearly tripping over the chair piled with cushions so that Ethan might reach the table. Closing his eyes in repressed irritation, he walked around his nephew and made his way over to the platters of food. Dishing up a large serving of eggs and ham, along with a thick slice of toast, Perry made for his usual seat to sit down, then scowled in confusion at the wrapped package that lay in front of him on the table.

"What is this?" He knew his tone was hostile, but it was because he had a sinking feeling he was about to feel quite set upon.

Emma, who sat across from him, turned to peer down at the package he was pointing at with his fork. "It is a birthday present from Jane and myself. Sophia informed us of the esteemed event after dinner. Our family makes quite a fuss over birthdays, so we …" Emma shrugged as if to complete the sentence.

Perry's chest tightened in surprise, his jaw dropping open. It had been ten years since anyone had acknowledged his birthday. Ten years since he had walked in and found his father with the woman from the village. The last birthday that his father had made any type of sense before plunging into his pox-induced madness. Panic descended as Perry fought to suppress the memories of that day.

There was no fifteenth birthday! That day does not exist!

He had to repeat this in his mind a couple more times until his chest eased and the memories receded.

"I do not want it!"

The chatter at the table stopped as everyone turned to stare at him. His brother furrowed his brow with concern that Perry did not want or need. He needed to be left alone. To forget. And not to pretend that he was worthy of love or esteem. He was a dark soul and there was no hope for him. No bright future.

Emma reached over and grabbed the package. "We did not mean to offend you. We thought we were offering a pleasant gesture."

"Feeling guilty for your ingratitude, more likely," he sneered. He almost winced, but restrained himself. He sounded like a belligerent arse, but he needed these overtures of familiarity and esteem to stop.

Emma lifted a hand to rub at her brow and stared down at the linen with a disappointed air, causing his guilt to mount. He stood, almost knocking over his chair in his haste.

"Brother, this is my fault. I told them you would appreciate it. Please sit and have breakfast in peace." Richard's conciliatory tone was reasonable, but Perry was not. He stalked out of the room without a word, outraged that someone had reminded him of the date. Mortified by his behavior. Stricken with unwanted memories. He needed to find a drink.

* * *

PERRY SAT in the narrow library, staring at the brandy he had poured. Currently he was merely a man who had poured a drink before midday. But if he drank it … if he drank it … *If I drink it, I will be my father.*

His brother's recent crisis over that same issue a couple of months earlier suddenly made sense. Perry would pay any price to not become his father.

Light footsteps sounded on the parquet flooring to announce her approach. He knew who it was without looking back.

"Did I do something wrong?"

Perry dropped his head into his hands. "No, Emma."

"Oh."

He exhaled deeply. "My birthdays have never been joyous occasions. I do my best to forget them, so you took me by surprise and too many unwanted memories troubled me at once."

Her skirts rustled as she came closer and slid into a chair next to him. Perry breathed in the fragrance of chamomile and wildflowers, and the darkness slowly unwound, his muscles easing until he lifted his head to stare sightlessly at the book-laden shelves. Clenching his jaw, Perry preempted Emma's response. "I apologize for my ingratitude. It was thoughtful of you."

"Thank you. I am sorry your birthdays have been so horrid."

He curved his lips into an empty smile, continuing to stare down the tomes to no avail. They just sat there, unperturbed by his lethal glare.

"Will you give us lessons today?"

"I shall."

"If you would rather take the day … although it is raining, and—"

"I would rather remain busy."

"Oh."

Perry was unaccustomed to Emma acquiescing in this manner. It made him uncomfortable. Next, they would settle into an amicable friendship, which would be one step away from seducing her. And that could not happen. He flicked his eyes in her direction.

"It is pronounced rain, by the way."

"What is?"

"You pronounced it *rah-ahning*. It is not. It is raining. Rhymes with Spain."

To his irritation, Emma failed to take umbrage. "Truly? I never noticed! *Rah-ahn* … Spain … *ray-ahn* … Spain … *raaayn* … Spain … rain … Spain." Her face lit up. "Did I say it correctly?"

"You did. Why is your hair still untamed?"

He saw her stiffen in displeasure. "The earl did not have anyone on his staff to assist us, so his man of business will be hiring a lady's maid."

"Ah, yes. My brother did little entertaining before he married. Except for single visitors of the female persuasion."

Emma scowled at his indelicate innuendo, just as he had planned she would. The moment of quiet companionship was terminated. She stood abruptly to leave the room. "I shall be in the breakfast room with Jane when you are ready."

She thumped out of the room, treading heavily in her ire. Perry grinned, feeling cheery all of a sudden. It was so delightfully easy to bait her.

* * *

TAKING hold of Perry's hand, Emma stepped into his embrace. He took several steps with her before sweeping her in a twirl until Emma trod down on his foot. Perry yelped, squeezing his eyes shut as his square jaw firmed.

"I apologize."

"You did it on purpose that time."

"Why would I do that?" she responded innocently.

"Because you are angry with me, and instead of expressing it, you have chosen to passively attack me every chance you get."

"Why, that sounds far too complicated to me. A much simpler explanation would be that I am clumsy and not very good at dancing."

Perry glared down at her, resentment written into every tense line of his six-foot-something frame. Emma sucked in her breath as she stared into those startling eyes, fascinated by the flecks of green and gold, even during their mutual impatience.

The music from the pianoforte came to a sudden halt. "I am so tired!" Jane's lament interrupted their eye combat. In unison, they turned to where Jane lay slumped on the pianoforte bench, her exhaustion evident.

"Are you still having trouble sleeping?" Emma's question held a note of confusion. It was quite unlike Jane to struggle with nocturnal relaxation. Or even relaxation during the day, if one thought about it.

"Ever since reaching London, I cannot sleep until the sun

rises. Perhaps it is the excitement of being here? I fear I cannot play another note!"

Perry's deep, intoxicating voice sent tingles over Emma's skin—again—when he spoke. "I need to practice the steps with Emma, so you can take a break from playing. Until she masters the simple steps of the waltz, there can be no advancement, so I will simply count it out for her while you rest."

Jane nodded, standing up from the chair to straighten her skirts. She looked slim and graceful, despite the weariness she complained of, while she loped across the music room to settle on a chaise lounge.

Turning back to Emma, Perry drew a deep breath as if to compose himself. "Can you make a sincere effort to learn these steps?"

"I am such a lummox, I shall never learn how to do this!"

He sighed. "Emma, the inability to dance is not an innate character flaw. It is simply a matter of persistence and practice. Granted, this particular activity is harder for you than most, but you can do this if you put your mind to it."

Emma inclined her head. She could make more of an effort.

Perry counted the beat in a low voice. "One, two, three —*hell and damnation*!" Perry released her to walk away several steps, suppressing his pain while Emma looked on.

"I apologize."

"We have been at this for an hour, and I swear you grow heavier every time you tread on my feet. For such a little thing, you are unbearably solid. Where do you pack all that weigh—" A strange expression flickered over his face as he dropped his gaze to her bodice and bit off the remainder of his words.

Emma looked down to see what he was staring at. Had she spilled tea on herself at breakfast? Stretching her neck back, she did her best to peer down her front to find what had captured his attention, then raised a quizzical eyebrow at him. Perry was now peering at his boots with earnest attention and muttering under his breath.

"Perhaps it is cumulative?"

His gaze found hers, his puzzlement obvious.

"Perhaps each time I step on your foot, the injury accumulates in intensity?"

"Perhaps," he snapped back. "Or perhaps you intentionally bring your foot down harder each time."

"Do not be ridiculous. I would never hurt you on purpose. Tell him, Ja—"

A nasal snore interrupted her. Turning to find her sister, Emma saw she was now fast asleep, her jaw hanging open in repose.

"Does your sister need a physician?"

"I do not know. She seems fine except for failing to sleep at night. Perhaps a little more excitable than usual, but mostly herself. I think the anticipation of the ball must be keeping her up." Just the previous morning, the earl had announced his intention to host a ball, the first to be held at Balfour Terrace—or any Saunton holding—since Richard had inherited the title. It was to be attended by friendly peers and allow her and Jane to practice their entrance to society among familiar faces. Familiar to the earl and Sophia, that was, not Emma and Jane. Jane had clapped her hands in gleeful pleasure at the news, while Emma had prevented a groan from escaping her lips. She had not wanted to sound ungrateful.

"I suppose she will fit right in with the usual Season schedule, then."

"Late to bed, late to rise?"

"Of course. No person of good breeding is familiar with early morning," Perry quipped.

"Well, that settles it. I do not belong here. I still rise early every morning!"

Perry frowned in disagreement. "It was a jest. Richard himself goes riding at sunrise since you arrived and Ethan is sleeping through the night."

Emma quelled her own irritation. Irritation that Perry still teased her. Irritation that she could not master the simple steps of the waltz. Irritation that she was so utterly distracted by the pleasure of being encircled in his powerful embrace that she simply could not calculate where her feet were supposed to land each time he attempted to tutor her. Not to mention irritation that she still wore her frumpy gowns, while he was so perfectly attired every time she saw him.

He looked especially fine, despite his sour mood, in his buckskins, snowy linen, and navy wool tailcoat, while she still wore her worn-out muslin. Pursing her lips in displeasure, she breathed in deeply through her nose to settle her nerves.

"If you will be patient with me, we can try again."

Perry walked back and placed his hand on her waist. Once again, her heart fluttered at the feel of his warmth seeping into her skin. Blowing a fortifying breath, she willed herself to concentrate as he took up her hand in his.

"One, two, three; one, two, three; one, two, three; one, two, three …"

Somehow, this time, perhaps in the absence of music to distract her, Emma stepped in time and they completed several repetitions without incident. As they drew to a halt, she laughed joyfully, looking up at him. "We did it!"

Perry bent his head to look down at her, a strange expression crossing his face as his eyes dipped to her chin. Emma froze in anticipatory silence, barely daring to draw breath as the moment stretched into eternity. As slowly as the movement of the sun across the sky, he lowered his head. In dizzying delight, she realized … "Are you going to kiss m*mphh—*"

All further words were cut off as his warm, firm lips found hers and Emma received her very first kiss.

Quivering delight spread from her lips, coursing down her throat and careening through her breast and into her belly where heated desire leapt into flames. Moaning in shuddering enrapture, she raised herself onto her toes to press ever closer to him. His spicy scent entranced her senses and fanned the flames rising from her midriff. Dropping her hand, his arms gathered her closer, bands of steel and muscle as he encircled her and lifted her off her feet to lick at her lips hungrily. Emma was dizzy with sensation, reminding herself to breathe, taking in air before losing herself further into the maelstrom as his tongue coaxed her lips apart to sweep inside her mouth and her hands stole over his broad shoulders.

She murmured in surprise when their tongues tangled. He tasted of coffee and fruit as he gave a low groan. This sign of his ardor intensified her own response until all she could think about was climbing him like a tree to wrap her knees around his hips and press as close as she could get. His hands moved down to cup her buttocks and pull her higher, where she felt the evidence of his hard arousal nudging against her center.

Dragging his mouth from hers, he slid along her neck to lick at the base of her throat, shooting frissons of hot sensitivity to pool between her legs where she throbbed with yearning.

"I have dreamed of this …" he whispered in her feverish skin as he nipped at her clavicle, scraping his teeth and awakening a new tide of passion as her head rolled back to allow him better access. She barely recognized her own self as she keened in pleasure, instinctively rubbing her core against his hardness to assuage her craving for him as his tongue dipped to lick at the swell of her breast, then swirled beneath the fabric as he sought more.

A loud snore caught Emma's attention. In a daze, she remembered her sister—her innocent, younger sister—was just fifteen feet away and could awaken at any moment. Her body screamed in denial as she lowered her legs, awkwardly pressed against Perry while he sluggishly raised his head. His eyes were glazed with lust as they slowly regained focus to find her.

A look of rousing horror crossed his visage as he carefully lowered her. Her toes found the floor while she continued to gaze up at him and he down at her. Slowly, he stepped back to release her and, for several moments, they just stared at each other.

"I … shall … see you tomorrow … at breakfast." With that, he sank into a tense bow before bolting out the door. Emma watched his exit with dazed delight, lifting her fingers to stroke her swollen lips in bemusement.

She had fervently wished to be the object of his desire if even for a few moments, and it would seem that she had received far more than she had bargained for when she made her plea to the universe.

Perry definitely wanted her. Desired her.

Now that she possessed such knowledge, she would need to ensure she did not act on it. He was a rogue, and he would never pursue an honorable courtship with her. If he were ever to marry, it certainly would not be to a country mouse with tangled hair and atrocious style. It would appear she had wished for fire, and now … now it threatened to consume her.

CHAPTER 10

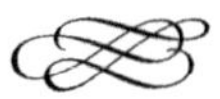

"A real man does not concern himself with the feelings or emotions of women or other inferiors. It makes him appear weak. Fear not, son, I will teach you to be a true gentleman."

July 1810, the late Earl of Saunton to his son, Peregrine, on his fifteenth birthday.

* * *

"I am warning you, Emma! If you snap at me one more time, I shall plant you a facer and you will have to explain to the Balfours why your eye is blackened!"

Emma sighed heavily and slumped back in her chair. "I am truly sorry."

"I must confess it flabbergasted me when you insisted we sit in the drawing room and *embroider*. You hate to embroider. Is that why you are such poor company, or is there another reason?"

Emma stared down at the mess of threads bordered by

her embroidery frame and chose to obfuscate. "It is so frustrating that I never improve at this."

"You never improve because you attack it in the same ill-advised manner each time you attempt it. If this were any other subject, you would take a moment to reflect on how to approach it differently, with patience, but we both know you have no interest in needlework."

Emma had hoped it would distract her from the passionate embrace with Perry after reading had failed to alleviate her frustrations. Jane was correct. She had attacked it in a frenzy while maintaining a stinging conversation with her blameless sister. Carefully, she picked at one of the threads to remove it.

Jane lowered her head and continued on her own needlework, which looked faultless. "So, the embroidery is the reason for your foul mood?"

Emma licked her lips. "Of course."

"So, it has nothing to do with the fact that Perry left during our dancing lesson?"

She hesitated. "Of course not."

"Or that he kissed you?"

Emma stabbed her thumb with the needle, dropping her embroidery frame as she flushed in embarrassment. Her eyes downcast, she mumbled her response. "How do you know that?"

"I was only pretending to sleep for the final few moments. I pretended to snore as a means to discreetly interrupt when it was obvious the two of you were losing control."

"Thank you."

"My pleasure. I knew there was something between the two of you. But what does it all signify? Will he court you?"

Emma groaned and dropped her head into her hands. "That seems rather farfetched. He is a rogue, after all."

"Not that farfetched. The earl had a terrible reputation,

but it is clear he is reformed. He spends all his time with Sophia and Ethan when he is not engaged in business matters. Who is to say that Perry is not prepared to follow his brother's example?"

Emma raised her head to contemplate the Monnoyer still life above the fireplace. It was exquisite in its fine detail of a vase of trailing flowers. The riot of petal colors from blossom pink to turkey red and deep burgundies were unarguably lifelike, and the piece was one of her favorites at Balfour Terrace. She imagined what she might look like in a gown of such rich color while she tried to straighten out her thoughts.

"I dare not hope for such a thing. I cannot allow myself to fall in love with a man I cannot rely on. It would break my heart."

Jane tilted her head. "That is a possibility, then? That you could see yourself falling in love with Peregrine Balfour?"

"I admire him despite his excesses. He is intelligent and ... he possesses so much potential, if he could only apply himself."

"Oh, my goodness. I would never have thought of such a man for you, but now that I have seen you together, it is clear there is a deep connection. Perhaps ..."

Emma waited, but Jane left her sentence trembling in the air like the rain clouds to be seen through the windows. "Perhaps?"

"Well, you love lively debate and he is an enigma—a challenge, if you will. As for his interest in you—you are steadfast, loyal, and the epitome of reliability, so perhaps the orphan in him seeks your attention."

"Orphan? You are so fanciful, Jane."

"The man was barely five years of age when his mother passed away, and his father died when he was still a lad. Perhaps he was one of those boys who was kept in the nursery, and his father neglected him entirely. Is it truly inconceivable that Perry is starved for love and affection? Not to mention, we both know there is something dark in his past based on his temper at breakfast this morning. Who has their day ruined by receiving a gift? There is a compelling story to explain that odd behavior."

Emma squinted at Jane in amazement. "When did you grow so insightful?"

"I am a woman now. You just never noticed because you think of me as your little sister. I have grown up surrounded by a loving family, but I can observe that other people have not been so fortunate to enjoy parents like ours. One day, I hope to have a large family of my own. The Davises have much to bring to the world in how we approach life."

"Yes, you do have much to bring, Jane. I apologize if I have condescended to you at all."

Jane waved her frame in the air. "Forget about it. It is the natural order of things for big sisters to mother their younger brothers and sisters. But do not think I did not notice your deflection, Emma. I stand by my assertion that you have much to offer the gentleman. It would not surprise me if this relationship develops despite your best intentions to protect your pride."

"Pride!"

"Sister, it is not a secret within our family that you are so concerned with embarrassing yourself that you do not make any efforts to socialize. You are intelligent and enterprising, but you could be more adventurous about pursuing your own path outside of Papa's interests."

Emma's jaw dropped. "What the blazes, Jane?"

Jane shook her head in reproach before setting aside her frame and needle to pick up the cup of coffee on the table. Sipping deeply for several moments, she put the cup back down on the saucer. "It is not ladylike to curse. Mama made me promise I would encourage you to meet gentlemen and to try new things."

"What? She made me promise to protect you!"

"We both have our orders, then, do we not? I believe you should take a chance on love."

"Jane, I appreciate you are an optimist, but I cannot give my heart to a man who cannot love me back."

"Nothing ventured, nothing gained," her sister rebuked.

Emma could not restrain her regretful exhalation. Jane was giving her terrible advice because they both liked Perry and her sister thought there was a future for them. His antics earlier that day proved he had no intention of courting her, running from their embrace like a scared rabbit. No, she needed to stick to her plan to assist Jane in meeting an eligible young man and then return to the safety of Rose Ash Manor, where she would assist Papa with the new estate.

If fantasies of spending her life with the enigmatic Perry teased her thoughts with what could be, she would firmly brush them aside to where they belonged. Buried in the deepest recesses of her mind.

* * *

TRAFFORD WAVERED on his feet as he completed his recital, throwing his arm around for emphasis and raining drops of wine onto Perry's head in drunken enthusiasm. A couple of the men surrounding the table gave a halfhearted clap, to which Trafford took a bow and then collapsed heavily into his chair, which creaked in protest.

Perry stared into his own burgundy beverage, feeling miserable. Again. He wondered what Emma was doing right now.

As his cronies broke into an amicable argument about whose poetry was the best, Perry groaned. This evening was getting worse with every passing minute. If he could trust himself near the young woman, he would be at home enjoying her company. But he could not infect her with his dark offenses. Everything—everyone—he had ever touched had withered and died. It was why he smothered himself in glib relations with people who were not important. The only constant left in his life was his brother, who had somehow survived his association despite the stain of Perry's presence.

He could not be responsible for destroying the light he perceived in Emma's determined spirit, which meant he must stay away lest he steer her down dark paths. To repeat the mistake he had made ten years earlier with the woman from the village near Saunton Park would condemn his soul to hellfire.

His breathing cut off for a second as guilt hit him. *Blast, stop thinking about that!*

Brendan Ridley leaned forward to whisper, "Is it just me, or are these evenings becoming asinine of late?"

Perry huffed. "Perhaps. Or is it our own state of mind that is shifting?"

"Hmmm … I do not know, but after our carousing a couple nights ago, I felt wretched. I do not even recollect why I drank that much."

Perry twisted his lips in regret. "I am afraid that may have been my fault. I was in a foul mood, and I encouraged several drinking games in a bid to drown my thoughts."

Ridley pulled a face, clearly attempting to recall the details of that night as the lamplight glinted in his brandy eyes. A close friend of Richard since their days at Eton, he and Perry had become friends by default. Now they were related because Ridley's sister had married their cousin, the Duke of Halmesbury, two years earlier. He was a good chap, despite his pursuit of shallow pastimes. Not that Perry was in a position to criticize him for that.

Running a hand through his chestnut hair, Ridley drew a breath. "Did we go to Balfour Terrace that night?"

"We did."

"Blazes! The entire evening is a blur. I cannot recollect what we did there!"

"Not much. We were only there for a few minutes before we left."

Perry grimaced when he was jostled by one of their companions standing up in a clumsy fashion to recite another—terrible—poem. When he looked back, he found Ridley looking perplexed and about to speak. "Why are you so maudlin, friend?"

"I am thinking about a woman."

"Oh, I can help you with that. I ran into Lady Slight, and she was talking about you. Apparently, you spent a memorable night together last month?"

Perry stretched his neck to relieve his muscles. "It was … pleasant." Certainly not memorable.

"Well, that is not how the widow remembers it. She would be most delighted to receive a visit from you. I found myself quite unable to convince her to allow me to visit in your stead. That delectable ace of spades appears to be quite infatuated with you. If you need a woman, I am sure she will be receptive."

"I did not mean I was thinking of women. I meant a specific woman."

Comprehension crossed Ridley's face. "Ah. There is a specific young woman who has caught your attention?"

"There is. But there is nothing to be done about it." Perry was astonished to find himself relieved to speak about Emma for the first time. He could never reveal his attraction to his brother. The earl would immediately take steps to separate them, and rightly so. But Perry was not quite ready to sever his connection to her.

"She is unavailable? Do I know her?"

"You met her the other night at Balfour Terrace."

Ridley's face scrunched in concentration. "I do not recall meeting anyone. Why was she at the Terrace? I thought Saunton was not allowing loose women at the family home?"

"She is not a loose woman. She is a houseguest. The earl and countess are hosting her for the Season."

Ridley appeared shocked as he sat back in his chair to stare at Perry, his mouth agape in horror. "Never say you are enamored with a young *lady*?"

Perry cleared his throat uncomfortably. "It will pass."

"Blazes, Perry! I hope so! You are younger than me. Please do not tell me you will fall victim to the parson's noose and leave me alone with these idiots?" He threw his arm out to indicate their fellow drinkers, who were too soused to notice their conversation.

Perry forced a false snicker. "Of course not. It will pass. No young lady deserves the likes of me."

A flicker of concern passed over Ridley's face at the self-disparagement, but Perry hurried to change the subject and raised his glass in a toast before Ridley could ask questions.

* * *

"ONE, two, three; one, two, three; one, two, three." As the music ended, Perry drew to a halt.

When they stopped fully, Emma's face lit up, her black eyes shining as he released her to step back. "I did it! I completed the entire set!"

"You did. You were remarkable."

"Thank you so much, Perry! You have been a wonderful instructor!"

"I concur," Jane interjected from the pianoforte. "I have

tried to teach Emma many times, to no avail. You have performed a miracle."

Perry carefully hid his pleasure at the praise. "Emma deserves the praise. She has worked very hard on this for days."

"I could not have done it without you. You are ... an excellent dancer." Emma dropped her gaze, coloring in her shyness. Perry's heart raced. Was she thinking about the kiss from a few days earlier? He himself had struggled to keep it from his thoughts, avoiding any time alone with her lest he be tempted to seduce the innocent young woman who responded with such fiery passion. The gentleman who married her would be fortunate indeed.

A feeling of disappointment at the thought of her with another man was swiftly squashed. Perry was determined to help Emma find a beau who was worthy of her, which was why he had been on his best behavior the past few days while they navigated her dancing troubles and visits to Signora Ricci's for fittings. Emma must marry a true gentleman who deserved her, then she could have children of her own to dote on. He would not—could not—be the cause of her downfall. Rather, he would play a role in her success.

"If we are finished for today, I would dearly love to take a nap?" Jane interrupted the silence pointedly.

A slight frown marred Emma's forehead. "You did not sleep again?"

"I did not. Who can sleep when we have our first ball so soon?"

"You do not want to attend with dark circles under your eyes!"

"Of course not. That is why I wish to lie down." A mischievous glint entered Jane's eyes. "In fact, you finish discussing any further preparation for the dances, and I will leave you to it."

Perry narrowed his eyes. Was Jane attempting to leave them alone? He watched with suspicion as the tired younger sister left the music room rather hastily. He had the distinct feeling she was matchmaking with her transparent maneuver to leave Perry alone with Emma.

I am alone with Emma!

He closed his eyes in agony. Their affinity had been building for days during their lengthy instruction, with her sister to act as a chaperone between them. Perry realized his breath had grown shallow since Jane had departed the room. He wanted to leap on Emma like a ravening beast. The recollection of their ardent kiss was a physical sensation on his lips and tongue. He could practically taste her, the memory was so vivid.

He steeled his nerves. It was imperative that he get away from her. Immediately. Perry started toward the door.

"Are we ever going to speak about it?" Her voice was low and tremulous, stopping him in his tracks as if she had shouted the question.

"Speak on what?" He kept his face averted. He could not look at her, his wild creature with her nest of black curls, eyes that bored a hole through his soul, and a sharp mind that was brimming with extraordinary knowledge. If he laid eyes on her alluring form, he could not remain honorable without a chaperone between them to stay his ardor.

"The kiss … our kiss." Her declaration was so soft it was practically inaudible.

He swallowed hard, trying to think how to respond. They were not meant to be alone together. He had no words prepared for this eventuality.

"Jane thinks you could be honorable. That you might court me if you were encouraged to do so."

He almost wept with longing. *Remember what happened the*

last time you allowed someone close? You destroyed their future, you despicable blackguard.

"You think I am dishonorable?"

"I do not know. I think you are invested with much potential, but you bury it so deep that only the most astute of observers can see it."

He flinched in disbelief. Potential? Him? She might be a veritable genius, but she knew nothing about him or his proclivities.

Spinning on his heel, he stalked back to lean over her. "I am acting with honor, Emma! I have stayed away from you, have I not? There are no hidden depths to explore. What you see"—he raised his arms to present himself—"this is all there is to me. So, no, we shall not discuss what happened, and we certainly shall not spend any time alone."

With that, he stormed into the hall. He had caught the flash of pain in her eyes, but he had to hurt her in order to protect her. She did not know what hell she would invite into her life if they pursued their attraction.

CHAPTER 11

"He died. Did I forget to mention it? My memory is not what it used to be."

July 1811, the late—and frail—Earl of Saunton, to his son, Peregrine, on his sixteenth birthday, in response to a query about his maternal grandfather.

* * *

After the dancing lesson, Emma did not have time to think about her interaction with Perry or ponder his remark on his lack of depth. The first delivery of their gowns had arrived, much to her relief. The Duke and Duchess of Halmesbury were coming to dinner, and she had been terrified that she would be forced to wear one of her frumpy gowns, despite Signora Ricci's assurances of timely delivery.

The countess had arranged for her lady's maid to assist Emma and Jane to dress for dinner, a complicated feat for one abigail to see to three women. Sophia had adjourned to her rooms early so that there would be sufficient time for everyone to prepare.

Emma lifted her hand to toy with an errant curl. She hoped Miss Toussaint could repeat the prior miracle with the hair tonic, despite the limited time at hand.

Ethan moved a chess piece on the board between them, his little face screwed in concentration. Peering at the pieces carefully, he finally let go of the knight to complete the move. The moment he was done, he looked back up at her to continue his story. "… Papa made sure we were completely alone. And then"—Ethan looked about to ensure no one could overhear him, dropping his voice—"he galloped in Hyde Park!"

"What? The two of you were very naughty!"

"Papa said it was sunrise and the park was mostly empty, so we could risk it for a few moments."

From across the room, the earl raised his head from the book he was writing in. "Ethan! That was intended to be a secret." Richard's tone was light, despite the admonishment. "Now Emma will think we are ne'er-do-wells who flout the rules of Hyde Park."

Ethan frowned in perplexity. "What is a *nair-air-dwell*?"

"It is a little boy who makes his papa look like a scoundrel in front of the ladies," his father replied with a fake sigh.

"What is a *scown-drill*?"

The earl chuckled before rising to his feet. Striding across the room, he leaned down and picked Ethan up, who squirmed and giggled in protest as he was lifted from his chair. "Papa, I am in the middle of a game!"

"Chess is for little lads who keep the secrets they promised to. We will leave Emma alone so I can give you the word lessons you just asked for."

"Are we really *nair-air … dwells*?"

"How about I explain what it means and then you can decide for yourself?"

Emma observed their interplay with a fierce pang of longing. Would Perry have a son one day? If so, would the boy look like Ethan, with his dark locks and striking green eyes? A lump formed in her throat. Would *she* ever have a son of her own? Pressing her lips together, she frantically sought for something to distract her thoughts before she displayed embarrassing emotion. Hopping to her feet, she summoned Jane to join her in their rooms to await their turns with Miss Toussaint.

It was two hours later when she moved her head back and forth to see her hair at different angles in the mirror.

"You look so beautiful, Emma!" Jane's voice was suspiciously muffled.

"Are you crying?" she responded in consternation.

"It is just … I have never seen you … Sophia!" Her sister implored the countess to intervene.

Sophia came to stand behind Emma, her reflection appearing in the mirror as Emma continued to stare at herself in disbelief. "Signora Ricci is an artiste. The cut of the dress perfectly suits your figure, and that color, Mazarine blue silk …" Sophia bit her lip.

"Are you going to cry, too?"

"You just look so beautiful," mumbled the countess, her eyes glistening.

Miss Toussaint had tamed Emma's hair into a cascade of glossy curls mounted in an elegant coiffure. Along with the deep blue silk of the gracefully draped gown, Emma admitted to herself that she had never looked so comely, despite her mild discomfort at the low-cut bodice which revealed the upper slope of her bosom. She was fit to meet a duke, a peer second only to the royal family itself.

"If you are concerned about meeting the duke, do not be.

He is the kindest gentleman of my acquaintance. He and the duchess are fully aware that this is a practice dinner for you and will do everything they can to set you at ease." Emma smiled at Sophia in the mirror. The Balfours had turned out to be as generous and warm as her own family and, despite her misgivings, she was grateful for all they had done.

"Thank you … for everything," Emma said to Sophia's reflection.

The countess looked close to tears again, taking a moment to clear her throat. "It has been our great pleasure, Emma. What you did for Ethan can never be repaid. The earl is … so … utterly relieved that his unintentional neglect caused no permanent harm to his son." Sophia patted her own stomach, a protective gesture Emma had observed her do several times. "A family like yours cherishing our boy until we learned of his existence is the most fortunate outcome one could wish for. You nurtured his character and his genius."

Emma gave a tremulous smile, blinking tears from her own eyes.

"Goodness! Look at us. We are turning into watering pots! We should go down and prepare for the arrival of the duke and duchess!" Sophia wiped her eyes before shooing them from Emma's bedroom.

Smoothing her skirts, Emma hoped Perry would be at dinner, despite her determination to stay away from the rogue. If he had desired her before tonight, what would he think when he saw her so elegantly attired? Her vanity could not be denied. She wanted to impress him.

The evening began without incident. The duke had turned out to be a warm, composed gentleman with the appearance of a Viking god, towering over the earl and even Perry, who were not men of small stature. The duchess was a warm young woman whose unusual brandy eyes glinted in the gaslights, and she smiled frequently. But Emma had barely noticed them after Perry entered the drawing room where they congregated before dinner was called. His emerald eyes had found her and, to her great gratification, had remained fixed on her for the rest of the evening.

They sat together at dinner, and he engaged in animated conversation with her while they waited for the courses to be served. Despite her earlier decisions regarding the handsome rogue, she responded in kind, blossoming at his obvious admiration and feeling beautiful for the first time in her young life.

"Thank you, Timothy, but I will not have the soup tonight." Perry's proclamation was stated with confidence, his mellifluous voice causing the entire table to pause mid-conversation and stare at him. The footman stood frozen in surprise, gripping the bowl of soup he had been about to place on the table in front of Perry, and obviously uncertain what to do. Perry smirked knowingly at Emma before he took mercy on the servant. "It was a jest, Timothy. You may leave the soup."

The footman visibly exhaled in relief, lowering the bowl before stepping back deftly. The other diners resumed their conversations while Emma used the back of her fist to thump Perry lightly on the side of his thigh under the table. Lowering her voice, she whispered, "You did that to make fun of me!"

Perry grinned, his square face youthful in the low light. He was unusually relaxed, letting his guard down more than she had previously seen him do. "I merely provided a demonstration of what would happen if you ever disdained the soup."

Emma pressed her lips together to withhold the giggle that threatened to escape. "In that case, Sir Galahad, I thank you for saving me from the very worst of embarrassments."

"Heaven forfend, you commit social suicide by turning a bowl of broth away."

The giggle escaped, and Emma laughed out loud. Fortunately, she was sharing her dinner with family and friends, so no one showed any sign of rebuke as they sipped their soup from the sides of their silver spoons.

* * *

PERRY WAS ENJOYING dinner with Emma at his side in the lavish dining room. Not in his feigned manner he had cultivated over the years to hide his thoughts, but truly enjoying her company. When he entered the drawing room earlier, he had immediately seen the difference in her demeanor.

His wildflower had found her confidence, and although she looked utterly lovely in her new evening gown with her hair expertly styled, it was that newfound assurance that had entranced him. She was incandescent, and he had immediately been drawn to her side, taking a moment to arrange to be seated beside her for dinner.

After his jest with the soup, she had thumped his thigh, and it was all he could do not to reach down and grab her hand with his own to stroke her fingers. Her bare fingers, for she had removed her gloves for dinner.

Perry quelled the primal surge of lust at the thought of her naked skin beneath his. He feared his fascination was evolving into an infatuation, but he could not find the strength to withdraw despite his best intentions to avoid her. He was a moth drawn to the flame of her unbridled vivacity, and it was only the presence of others at the table that prevented him from pulling her into his arms right there in the dining room to taste her lips once more.

Emma leaned in to speak. "Did you notice that Jane and I both sipped the soup from the side of our spoons? Without instruction or supervision? I think we might be prepared to eat dinner without you present, Perry!"

Perry chuckled at the remark while he fixated on the sweet curve of her neck. His breath sharpened, and it took all his will to not allow his eyes to fall to the swell of her breasts so elegantly framed with blue silk. Leaning back to compose himself, he noticed the duke observing him from the head of the table where he sat diagonally across from Richard. Halmesbury smiled before turning back to reply to the earl.

Perry realized he had not responded. "So, it is your assertion that you are prepared for an evening without my company, Miss Bluestocking?"

"I am certain I could manage," she responded pertly.

"But would you want to?" Perry's question was laced with humor, but he hungered for her answer.

Emma stilled, then glanced at him with a serious expression. "No. It is better when you are present."

His heart stopped in his chest at the earnest confession, then he deliberately inhaled her chamomile scent that had been delicately teasing his senses since the evening had begun.

* * *

Emma sat on her bed later that evening, still thinking about her altercation with Perry earlier that day. It pained her that he seemed to think so little of himself, and she wondered what the cause of it was. He had been a marvelous tutor these past days, so she knew he possessed persistence, and his presence had given her the confidence she needed to overcome her lack of grace. As the ball approached, Emma now believed she could get through the event without experiencing significant misfortune.

There was no doubt in her mind that the gentleman

possessed potential. The true issue was that he had no intention of maturing, which was why it was imperative that she stay away from him. Emma had no desire to have her heart trampled. As it stood, she was perilously close to imagining herself in love with the unattainable beau. Jane was foolish to encourage her sentiments. And Emma was foolish for listening merely because she wished it were possible that he would come up to scratch.

Her fingertips played along her lower lip where he had licked in his passion. She had never imagined such intense, consuming fire existed.

Emma dropped her hand, sighing deeply. Contemplating impossible futures in the manner of a heroine from a gothic novel was not a worthwhile pursuit. It was all so melodramatic. Jane needed to meet a gentleman and then Emma needed to go home so she might return to her real life, not this imaginary world in which a maiden and a rogue surmounted the obstacles in their path to achieve everlasting love. *This is Elizabeth and Darcy's fault for planting such notions in my head!*

She had relished her moment basking in the glow of his attentions, but now it was time to be realistic and put aside foolish dreams.

Rising to her feet, Emma tightened the sash of her wrapper and walked to the door. She needed to find a new book to divert her thoughts. Clearly, a night of tossing and turning was imminent unless she sought a distraction. Turning the handle, she pulled the door ajar.

"What the living blazes!" Emma clapped a hand over her mouth, hoping her screech would not waken the other inhabitants of the family hall. This matter was private, after all.

Perry, framed in the doorway, stared at his Hessians. "I could not stay away any longer."

His jacket was missing, and his shirt hung loose to expose the column of his throat. His sleeves were rolled up to reveal thick forearms covered with a smattering of fine sable hair. Emma had to clench her hands to stop from reaching out to feel his golden-brown skin beneath her palms. She could barely make out what he mumbled to his boots because her pulse quickened with a rush of joy, while her conscience shouted warnings at the back of her head.

PERRY HAD STRUGGLED with his conscience since dinner. Emma had been a temptation since he met her, but now that she was artfully attired and self-assured … she was devastating to his state of mind. Her mere presence lifted his spirits, and her habit of dressing so poorly had been his only meager defense from losing his scruples altogether.

He had tried to walk down the hall to leave and find his friends—any distraction at all—but on the way out, his boots had led him to her door without him making any conscious decision. He had been standing in a quandary for some time when he heard her approach from the other side and open the last remaining barrier between them.

He could not find it in him to turn away. Staring at her slippers, he attempted to explain his mortifying lack of honor.

"I could not stay away any longer." It was the second time he had said it, but Emma had not yet spoken. Silently, she opened the door farther, and he stepped into her room. Carefully, she closed the door behind him and turned to stare over his shoulder. Chewing on her lip revealed her tension.

"What is this? Between us?"

"I do not know," he replied. "It is powerful, is it not?"

"Not unlike the orbit of the moon around the earth." Emma's response was so quintessential to her character, Perry could not help the smile that crossed his face. Had he ever smiled so much? Since Emma had walked into the drawing room at Rose Ash Manor, he simply could not help himself. He was positively cheery since he had first encountered her.

Raising a hand, he took hold of one of her trailing black locks. "You looked beautiful this evening. A true maiden of the *ton* ... except ... well ... you." Perry restrained a grimace. He hoped she understood it was a compliment. That she was far better than any maiden of the *ton*, in his estimation. His elegant manners and silver-tongue had been fading since he first encountered this glorious creature in Somerset.

Huge coal-black eyes found him in the low light. "Do you mean that?" Emma seemed pleased, to his relief.

"Oh, Emma, if you only knew. My defenses are crumbling, and I can no longer protect you from myself."

A frown of confusion marred her heart-shaped face. "Protect me? Whatever do you mean by that?"

But Perry refused to think about his past. He stepped forward and slowly lowered his head, giving her a chance to deny him if she would.

Finally, his lips made contact with her exquisitely soft mouth, his heart beating faster in his chest. His fiery bluestocking was moonlight and shadows, a whimsical blend of chamomile and wildflowers, and he could no longer restrain his passion. She moaned her desire against him, the only invitation he needed to work an arm around her while his free hand tore at the sash of her wrapper. His tongue found hers and she responded, as before, with enthusiasm, her arms winding around his neck and her fingers combing through his hair to send frissons of sensual delight to course through his body and gather in his groin. He must touch her, taste her, but somehow he would find the strength to stop, to not sink into the warm clasp of her body, because he could not ruin her future as he had done before with—

"Emma, sweet … feisty … Emma." He groaned between deep kisses before leaning down to lift her in his arms, followed by the muted thunk of her slippers falling to the floor. His woman looked up at him with glazed eyes, swollen lips, and trusting adoration, and his profound yearning nearly overpowered him. *I wish she could be mine. Forever.* But that was not to be. He had this moment with her and then he must finally let her go so she could find the future she deserved with a man worthy of her.

HE TASTED of wine and mint, Emma had discovered while their lips molded together in a deep, drugging kiss. She burrowed against his hard chest, enjoying the feel of Perry's strong, muscular arms banded around her as he strode effortlessly toward her bed. They had not discussed where this night would lead, and he had made no promises, but she could not find the will to resist him. She held no hopes that she would ever find another gentleman so appealing, so if there was no future to be had with Perry, she would simply return home as soon as Jane was settled.

Emma had been fighting her attraction to the charming rogue since she first laid eyes on him, but she could no longer fight what her heart and her body cried out for. Deep in her soul, she trusted Perry even as he spoke of not trusting himself. No matter what happened, she knew he would ultimately do the right thing. She would follow where he led because to do anything else was to invite a lifetime of regrets and wondering what it would have been like to be with such a unique, incomprehensible man. And, despite his self-deprecation, Perry had more honor than he gave himself credit for.

Emma could hear his heart pounding hard in his chest through the linen of his shirt rubbing against her cheek. Perry reached the bed to lower her onto the sheets. She had thrown the counterpane aside when she left her bed earlier to pace her room and think about the very man now standing over her with heavy lids and rasping breath as he propped a knee close to her thigh so he might bend to kiss her once more. His intense eyes mirrored her own thick, coursing desire as she reached up to press her mouth closer.

Perry placed one hand to balance himself over her, but the other … the other found the top edge of her night rail as his lingering fingertips grazed back and forth over the rise of her shuddering bosom. Emma felt her nipples pebble in aching reaction, throbbing for his touch as he carefully slid his hand in to affectionately cup a breast which to her had always been a source of embarrassment—how could she be so slight of frame and yet have such prominent … assets?

"You are magnificent …" His whispered admission against her neck sent a tendril of heat dancing across her skin, causing her to shiver at the unexpected sensation. As he massaged her areola with his thumb, he pressed light kisses along her jaw. She bucked with agitation. "Shhh … be patient, termagant. We will be taking our time."

With that, he carefully undid the tapes at the front of her night rail so that his mouth could follow the path of his hand, revealing a turgid nipple which he leaned down to flick gently with his velvet tongue. Emma moaned loudly, finally understanding the role her plump globes played in the art of lovemaking as she arched up, keening in heady agreement. When his warm hand stroked over to caress her other breast through the thin cotton, while continuing his ministrations on the first by swirling his tongue over the stiff, pleading peak, she cried out, all thought vanishing. She could only feel. Feel his heavy weight, his determined mouth, his firm jaw, and the rasp of the stubble on his cheek as he groaned against her skin. "My God, Emma, your breasts are even more lovely than I imagined."

Imagined? It flashed through her mind that she had caught Perry's eyes dropping to her bodice on more than one occasion. Had he been fascinated by her bosom?

Zooks! In that moment, she comprehended just how naïve and innocent she was when it came to men and seduction. She had had an inkling he was interested in her physically, but this new realization cast light on several of their interactions in the past, including the day that they met. Perry had desired her from the first!

Newfound confidence filled her, bubbling up into her head as a giddy sense of delight. A sense of empowerment. She was desirable!

It gave her the courage to lift her trembling hands and grip his large, well-formed biceps through his clothes, flexing her fingers to feel the powerful muscles and leashed strength.

Perry exhaled roughly in pleasure when she smoothed her hands up to knead his broad shoulders, his breath sawing across her dampened breasts to send fluttering shivers tingling in every direction. He rose suddenly, to her dismay. Was he leaving?

"I need to see you!" He clenched the top edge of her night rail and ripped the garment all the way to the hem with a loud rending of fabric. Even Perry appeared surprised as he stared down at the tatters in his hand. "Well, that was surprisingly easy?"

Emma blushed despite her astonishment. "It is an old one I brought with me that has been through many washings. We forgot to order new ones when we saw Signora Ricci. But how will I explain its state, you … you … heedless barbarian?"

But Perry was not listening. He had dropped the two halves of the night rail, his impassioned gaze shifting to explore her exposed body. His eyes lingered on her heaving breasts before slowly shifting down her belly to—

Emma yelped and crossed her legs as he stared at the apex of her thighs, lifting a hand to cover herself. He caught her hand in his before extending the other to gently graze his fingertips over her belly, brushing over the black curls shielding her mound. She shivered and squirmed in the wake of the trailing heat from his searching touch. It was difficult to move with her wrapper and now her night rail draped to either side of her, inhibiting her arms.

Perry relentlessly stroked gently over her swollen seam, back and forth, back and forth, until Emma could stand it no longer and her legs parted in mute invitation to further his exploration. "Oh, Emma …" He leaned down and lathed one puckered nipple until she thought she would swoon with heady desire, all the while he slowly traced the slick folds of her crevice with a curious finger to brush over a particularly sensitive spot that made her toes curl. Her mouth fell open in a wail, but he hastily moved up to capture her mouth in a kiss as he continued his tantalizing touch.

"Shhh, lovely Emma. We do not wish to be interrupted, do we?" She opened heavy eyes to look up into his riveting green irises, mutely shaking her head and gratified to see he was as flushed and bemused as she had never seen him. With that, he came down over her body, his knees edging her knees open to bring his firm hardness against her. With only his breeches to separate them, she rubbed against him in wicked delight as he continued to kiss her, his tongue entangling with hers once more.

Slowly, he moved down to kiss and lick her straining

nipples, before moving down to place kisses lower and lower down her belly. Pleasure pooled and throbbed between her thighs as she moved rhythmically against him until she felt him press a kiss to the top of her mound.

Emma froze. "Are you—"

"Shhh …" Perry's heated mouth found her crease, his breath sending tingles to the sensitive spot he had found earlier and, to her dismay, Emma lifted her hips to encourage him as his tongue swiped her folds. The sensation—the indescribable sensation. She slapped a forearm over her mouth to release a muffled squeal of amazement at the shooting sensation that overpowered her. His hands gripped her hips, and he lifted her further to repeatedly explore, lick, kiss her melting core. Emma whimpered in muffled delight until white-hot sensation overcame her, and wave after wave of unadulterated pleasure hit her until she lost all notion of where she was.

CHAPTER 12

"Perry, it is most unusual that you have never left home to attend school like other boys—men—your age. As the new head of the household, I ... I wondered if you had any thoughts regarding your future?"

July 1812, Richard Balfour, the newly titled Earl of Saunton, to his brother Peregrine on his seventeenth birthday, two days after their father passed away.

* * *

Emma woke midmorning and stretched her body out in pleasure. Perry had cuddled her after her climactic event, nuzzling her temple and stroking his fingers over her naked body until she had fallen asleep. Now she awoke alone to the joy of having spent a passionate night with the man she loved.

Love?

Emma sat up in horror. Was she truly so stupid to have fallen in love with an incorrigible rake?

Oh, Lord!

She dropped her head in her hands.

Perhaps he felt the same? After all, he had stopped short of taking her virtue despite the obvious discomfort it had caused him.

Or had Perry stopped short because he did not want to ruin her for marriage to some other young man?

Her feelings of happiness dissipated to worry. How had she allowed her heart to become engaged? If Perry had honorable intentions, he would court her openly. Maybe he had plans to? Maybe he stopped short in order to honor her with a proper courtship?

Emma prayed for fate to be kind to her, for Perry to be kind, for their blossoming relationship to bear fruit, but her hands trembled as she acknowledged her fear that the man she loved would not pursue the connection that had formed between them. That the incomplete act was a sign he would not allow things to progress any further.

As she sat hunched over with the crumpled counterpane draped around her hips, Emma caught sight of her naked breasts. She was still in the torn night rail and wrapper! Scrambling from the bed, she gathered the pieces in her hand, staring at them in a quandary. What was she to do with the garment? There was no explaining its current condition, and if she threw it out, the servants would gossip.

She drew the wrapper off and then the rail, which she draped on the bed. Putting the wrapper back on, she grabbed the rail and tore a wide strip. Her mind racing, she continued to tear the strip into handkerchief-sized pieces. Her plan gave her a distraction from her thoughts, so with gusto she continued to tear the cotton. At worst, the servants would think her impulsive or eccentric, but no one would suspect she was hiding a scandalous night in the arms of the incorrigible Perry.

A soft knock sounded at the door behind her. Clapping a hand to her chest in surprise, she exhaled in relief that the night rail was half obliterated, a small pile of handkerchiefs on the bed.

"Come in!" she called.

The door swung open to reveal the countess, impeccably dressed in an indigo and cream day gown that perfectly complemented her coifed red-blonde hair. Behind her, Jane tottered in with dark circles under her eyes and a weary slump to her shoulders.

"Did you fail to sleep again, Jane?"

Her usually cheerful sister sighed heavily. "I really do not understand it! I have never had trouble sleeping before. Being in London must just be too exciting. The only time I seem to sleep is in the afternoon, when sheer exhaustion finally causes me to pass out."

Emma scrunched her face in commiseration.

"I offered to send for the physician, but your sister says there is no time today." Sophia's voice contained concern.

"No time?"

Sophia broke into a broad smile. "That is why we came to find you! There is a delivery from Signora Ricci, and the new lady's maid is downstairs. I wanted to send her up to help you prepare for the day, but then the garments arrived, and I thought we could have you and Jane try them on so we can judge whether they are to our liking."

The thought of new gowns cheered Emma up. Perhaps she could lure Perry into courtship? He had responded in a gratifying manner to her appearance the evening before, so perhaps enticing him further would overcome any misgivings to wooing her with a mind to marry. Emma knew it was unlikely, but the romantic in her could not resist hoping for a happy ending, despite her suspicions regarding his intentions.

"I shall dress so we can breakfast, and then that sounds delightful!" Emma attempted to squash the internal voice that taunted her. *You wish to see Perry at the breakfast table, you gullible chit!*

"Uh ... Emma ... What are those?" Jane pointed at the pile of cotton squares on the bed alongside the remaining half of her night rail.

"I ripped my rail by accident, so I thought I shall turn it into practice for my needlework."

The countess crinkled her nose in subtle confusion. "We have fabric for you to practice with, Emma. I can request it to be brought to you."

Jane might appear tired, but she managed a healthy dose of skepticism as she stared at the squares. "Practice needlework? Perhaps Sophia should summon the physician, after all?"

Emma grasped desperately for an explanation to placate her sister's mistrust. "I mastered the waltz. I thought I should make a fresh attempt at embroidery! However, no need to waste good fabric on my shaky hand. I will practice on these before I waste good cotton."

"Very thrifty of you, Emma. The gentleman who marries you will be fortunate, dear." Sophia did not seem entirely convinced of Emma's sanity, but she attempted to sound encouraging.

* * *

Perry ran his hand through his hair in agitation. He had left Emma's rooms before sunrise. Before servants could observe him. There had been a moment out in the hall when he thought someone might be there with him—might have seen him. He had stood in silence for several minutes, listening until he had grown certain he was mistaken.

In his rooms he had dressed for the day, leaving the townhouse as the first rays of sun lit the quiet Mayfair street outside. Then he had sought out his clubs to find sustenance, which he had picked at halfheartedly.

Perry could not believe he had found the strength, the sheer power of will, to stop making love to Emma. His only boon had been that he remained fully clothed and had not felt her delicate touch on his naked skin. Her feminine scent alone was taunting him—he repeatedly imagined he could pick out her fragrance.

But he could not take her virtue. It would rob him of the last remaining vestiges of self-respect he had clung to all these years since that night—

Perry inhaled in a rush. *Do not think about that night!*

Stretching his neck to ease the tension in his muscles, he rubbed a hand over his tired face. He could not steal Emma's virtue, was the point. And he could not pursue her or woo her because she deserved better than a scoundrel. Even now, he wanted to return to her side, but he must stay away lest he do something regrettable. Next time they met, he must be ruthless. Cold. Arrogant. He must upset her so greatly that she would sever their connection on his behalf. It must be done to protect her, because if he did not drive her away, he would inevitably give in to his base impulses and find his way back to her door.

"Are you listening?" Trafford demanded.

Perry addressed the table with his response, too despondent to lift his head as he glared at the surface of the furnishing. "Of course."

"Then why have I repeated the same questions thrice to no avail?"

Flushing, Perry straightened in his seat. He had been out for hours now to avoid Emma. A window revealed that night had finally fallen and soon Emma would be in her room preparing for bed. *Where you cannot join her, you treacherous lech! You cannot ruin another innocent maiden without losing your sanity.*

Especially not if the maiden in question was the unique, intelligent, fragrant Emma.

"I apologize. I was woolgathering due to lack of sleep." The agony of staying away from her all day was a physical affliction. *If only ...*

"Blazes, Balfour! You have become foul company ever since you left on your errand to the country."

Perry blinked, returning to the moment. He dug deep to find a sarcastic smile, raising his head and wine in toast. "I do not know of what you speak, Trafford. I believe your new woman is making you melancholy and now you reflect your issues on me." With that, he swallowed the beverage continuously until he had drunk every last sip, before bringing the glass down with a distinctive clink on the table. "What do we do tonight, gentlemen? The night is young and so are we!"

Trafford blinked at the abrupt change in mood and velocity, which Perry ignored, along with the questioning look that Brendan Ridley threw his way.

Regrets be damned. He would find pleasurable pursuits to distract him from his maudlin yearnings and memories. He was the licentious son of the Earl of Satan, and it was time to behave so.

ON THE THIRD morning of eating breakfast with no sign of Perry again, Emma finally accepted that he was abandoning her. The feckless rogue had become frightened of their connection and now resisted it. She should be thankful he had left her virtue intact, she told herself as she picked at her breakfast. There was no ruin. No possibility of a babe. It was poor consolation.

"Where is my damned brother?" Richard growled at his wife in a resentful tone. "I thought the time of vanishing for days was over, but yet I have not seen him in three days! He promised to assist the young ladies with their dance instruction, and now the ball is only days away!"

"He is sleeping in his bed at night," soothed Sophia. "I know he worries you, but he is coming home. Albeit at strange hours."

The earl pulled a face of query. "How do you know that? I rise at sunrise every morning, and I do not know that. I need to speak to the infernal rascal, but he evades me at every turn!"

"The servants have informed me that by the time they enter his rooms at sunrise, his bed is unmade." The countess had modulated her voice as if coaxing a child, clearly attempting to smooth her husband's ire.

"I have something of import to discuss. His behavior recently is beyond the pale, and I am quite losing my patience with his antics." The earl's tone remained belligerent.

"Richard, do not scare our guests." Sophia flicked her eyes toward Jane and Emma with a small tilt of her head.

He drew a sharp breath, reminding Emma of her own tempting rogue in his frustration. The earl's customary affability was not in evidence this morning.

"Emma learned a great deal from Perry. I can practice with her and teach her the rest now that she is so far along," Jane ventured. Emma was relieved to see color in her cheeks as her sister sipped on the coffee she had become so fond of.

"I agree. Jane and I have tried on our new gowns, and

Betty has mastered the art of my wild hair." Emma raised a hand to rub one of her improved glossy locks between her fingertips. Their new lady's maid had initially been daunted by Emma's nest of curls, but the more experienced maid, Miss Toussaint, had provided Betty with the hair tonic and shown her how to manage the unruly locks. "Today we shall practice the full set together. Do not worry about us." *Nay, worry about your brother and unearth him so we may all feel better.*

Emma's protective instincts were on high alert. Perry struggled with something, and he needed assistance. This prolonged absence proved her suspicions. Although she missed his presence, it was concern for him that most unsettled her musings.

Perry was a man haunted by unnamed demons, and she had been selfish to not notice or attempt to assist him. She had been too distracted by his handsome visage, not to mention lustful in her desire to share his kisses. If she had truly cared more about his happiness, instead of pursuing her own pleasure, she would have demanded to understand what tortured him so. It irked her to feel disloyal to someone she cared for, even as she felt betrayed by his absence. Why did he feel he must protect her from himself?

She could not deny the worried feeling in her belly, nor the flashes of vexation that scurried across the surface of her skin. Rising from her chair, she decided keeping busy was the best course of action. "Shall we go practice now?"

Emma had formed a plan, and she needed to keep her attention occupied until it was time to execute it lest she go mad from her errant thoughts.

THE TALL CASEMENT clock down the hall tolled twice as Perry entered Balfour Terrace, exhausted. He had kept up a steady schedule of riding, carousing, debating, and anything else he could think of to occupy his thoughts. Anything to avoid finding himself at Emma's door. The next time he crossed her threshold, there would be no stopping himself. The sweet serenity of cradling her in his arms after he had brought her to pleasure still lingered, mocking him with what could be if only he were an honorable man. If he had not ruined a young woman's life and driven away anyone he had ever cared for.

He would lose Richard, too, if he wrecked Emma's life. Perry was certain Richard would never forgive such a transgression against a young woman he considered to be family. Thank God his brother did not know about— *Stop thinking about her!*

Perry had run from his past and concealed his inadequacies for so long with sarcastic smiles and mindless pleasures. Defeat wearied his soul. Then his brother met Sophia, had a change of heart regarding how he lived his life, and made reparations. Perry had pretended he was amused by his brother's stumbling efforts, but truthfully, he had witnessed Richard's progress with bated breath.

He had dared to hope for a fleeting moment—or rather, a couple of months—that he might somehow make reparations for his own past misdeed and pursue his own enlightened future. Then he had met Emma and accepted the painful truth of his terrible past as the devil's apprentice, destined to be an irremediable spawn of hell.

In contrast with his brother, who was a leader of men, well-respected and liked, Perry was nothing. Had done nothing but destroy a young woman's future. He could see no path out, and he dared not confess his past lest his own brother turn from him in disgust and he lose his last remaining connection to anyone who cared for him.

The fear was not unfounded. Their grandfather had lost faith in him as a boy, fading from his life in damning condemnation of his younger grandson after Perry had pleaded with him to remove him from Saunton Park—*Satan Park*—to live at his home in Shepton. His grandfather had assured him he would assist Perry, who had been desperate to get away from his father's influence. The old man had been the only remaining light in Perry's life after his brother had stopped coming home four years earlier, instead favoring visits with Brendan and Annabel Ridley.

Instead of fetching Perry to his home, their grandfather had stopped visiting altogether, clearly losing interest in him. Perry never saw the old man again. The late Earl of *Satan* had eventually informed him that the beloved figure from his childhood had died.

To that day, Perry knew not what had happened, why his grandfather had abandoned him to his fate, but he had never had the fortitude to ask Richard about it. He feared he would learn that his brother's relationship with their grandfather had continued uninterrupted, which would mean Perry truly had been abandoned as a hopeless case.

There were many things he did not have the fortitude to discuss with Richard. His fierce gratitude for his brother, his only remaining family, commanded Perry to avoid any missteps that might lead to yet another estrangement. He knew he was a coward, but if Richard turned away from him, Perry would truly have nothing meaningful left in his life.

Christ, these maudlin thoughts are killing me. Perry longed for the days when he had moved numbly through life without a care. A door to his memories had been opened, and he could not seem to force the door shut, no matter how much wine he drank.

Perry looked up from his thoughts to find his legs had found their way to the family wing. Emma's door loomed to the right. Moving forward, he gently placed a palm on the wooden panel, imagining Emma in the room beyond. He wondered if she slept or if she was awake like him. His entire body yearned to join her and reexperience the peace of holding her in his arms, listening to her low breathing as she fell asleep in sated pleasure, but he could never return to that moment. It was yet another memory to haunt his waking hours, but he must protect her from himself at all costs. He would lose his mind if he extinguished her light like he had—*No more! You must forget that night!*

Perry forced his feet to move in the direction of his room. He would sleep for a couple of hours and then force himself out of the townhouse again. The only reason he returned home at all was to feel that he was still somehow connected—still somehow part of a family—even if it was a tenuous connection that was sure to inevitably end regardless of the care he took to maintain it. This situation with Emma proved his dishonorable nature, and eventually, his brother would come to realize Perry was a lost cause.

Well-done for curtailing the maudlin thoughts, Perry.

He just needed to keep his head down and wait for Emma to be gone, at which point he could resume his life and avoid making any mistakes. The next time he saw her, he would ensure he did something so unforgivable that she would be the one to keep her distance. *Unforgivable.* He could nearly taste the bile from his churning stomach. The ball would be his opportunity to ruin their connection in a manner so permanent, there would be no risk of him ever causing her harm.

Giving Emma up was the only method to ensure he saved the young woman from his dark influence, maintained his relationship with his older brother, and kept whatever pieces of his soul he had left to protect. Feeling more certain of his plan to keep Emma safe, he opened his bedroom door and stepped inside. His heart leapt from his chest. He was not alone.

"I have been waiting for you."

* * *

When the countess mentioned that Perry had been returning home in the early hours, Emma recognized an opportunity to repair her insensitivity. She was determined to assist the young man who had captured her heart.

Long after the family retired for the night, and too nervous to read, she had simply prepared what she would say, fidgeting endlessly with her wrapper and hair in an agitated fashion while her mind whirled.

Emma's hand flew up to clutch her chest in surprise. The door had opened without warning. Biting her lip with nervousness, she hopped down from the tall bed to stand at the foot of it and gaze at the gent across the darkened room.

"I have been waiting for you." *Truly? So much for preparation.*

Perry looked worse for wear, yet her heart ached to see him after his continued absence this many days. He closed the door behind him. Reminding herself that she was here for his sake, not her own foolish heart, Emma threaded her fingers together to still her nervousness.

"I see that." His tone was distinctly cold. Her confidence—whatever shreds of it she had brought into his room with her—evaporated as her shoulders drooped. Perry had accused her of being feisty, but she was so far beyond her limited experience, she had nothing to draw on to feed her fire.

"I wanted to ... verify that you were all right?" Emma knew her question was weak, but what was she to say in such a situation? They had made love, or at least he had made love to her, while he silently struggled with unnamed evils, and now she dared to offer solace to a man who had been her adversary since they had met. What was this between them? It followed no logic, their strange relationship. The only comparable analogy she could draw was that, despite their sexual attraction, in her mind Perry was family somehow, and family required loyalty.

"All right?" His frosty tone froze the breath in her chest. Emma squared her shoulders and exhaled. This was a matter of integrity. She needed to follow her conscience to do what was right by him, whether or not he welcomed the attentions.

"It occurred to me that you have had something on your mind, but I was so taken with … you … that I failed to offer my assistance."

"Your assistance?" He barked a humorless laugh. "You cannot help with what ails me, Emma. You should go to bed."

Emma welcomed the rising frisson of annoyance. It fortified her spirit. This, she was familiar with. "I am very learned, and I assist my father with estate matters. He often discusses issues with me. And Sophia has told me many times that I did an exemplary work raising Ethan and fostering his intelligence. I may be young—innocent, even—but I am logical and good at solving problems. I … like you, and I wish to offer my assistance with your troubles."

Perry's face was stiff as he stepped forward. "Get out of my room."

Her courage began to fail. "Why, Perry? What have I done to upset you so?"

"Your presence upsets me."

Emma's resolve crumpled. The man who held her heart in his hands had never sounded so icy, so deliberate, so … hurtful.

You have made your offer of help, and you no longer owe him anything.

Knowing that behind this rude, ruthless behavior, Perry was hurting, was a small comfort, but nevertheless, she needed to protect herself from any further heartbreak. Firming her jaw, Emma gave a curt nod and moved to the door, jumping in surprise when Perry's hand snaked out to grasp her wrist as she passed him.

"Emma …" His voice was strangled, tortured, and Emma knew she had been correct. The rogue hid pain behind his elegant manners and sarcastic smiles. Her heart ached for him, but what could she do if he would not speak about it? She waited, certain he could feel her pulse leaping where he held her. "Emma …"

With that, he turned toward her, using his grip to tug her into his arms. His lips descended to seek hers. Emma gasped, then lifted on her toes to kiss him back as relief and desire coursed through her at the touch of his mouth on hers, but he pulled his face away and buried it into her hair to breathe deeply. "You always smell like freedom. My sweet, fiery Emma."

Emma listened to his heart thudding in his chest while he stroked his arms up and down her back, embracing her as if he were a drowning man and she the tether that would bring him to safety. It broke her heart to sense his agony. After a few moments, he sighed and pulled back to release her and step away.

"Will you be at our ball?"

There were several moments of silence. Emma wished she could see his face, read his expression, understand what troubles he shouldered. "Of course I will be there."

His tone was odd, mounting Emma's misgivings that she had failed him in some manner.

"Will you dance with me?"

A long pause. "Perhaps. Goodnight, Emma."

Dismissed, she departed, casting one last glance to her beloved rogue before gently closing the door to stand in the hall and wring her hands in frustration. For a moment, she had made some progress with him, but then the moment had evaporated to leave her more worried than before.

CHAPTER 13

"You are an amusing fellow, Balfour. Care to join us for a drink?"

July 1813, Lord Julius Trafford to Peregrine, on his eighteenth birthday.

* * *

Emma woke the day of the ball to a heavy shower of rain, the downpour deafening while thunder shook the windows in a rattle of glass. Was it foreboding of the day to come?

Chewing her lip, she lay in bed, staring at the ornate cornices framing the ceiling to consider the cause of her anxiety—Perry's strange mood the night before. She missed him fiercely, but that was secondary to her worry that he suffered some great burden. If only dealing with a grown man was as simple as talking to a lad of four years old. If Ethan was troubled, she simply picked him up to sit on her knee and asked him what bothered him. But Perry was an adult male with complex thoughts and problems he did not wish to discuss. Emma had the instincts to help, but none of the knowledge or fine understanding of what made a man act the way he did.

Emma shook her head in disbelief. *I shall become a downright lie-abed, worrying about that enigmatic fool.* She should be concerning herself with preparations for the ball that evening. Decision made, she threw the counterpane aside, along with her gloom, and rose at the same time that she heard a soft knock on the door. Betty had arrived to assist her.

The rain stopped, and the sun made an appearance while the day passed in a whirl of activity. The countess saw to the final details of the ball while a horde of servants and merchants ran through the ballroom and first floor of the large townhouse. Flowers were delivered, and silver candlesticks with thick stalks of beeswax were placed in strategic locations to increase the lighting. Balfour Terrace boasted gaslights, which were an expensive oddity within private homes, but there were shadowed corners to fill and the candlelight added a certain ambience. The earl liked his comforts and was renowned for having tripled the Saunton wealth, so Emma could not disparage what he spent for those comforts.

Windows were cleaned until they shone; furniture polished, floors swept. A whirlwind bustled past Emma and Jane as they discussed points of etiquette and practiced their dancing in their new stays, gowns, and slippers. Emma was determined to not slip, trip, or stumble because of unfamiliarity with her clothing and accessories, so she made Jane go through the motions of the evening.

At midmorning, the countess joined them for tea and refreshments in the music room, away from the flurry of preparations.

"Emma, I think the evening will go well, but I have a

confession to make." The countess fidgeted with her hands. "It is rather a small ball by high society standards. A hundred or so of the people we like best ... I admit I become anxious in large gatherings. I was willing to invite more guests, but Richard insisted we keep the list manageable so it would not unduly distress me."

Emma's mouth fell open. "You get anxious? But you always appear so perfectly charming?"

"I have years of practice, but yes. There are situations that make me nervous."

"I feel terrible. We would have forgone the ball altogether, Sophia. There was no need to put yourself through this!"

Sophia crinkled her nose, tilting her head at Emma remonstratively. "It is our great pleasure to introduce you and Jane to society after all you did for our family. I only meant to apologize that it will be smaller than you might expect."

Jane leaned forward to clasp the countess by the hand. "I assure you, Emma is quite relieved she need only contend with a hundred guests. Any more than that, and it would be quite intimidating for us. Our country assemblies are not ... so grand as what we see unfolding downstairs."

Emma gazed at her sister in admiration. As Jane had stated not so long ago, she had matured despite the family's tendency to view Jane as a little girl. She was becoming an elegant, beautiful woman who would soon attract many suitors. Emma supposed she had attracted a suitor of her own, just not one who wished to court her. Melancholy returned to settle on her like a gray blanket of gloom and spoiled the pleasurable moment.

"Thank you, Sophia. It was my great pleasure to take care of Ethan, and I—we—appreciate all of this extra effort to include us in your family. It was difficult to lose Ethan so abruptly, but now that I see how you and the earl care for him ... I am more than satisfied that he is in excellent hands with loving parents to prepare him for life."

Sophia smiled, a handkerchief magically appearing in her hand. "I will warn you girls, one day when you are with child, the smallest thing could set the tears running." She sniffed, dabbing at her stormy blue eyes before she tucked the fabric away and rose. "I must return to the arrangements."

Once she left, Emma took charge of keeping them busy once more.

"Practice ball gowns? Truly?" Jane bemoaned as they walked up and down the music room in ball gowns not designated for that evening.

Emma wanted to be sure she could move as needed in restrictive garments. She would not fall on her bum in front of the earl's friends like she had in the carriage on the way to Signora Ricci. That day was the first time Perry had touched her with interest in his eyes—a memory she immediately pushed aside. Tonight was about ensuring Jane successfully launched and found herself a gentleman as soon as possible.

As feared, London was proving to be a negative influence on Emma's state of mind, and she needed to figure out how to get home again. Perry had walked away from their unusual connection, and Emma had no interest in finding another young man while she secretly craved his company.

So, she kept them busy practicing until the early afternoon.

"It is time for a nap," Emma announced once she was satisfied that she was prepared to attend the ball with passable grace.

"Zooks, Emma! You are a virago!"

"You do not wish to nap?"

"Of course I wish to nap"—Jane yawned delicately into her hand—"but need you be so imperious?"

"Determined."

"What?"

"I am not imperious. I am determined. Tonight will be a great success, and you will meet many young men who will wish to dance with you. You are as pretty as a princess, Jane."

Jane's tired face relaxed. "Thank you. I appreciate your efforts, I do. It is just that I am so tired and you are so demanding."

"I apologize if I have been curt. I am … distracted, I suppose."

"You are thinking about Perry?"

Emma averted her gaze when the mention of his name caused a twinge of anxiety in the region of her stomach. It would not do to reveal her reckless behavior with the handsome rogue. Especially now, when it was patently obvious that his intentions were not honorable.

How mortifying that she had allowed matters to get so out of hand. Had she really thought that Emma, the country mouse, could entice a devilish rogue to change his ways and settle down to court her? Her heart squeezed painfully at the thought of her beloved, annoying cad of a scoundrel. If only he would talk to her about what troubled him. What had Jane said about Emma needing a challenge? Perhaps selecting a challenge that she had the vaguest possibility of overcoming would have been wise.

"Why do you say that?"

"Because he did not leave our side, but after that dinner with the duke and duchess, he vanished. What do you think could have happened to chase him away?"

Emma's cheeks heated as she recalled the night of passion they had shared. "I do not know. You would have to ask Perry himself," she mumbled.

Jane gave a heavy sigh. "I had hoped the two of you … that you would find your own gentleman, Emma. The two of you were so animated together at the dinner. I was sure …"

Her eyes prickled, threatening her equanimity. She did not want to think about that wonderful night. Recalling the magic shared before Perry had severed their connection made her head ache and her throat thicken. There was nothing she could do if he was afraid to pursue their unique meeting of minds and souls. Nay, tonight was about Jane—while protecting her own heart from further abuse.

Yet, she could not help wondering whether Perry would make an appearance as he had promised he would while she led Jane up to their rooms for a lie-down. Her sister was exhausted, and Emma, too, had not slept well since Perry's abrupt departure from their daily routine. They would need their wits about them that evening when they met more than one hundred members of the *beau monde,* who the earl and countess had assured them would be a mix of suitable nobility and gentry.

* * *

SINCE THE BALL HAD BEGUN, Emma had kept an eye out for Perry's arrival. Sophia had introduced many distinguished personages who had all behaved with exemplary manners. Condescension had been minimal, and many of the guests were genuinely pleasant. Emma supposed that since Richard had brought his by-blow into his household, he had quickly learned which of his acquaintances were worthwhile to maintain relationships with.

"Emma, may I present Lord Lawson and his daughters?" Emma forced her gaze back to the present moment and found a swarthy gentleman with graying hair taking a bow. Sophia explained how the family was musically gifted—their musicales the toast of the Season. Emma smiled and made small talk with the sweet young ladies accompanying their father.

And the night continued, but Perry still did not appear. Emma held out hope for his arrival while she and Jane danced with several young men whom the earl introduced to them. She managed without incident and was pleased to see Jane enjoying herself, but as the night drew on, Emma suspected she herself would recognize few guests after this evening, due to her thoughts so entangled with a lamentable friend who did not keep his promises.

Eventually, after eleven o'clock, Emma was standing with Sophia, who was talking to her cousin, Miss Abbott, who had the appearance of a lively ethereal creature and chattered with optimistic enthusiasm. Emma quite liked the cousin, but her thoughts were occupied, as they had been all night, with the one person not present at the prestigious event.

Peering across the room yet again to search for his familiar face, she caught sight of rich brown locks over the heads of the dancers engaged in a minuet. At first, she thought she had found the earl, yet again to mistake him for his brother, but as the figure approached, there was a break in the crowd and Emma was elated to see it was Perry accompanied by Lord Trafford just behind his shoulder. Then her eyes settled on the woman on Perry's arm, and her spirits plummeted. Lady Slight, of tight gowns, red hair, and flawless fair skin, was draped to his side as if she were painted on him with oils.

Emma swiftly stepped away from her *tête-à-tête* to move behind a Corinthian column and gather her wits in the shadows.

He planned this. He must have. Attending *their* ball, filled with friendly faces to ease their launch into society, and he brought a woman of visibly low morals. He was flaunting her to ensure Emma knew … knew that there was no them. *No us. No special connection.*

His promise to attend, along with his evasion regarding

the dance they had once spoken of sharing, now made perfect sense. Perry had planned to inform her of his intentions, using the lovely, vicious Lady Slight as the means of delivering the message.

Emma leaned a hand against the marble cladding, steeling herself to return to the ball and pay no attention to him or his cronies. She would simply focus on Jane. Her sister stood a real chance of making a good match. Jane was lovely, clever, and pleasant, and Emma would ensure that her sister found a wonderful young man. A reliable one. She simply needed to ignore the baiting and keep her mind on Jane's happiness. If she could help Jane make a match, she could finally go home to her real life, where she was in command of her day—and her heart.

Her mind made up, Emma stepped out. The countess and Miss Abbott had moved without noticing Emma's absence. She swung her head around to spot where they had headed to so she might rejoin them.

"Well, well, if it isn't the country mouse." She turned to find herself face-to-chin with the redhead who had been brought into the ballroom to aggravate her. Emma's last vestiges of patience snapped at the dulcet tones of the wicked woman in the too-tight dress with the obscene display of bosom that violated Emma's sight. She had planned to stay away from Perry and his *friends*, but if she were to be directly addressed by the strumpet, she could not be held responsible for the consequences.

Emma welcomed the swell of anger in her breast, filling her with the resolve of righteousness. She knew how to defend herself.

"Rather a country mouse than—than—than an adventuress!"

The woman hissed in horror. "You little upstart bitch!"

"You courtesan!" Emma hissed back.

Perry walked up to interrupt. Emma suspected he had been observing from nearby because his timing was so meticulous. "Ladies, jealousy is such an ugly color," he drawled.

Emma took a deep breath. It felt so good to be near him despite the hurt he was inflicting.

Lady Slight smiled coyly. All evidence of hostility had vanished from her beautiful, empty face. "I apologize, Perry. I know the young woman is important to your family. We simply quarreled for a moment, no disrespect intended."

Emma repressed a growl at the disingenuous smile. But then Perry opened his mouth. "Lady Slight, come now. You are the widow of an esteemed viscount, while Miss Davis is simply the clumsy daughter of a tenant farmer who was gifted some negligible land in an unimportant part of Somerset. She barely possesses a dowry. You need not adopt any airs with her. Does she, Emma?" Perry threw a sneering smile in her direction, lifting an eyebrow in facetious query.

Emma's heart shattered into a thousand painful pieces, and her rush of bravado died.

She could not find the strength to even glare at him accusingly. Instead, she stood frozen, fighting back tears at his cruelty, as the blood drew back from the surface of her skin to leave her face, her lips, her fingers numb. She had already understood his message when he walked in with the wicked widow. There was no need to belabor his rejection with the cruel jab.

Emma had known it would be a mistake to come to London, that she would be an object of mockery, and she had been willing to withstand it for the sake of her loyal, wonderful sister who deserved a chance to realize her dreams. Because of the disloyal cad standing before her, she had changed her mind and hoped to be a success in polite society after so many hours of tutelage to build her confidence.

Now the man who held her heart broke it with malice and intent—it was all she could do to not fly at him in a rage, or simply fall into a weeping heap on the floor. Even Lady Slight had an air of pity cross her face at the cutting taunt.

The gentleman who had built her confidence, who had previously protected her from the wicked widow, now callously eviscerated her in the most public manner.

His emerald eyes watched her closely. The spiteful blackguard ensured that the verbal dagger he wielded found her heart to pierce it deep. Emma could not respond. She was too startled to, while her throat thickened with unwanted emotion. No one she had ever considered dear to her had ever attacked her so viciously. He knew what to say to hurt her most, her deepest insecurities, and used them as a weapon against her. How did one defend against such an unwarranted aggression?

Finally turning away, he proffered an arm to Lady Slight, who hesitated and then smiled in acceptance. "Come, Lady Slight, the country mouse has been struck speechless. We should not waste our time arguing with her when there is much pleasure to be had."

Emma watched them walk away, the pain in her chest expanding until the entire room disappeared. All she saw was him. Walking away. With … her—his new paramour.

Had she herself even qualified as a paramour? They had only shared the two kisses and the one night of passion. Had she simply been a mere dalliance?

Emma tried to think what she should do, but she could not find her feet to move or catch hold of a thought to follow it to a decision that would lead her away from the spot she was rooted to.

"May I have this dance?"

It took several seconds for Emma to register that the Duke of Halmesbury, the blond Viking who had joined them for dinner the prior week, was talking to her. The earl had introduced him as a cousin, had he not?

The duke bowed and straightened, holding out a large, sun-bronzed hand. "Please, Miss Davis. It will limit the gossip."

Emma realized heads were turned in her direction. Members of the *ton*, in their silk gowns and evening finery, were staring at the scene that had unfolded, but now she stood alone, gawking at the departing couple who had just trampled over her heart. Which meant the spectators now stared at her.

From a distance, she saw her hand raise from her side to accept his request. Numb, she still felt silly as one of the most petite women in the room sweeping into the dignified embrace of a waltz with the tallest man she had ever laid eyes on. His Grace topped six feet by several inches.

Funny what your mind focuses on when you are in shock.

Emma dared not blink, or think about what had just happened, or the tears would flow until she was a weeping mess.

As if reading her thoughts, the duke lowered his baritone to prevent being overheard. "I have never seen Peregrine so lighthearted as he was at dinner the other night. I was quite hopeful for him. But now I see he is acting the arse."

Emma's eyes widened in surprise.

"Come now, admit that is what you were thinking."

The show of support, along with his dry humor, caused her lips to twitch into a slight smile. *Oh, good. I live yet. I did not die moments ago.*

The duke watched her carefully, a thoughtful expression on his broad face while they twirled about the ballroom.

"Forgive me for my impudence, but have you considered that he is afraid?"

"Afraid?"

"Of you? Of what you represent? Great joy is accompanied by the possibility of great tragedy."

Emma swallowed the lump in her throat so she might respond. "I know it is fear. He could not truly prefer … that woman."

"Brava, Miss Davis. No, he does not prefer Lady Slight. The young woman is a pretty but mostly empty package. I believe the theatrics were merely a show for your benefit." It was a relief to hear her suspicions echoed by such an astute gentleman.

It felt a relief to talk about her secret infatuation, as well. Even if the duke was a stranger, he had a warm, comforting manner about him. "What do I do?"

His gray eyes contemplated her for several moments before he spoke. "It will not sound intuitive to you—you most likely will not appreciate my assessment."

"Please?"

"Do you know how Russia defeated Boney's invasion in 1812?"

Emma furrowed her brow. She had read an account of the Russian Campaign once. "A tactical retreat?"

"Just so, Miss Davis. A tactical retreat is frequently employed in chess. I believe you play?"

"You think I should leave? Do you mean return home? To Somerset?"

"I do. It is that or flirt with another man, but I do not believe that is fitting with your esteemed character. I believe if you leave, Peregrine may realize what he is giving up. He is clearly a man in torment, standing at a crossroads. In your absence, he will quickly rethink his course, if it is meant to be."

"How would you know that?"

The duke looked across to where his elegant duchess stood talking to Sophia, affection obvious in his gaze. "Because all men are arses at some point. Absence makes us realize what we stand to lose if we do not act. Sometimes the best move is a retreat to lure your opponent in. If Peregrine loses you altogether, without warning, it will force him to reconsider the decision he is attempting to execute … I saw how he looked at you. I think there is an excellent chance he will seek you out."

Emma considered the advice. The direct approach had failed, so perhaps Perry needed to be … lured.

"Thank you."

"No, thank *you*. I always found my younger cousin charmless, cold even. But since the earl's recent marriage, he has seen fit to share some details of their youth, and I fear I now understand too much about what might trouble Peregrine. I wish I had known the extent of their troubles so I might have interceded, but I had inherited a dukedom while I was still at Eton and I had troubles of my own to see to, so I did not observe that they struggled with serious issues in their household. I would dearly love for Peregrine to have a chance at happiness. It was … uplifting to see him genuinely amused at our dinner."

Emma had previously read of His Grace's philanthropic work and knew he had an excellent reputation. The kindness he showed her now proved his reputation was earned.

"I appreciate you stepping in."

"You are practically family now, Miss Davis, and I have spent time with Ethan, so I know firsthand that you are an exceptional young lady. I believe Peregrine will need you at his side to find his way, much the same as his brother needed Sophia to heal. I … hoped to dissuade you from giving up on him prematurely."

Emma gave a tight smile, gratified by the kind words. "It is tempting to wash my hands of him, but I am not easily dissuaded from my loyalties."

"And if he betrays you tonight? With the widow?"

"Then he is not the man I hoped he was."

The duke smiled with concern in his eyes. "I hope Peregrine realizes how fortunate he is before it is too late."

Emma mused over his words. Once the dance ended, the duke returned her to Sophia's side before bowing and departing to join his wife.

Emma smiled and laughed, continuing the evening in a daze of manners and small talk while she thought about returning home.

If Perry failed to follow her, she would need the distance to mend her heart. It was clearly the only choice for her to take. Richard and Sophia would take care of her sister, and she—she would retreat.

Emma sat through supper, laughing with a young man who was friendly. If anyone asked her what they had discussed, she could not possibly have told them. She was simply acting on necessity, but her mind remained occupied with plotting her departure from London. At the end of the evening, with her head held high, Emma finally retired to the family wing with Jane at her side. Fortunately, her sister was too tired and excited by the evening's events to notice anything amiss.

When she eventually reached her room, Emma undressed with Betty's assistance, but as soon as the door shut behind the departing maid, Emma sank to the floor as silent sobs racked her frame. Wrapping her arms around her knees, she pondered how the very best of nights, with the heights of unexpected, unannounced love, had been shortly followed by the very worst of nights. Perry refused to return her sentiments. She felt like a herd of elephants had trampled over her chest.

As she had suspected, she was too gauche, too naïve to survive the *ton*. She had nearly lost her virtue to an irredeemable rake.

Except he had left her virtue intact?

Somewhere deep down, Perry was a good man, but he was clearly afraid of deeper connections. Tonight's cruelty was about sending her a message. She knew the scoundrel well enough to realize their connection had frightened him as His Grace had suggested, and now he was withdrawing in the most painful manner.

Like Icarus, she had flown too close to the sun and her wings had melted away to leave her tumbling back to earth with no one to catch her. It was time to go home and put the pieces of her broken heart back together.

Perhaps Perry might follow, but despite the duke's optimistic outlook, she dared not hope for such an eventuality because the disappointment if he did not … it would be too great to bear.

CHAPTER 14

"Your turn to buy a round of drinks, Balfour."

July 1814, Lord Julius Trafford to Peregrine, aged nineteen.

* * *

Emma could not sleep. Not a wink. Close to sunrise, she rose and opened her door to the family hall so she might hear when the earl made his morning movements.

As the first light of the day appeared, she heard footsteps out in the hall. Darting out, she saw Richard striding away in his riding attire. "My lord, could I speak with you?"

Richard turned back. "My lord?"

"I apologize. I am anxious, Richard, and it slipped out."

The earl compressed his lips, worry crossing his face as if he suspected what their conversation might be about. "Shall we go to my study?"

"Betty has not come up yet. Will it be all right if …" She waved a hand over her nightwear.

"Yes, come downstairs in your robe. I shall send for some tea and biscuits while we talk."

Emma joined the earl at his side and together they descended to the lower level, crossing the entry hall to enter his study in the hall beyond. There Emma sat in one of the ivory armchairs, sitting on the edge of her seat and twisting her hands nervously in her lap while she tried to think what to say.

"Is this about Perry?"

Her lips quivered at the unexpected question. Keeping her eyes downcast, she wiped a tear from the corner of her eye. "I must return home this morning."

The earl sighed heavily. "Could we speak candidly for a moment? I heard about the scene with Perry. I … know the two of you were forming a bond. Halmesbury told me … well … did I do you a disservice by inviting you to London?"

She relented. Clearly, the entire family had an inkling of what was going on. "I appreciate what you have done. You have been most gracious, and I have no complaints. I enjoyed seeing Ethan and knowing he is doing well."

Richard looked relieved. "Perry is a good man, but my father was most unkind to him. Something the duke says I must discuss with Perry despite his reticence, so I might understand what happened while I was away at school. *Blast!* I would haul Perry out of bed and force the two of you to talk this out, but I suspect that you leaving is the best method to bring him to his senses."

Emma could not comment on that. She had already decided to not get her hopes up. "I wanted to inform you of my decision to leave and ask that you would take care of my sister. I do not wish to stand in her way."

"Of course! We … I owe you everything, Emma. I will protect Jane with my life and ensure she meets only the best of men."

Emma nodded. "May I beg the use of one of your carriages?"

"We shall send you with two. You have that wardrobe to return with, and I will send extra footmen to ensure your safety. Obviously, Betty will accompany you to Somerset."

"That is unnecessary!"

The earl took on the commanding air of a lord accustomed to having his words followed to the letter. "Emma, you need a chaperone to accompany you, and Betty is your lady's maid. I shall find someone else for Jane."

Emma snorted. "A lady's maid at Rose Ash Manor! You jest!"

Richard became positively parental. "I do not! I shall pay her wages, but someone must take care of your new gowns and escort you home."

"But … it is far too extravagant."

"Young lady, it is my prerogative, not to mention my duty, to provide employment. Betty was hired to take care of you, and now a fortunate young maid will be hired to take care of Jane. I know you are aware of economics, and I am confident you would not wish to prevent another young woman from being hired."

Emma clamped her mouth shut. She had never realized that Betty must consider herself lucky to have found employment in a stable household. And now, yet another young woman would find a place tending to Jane. She recalled her mother's words before they had left for London. Not everyone was so blessed to be born into a happy and successful household such as the Davis family's, and the new position would be a wonderful opportunity for someone. "I apologize. I suppose there is more to estate management than I had considered."

Richard smiled broadly. "Excellent! I shall have your

trunks packed and inform Betty that she will be responsible for you during the journey home."

"Thank you … Richard. For all you have done. I enjoyed visiting your home, despite everything."

He contemplated her for several seconds, visibly struggling with something he wished to say. "I think I will see you soon. If I do not, my brother does not deserve you. In which case, you may return for a Season anytime you wish."

She rose to leave.

"Emma? If there are any … consequences … to your stay, you are to inform me. I shall command Perry up to scratch, if necessary."

Emma raised her brows in confusion. "Consequences?"

Richard's gaze flicked away uncomfortably. "Yes. You will inform me immediately if there are any … consequences to your stay in my home?"

"I suppose," she agreed, unsure what he meant by the cryptic question.

"You promise?"

"I … promise," she responded in an uncertain tone. The earl gave a firm nod, which Emma took to be the end of the conversation. She walked away.

Emma located Ethan in the nursery to say her goodbyes. To her relief, he took the news well, apparently much more settled into his routine now that she had visited him and sorted out the issues that had troubled him. They parted with good cheer and her promise to show him around Rose Ash during his future visit.

Then Betty and the servants packed her trunks while Emma and Jane made a tearful farewell.

"I cannot believe Perry said such cruel words to you." Emma had been forced to explain the reason for her departure.

"He is reacting out of fear. Not unlike when one of the cats has been injured, yet spits and hisses when we try to help. But if he will not allow me to approach him, then I have no choice but to withdraw. I will not expose myself to further hurt. You can use a bag to overpower a small creature so you may assist them despite their fear, but I am afraid I have no bags large enough to overpower Perry." Emma gave a wan smile at the joke.

Jane thought about the analogy, her head cocked to one side. "He is still a wounded child at heart, is he not?"

Emma nodded gravely. "The duke and the earl both alluded to a very troubled youth. It appears your assumptions were correct, clever Jane."

"Are you sure about returning, Emma? Perhaps if you give him time, Perry will realize he has made a mistake?"

Made a mistake? He could be making a mistake at this moment. An unforgivable one. Emma's thoughts were sour because she had spent her torturous, sleepless night trying to suppress imaginings. Imaginings of Lady Slight sprawled out on a bed while Perry serviced her with his mouth. Imaginings of him undressing to reveal his powerful masculine form and the fascinating appendage between his legs that had pressed against her center during their one night of passion.

He had not undressed during their night together, but he would with the redheaded tart. Which had led to imaginings of him bedding the wicked widow properly, with a desirable woman rather than the clumsy daughter of a tenant farmer who knew not her place. Her understanding of what this entailed was vague and mostly based on witnessing animals rutting on the farm, which only made it worse somehow. *I am sure the widow is a much better bed partner than silly, inexperienced Emma.*

Emma forced the lump back down lest she choke on her bitter musings. "I am not equipped for this, Jane. My heart is broken—I need to get away from Perry before he can hurt me further."

"Your heart? You admit you are in love with him, then?"

"I am. I was … I do not know. I am desperate to put space between us so I can gather myself back together and sort through my thoughts."

Jane's ice-blue eyes were welling with tears, her long sooty lashes damp as she clung to Emma's hands. "This was not how it was meant to be! He was meant to acknowledge your connection, and you were meant to be the first of us to make a match."

Emma enveloped her taller, graceful sister in a tight hug. Jane lowered her cheek against Emma's hair to hug her back fiercely. "You are such a romantic, little Jane."

"It is your fault! You introduced me to Elizabeth and Darcy. And that Edward Ferrars finally fulfilling his purpose and finding a way back to Elinor."

Emma huffed, wiping her own eyes. "They are characters in stories, you ninny."

"I know, but the author was most persuasive, and when I saw you with Perry—"

"You saw me with my Wickham, unfortunately. Not my Darcy, as much as it pains me to admit."

Jane's tears stopped. "So, your Darcy might still be out there for you to meet?"

Emma sighed. Given her lack of social grace and misfortune with men, it was more likely that Perry had been her Wickham and her Darcy all rolled into one infuriating package to torment her.

"Will you be all right without me, Jane?" It was time to change the subject and close the chapter of her life that would be forever named after an incorrigible rogue.

"Do not worry about me. Sophia and I get along well, and I met several esteemed young men last night, including a gent who owns land in Somerset, near to Saunton Park. The countess said we will move the household to the earl's country seat for a house party, so I shall be within driving distance of Rose Ash soon."

"I am so glad for you."

"Thank you for this opportunity, Emma. The men in Rose Ash are mostly too old, or not as well read as you and I."

"Oh, Jane. It was my great honor to create this opportunity for you, and I would allow my heart to break a thousand times if it would bring you happiness."

Emma enjoyed one last meal with her sister, Ethan, and the Balfours, and then departed midmorning for Somerset with a heavy but relieved heart. She hoped that when she reached home, the reminders of Perry would gradually dissipate, and she would no longer imagine him in the widow's bed.

* * *

WHEN PERRY FINALLY AWOKE, it was to the late afternoon sun. His head ached something fierce, and his eyes felt like pebbles—nay, boulders—rested under his scratchy eyelids. Groaning, he sat up to rub his face.

Which was when he realized he sat in rose-scented sheets with his chest on display. His heart stopped in horror. Had he drunk so much wine that he had fallen into bed with Harriet?

Somehow it seemed a terrible possibility, one that filled his belly with dread. Self-loathing, a regular companion since his fifteenth birthday, coiled through his gut. But this time it was stronger, more intense, than he had experienced in years. In fact, it felt worse now than the night he had spoiled that young woman's innocence with his selfishness. Carnal relations with a woman other than Emma was inconceivable.

"Well, good afternoon, Mr. Balfour." The widow purred from across the room, standing by a tray of refreshments laid out on a low table. "Would you care for some coffee?"

Perry nodded eagerly. Coffee should help with the deuced crapulous headache he had acquired.

The redhead poured a cup and brought it over. Perry took it and sipped tentatively. It had cooled a little on its journey to her bedchamber, so he downed it in relief.

Harriet hitched a hip on the bed to face him. Her silk wrapper gaped open to reveal her rounded breasts in one of those lacy *bon ton négligés* that did little to disguise the thrusting pink of her hardened nipples through the gold threads. Her breasts were as full as Emma's, but somehow Perry did not find this particular pair as enticing as he found the pair on his fiery bluestocking. He kept his eyes averted as best he could under the circumstances. Harriet's obvious attractions were no match for the passionate, innocent charm of his wildflower.

Perry swallowed hard, wondering why he could not recollect the night before. It seemed highly probable that he had bedded the widow, which made his heart squeeze painfully in his chest while the self-loathing in his gut ratcheted.

Yesterday, he had believed his plan to be a clever proposition, but now that he had seen the agony in Emma's eyes at his betrayal ... he was not sure he had done the right thing. The plan had been to protect her from himself, but now he awoke, tortured by guilt and concern over the wild young lady from Rose Ash while he lay in another woman's bed. *Perhaps I should have sought advice? If not from Richard directly, perhaps from someone else? But who would have provided me with discreet guidance on how to unravel this tangle?*

Perry's stomach dropped with the heavy certainty of his grave mistake. He should have spoken to Halmesbury. He was not close to his cousin, but the duke was renowned for having a good head on his shoulders and a charitable heart. Halmesbury had been the man to advise Richard on how to make reparations for his past in a manner to unburden his future, yet Perry had executed this dastardly plan without pausing to consider it might not be the best course of action.

Now it might be too late. He could not apologize to Emma if he had bedded the sultry baggage who was trailing her fingers down his naked chest. Perry caught her hand in his. Her touch, which had been so desired the prior month, made his skin crawl in rejection.

Better to know—how fucked am I?

"Harriet, did we ..."

"Swive? Not so much, darling." The widow purred, her red hair swinging forward as she grasped the counterpane at his waist and pulled it back. "See?"

Perry looked down and saw what he had not noticed—or felt—in his disorientation. He still wore his trousers.

The relief was so profound he risked swooning like a maiden back onto the pillows behind him. He drew a ragged breath, the guilt assuaging just a hair so that he could once more draw air into his lungs.

"I ordered sustenance. We can rediscover pleasure this evening, Mr. Peregrine Balfour." The redhead was a seductive siren, but another woman fully occupied Perry's heart, and there was no room left for a sensual widow.

My heart is occupied? What the hell does that mean?

"I am afraid I must dress and go home now, Lady Slight."

Harriet sat back abruptly, her bosom bouncing in what would be an alluring manner if Perry possessed an iota of interest, but he did not. This had all been a terrible mistake. Perry tried to think how to remove the widow and spring from the bed so he could make his escape.

"Never say you are enamored with the country mouse?"

"Enamored? No. Hopelessly besotted, wholly in love? Yes!" Perry's gloom evaporated instantly. He had been evading the truth for days.

I love Emma!

He must seek her out at once to apologize profusely and beg her forgiveness. Then he would seek the duke to confess the whole lamentable situation so that he may be advised on how to fix this terrible mess in the same manner that Richard had been fixing his over the past several months.

The widow hissed, her blue eyes clouding with rage. "That little chit! Have you gone mad? What could you possibly see in such a dowdy little creature?"

"A world of possibilities! New, undiscovered futures! Hope of becoming a better man!"

Perry grasped the counterpane and threw it aside. Harriet yelped in surprise, jumping off the bed to back out of the way as Perry sprang up to find his clothes. Then he grimaced. They were wrinkled and smelled of wine and roses. He would need to change before he spoke to Emma. Not even he would believe that he had not spent the evening frigging if he appeared in this attire. He must hurry.

I need to wipe that torment from her eyes.

What had he been thinking to wound the keeper of his heart in such a cruel and public manner? There was no explanation other than that he had taken leave of his senses.

It took nearly two hours to quarrel with the widow, learn the events of the night before, and then attempt to assuage her grievances. He would not have bothered, but he was concerned the woman would seek revenge against Emma, so he at least must make an attempt to tend to her wounded pride.

It was nearing eight o'clock when he finally reached Balfour Terrace. Just as he strode across the entry hall—the hall where Sophia or Richard could have been killed earlier that year because of Richard's own ill-advised past—Perry heard a commanding bark from behind.

"Peregrine Landry Balfour! I have been looking for you for days, you bounder!"

He paused, still facing the staircase in his haste. "I do not have time, Richard. I must change and then find Emma to apologize."

"That is regrettable, Perry, because Emma is gone."

CHAPTER 15

"We shall flip a coin to see which of us pursues the delectable widow, shall we?"

July 1815, Brendan Ridley to Peregrine, on his twentieth birthday.

* * *

Perry walked to the staircase and slumped down on the third step, his knees no longer able to function as he landed heavily.

"Gone?"

"She left midmorning"—Richard checked his pocket watch—"approximately nine and a half hours ago. I am afraid you have missed her."

"Gone where?"

"Home. To Rose Ash Manor."

Perry dropped his head into his hands as his optimism slowly shriveled away. "She was meant to stay and find another young man."

"Was that the plan? I venture that your understanding of the young woman is flawed."

Perry admitted he had known better. Had he really thought that fierce, loyal Emma would accept his attack and then turn around to court another man? If he was honest … he had not wanted her to find another, more deserving man. *He* wanted to be her man. His plan had been a computation of reactions and flawed tactics designed to ease his conscience. Truly, nothing he had done made any sort of sense. He had acted like a man driven by demons and had fouled up the only good thing to happen to him in years.

If he had been attempting to drive her into the arms of another gentleman, why the hell would he have humiliated her in public? At a ball held in her honor? *What was the plan, you cursed idiot? Make a public spectacle of rejecting the young lady so some gentleman who witnessed it, or heard about it from one of the guests, inexplicably found her irresistible?*

"Oh, my God! What have I done?"

"Plenty, by my count, but this is not the venue for such a discussion. You will accompany me to my study. Now!"

The earl had never used such a tone on Perry before. It was pure, imperious authority. With a sinking heart, Perry wondered if he had gone too far, as he had feared, and now his brother would end their connection like their grandfather had abandoned him in his youth.

Stark terror raced through his veins, and the only hope that Perry could grasp was that if he had gone too far, Halmesbury would assist him in repairing this tangled situation, as he had done for family and friends alike.

Perry followed his brother and sank into his customary position in the armchair that flanked the left of the fireplace in the study. Swallowing his fear, he stared at his Hessians in misery. Emma was gone, and he had angered Richard to such a great degree that he might lose both of them tonight.

Richard sat across from him in silence. A thick silence that wrapped the room in a cocoon as if time itself stood still.

"I have been trying to speak with you for several days. I saw you depart Emma's room the other morning. I prayed it was leading to something meaningful, but then I saw across the ballroom what appeared to be you giving her the cut direct with a merry ace of spades on your arm. Emma is an innocent young girl, and I must admit to my great disappointment that you robbed her of her virtue and then broke her heart so publicly."

"I did not steal her virtue."

Richard raised a skeptical brown eyebrow, his emerald eyes glinting with restrained outrage.

"We did … stuff, but her virtue is intact," Perry insisted.

Richard narrowed his eyes, contemplating Perry for several moments. "Why?"

"I could not do it to her. I am a second son with no prospects, while she is a revelation of womanhood. She deserves a perfect husband, and I have nothing to offer her."

"I see."

They sat in silence while Perry tried to read his brother. Did the fact that Emma still possessed her maidenhood lessen his brother's anger? Would he somehow come out of this evening still a member of this household? Still a valued brother?

The earl cleared his throat and, to Perry's relief, appeared calmer than before.

"Then it is time for us to have a discussion. Halmesbury has taken me to task for failing to converse with you … about our past—your youth—to uncover what ails you so. He says my failure to take more action has led to this stalemate between you and Emma."

Perry shook his head. "This is not your fault, Richard. I am responsible for my actions."

"I do not deny your ability to act on your own, but I do not think that was Philip's point. Recently, I have confessed some details of our youth to our cousin. About the earl—"

"Of Satan?"

Richard hesitated. "Quite. I think you should know that I shared with him some of my experiences. The two doxies in my bed when I turned twelve. Father's orgies. His pox and his decline. The mercury treatments and the mental confusion. That the earl kept you imprisoned at home, denying you access to school and family connections—"

Perry's head snapped back in shock. "Wait! What do you mean, family connections?"

Richard stopped and frowned. "You did not know?"

"Know what?" Perry felt ridiculous barking his inane questions out. *Did Richard mean ...?*

"Our grandfather tried to remove you from Saunton Park when you were fourteen. It horrified him how you were living—the spiteful tutors, our father's lecherous behavior, the strain he witnessed in you when he visited for your birthday. He said it should have been a day of great celebration. When a boy becomes a man. Instead, he found you in a terrible state. He demanded to take you home, but our father threw him out. As the earl was a peer, Grandfather Landry could find no one to assist him with this matter. He spent his last years attempting to gain access to you."

"How do you know this?" Perry's voice was hoarse. The old man had not abandoned him?

"He came to see me at Oxford just before he died. He told me what had happened and made me promise that once our father died, I would take care of you. See that you received the care and mentorship you lacked. Provide you with a safe haven and allow you to recover from the damage."

Perry ran a trembling hand over his face. "He did not abandon me."

Richard sat forward, his usually affable countenance wreathed with concern and puzzlement. "Abandon you?"

"The last time I saw Grandfather was that day I turned fourteen. I was … so desperate. Father was plaguing me with his attentions. Working to turn me into a *gentleman*, or what his twisted mind conceived was such a thing. I pleaded with our grandfather to take me with him, and he said he would see what he could do. It was the last I saw of him. Finally, when I was sixteen, I asked the Earl of Satan, during one of his last lucid moments, what had happened to the old man. He informed me that Grandfather Landry had died."

His brother slumped back in his chair, raising a hand to tug at his cravat with a pained expression painted on his face. "I am so sorry, Perry. I should have done more. I was so desperate to protect myself that I forgot I had a little brother trapped at home. I should have come home during school holidays, but after the doxies in my bed—"

"When you hid in the guest chambers for over a week?"

Richard nodded. "After that, I was too afraid to come home, so I started visiting the Ridleys for my breaks. Their father, the baron, was only too pleased to have the heir to an earldom visiting his home, so I took advantage and went there anytime I was due to return home. If anyone abandoned you … I am afraid it was me, Perry."

Perry stared at his boots. Reluctantly, he revealed the embarrassing gratitude he had clung to since Richard had opened the door to his cage during that desperate time. "You saved my life, Richard. When our father died, you gave me the power of choice over my life. Leaving for school …" Perry was too overcome to continue.

Richard swallowed hard. "I am glad to hear that. I still wish I had had this conversation with you before today."

Perry surreptitiously wiped his eyes. "But were either of us ready to do that before today? I will admit that your reparations to the women of your past, and Sophia's arrival in our home, were necessary steps to reach this day."

Richard nodded. "My ethics on the subject of family were beyond questionable until recently. I am not sure how much help I would have been before my marriage. But, Perry …"

He stilled in his seat, not daring to breathe lest Richard asked about what he was not ready to reveal to him.

"Is there something more behind your recent behavior? I understand you believed Grandfather abandoned you, but … I … it does not quite explain the dramatic antics, does it?"

Perry dropped his head, heat rising over his neck, his ears, and his face. He knew he was blushing fiercely, which would awaken Richard's suspicions, but he could not hide his reaction. "I do not know what you mean," he muttered into his poorly tied cravat. His stomach growled loudly, as if to accuse him of lying.

"Have you eaten today?"

Perry shook his head, still not able to raise it.

"Then we shall find you something to eat before we talk about whatever is causing this bizarre reticence."

Nodding, Perry stood up. He could not meet his brother's eyes as they left the study to walk to the kitchens, but he would take the reprieve of a meal to consider how to navigate their impending conversation.

EMMA AND BETTY shared a room at a quality coaching inn recommended by the earl to the coachman driving them in the lead carriage. Richard had insisted that the maid chaperone Emma, so she had decided to have her in her room, both for propriety and the additional security. A woman staying alone in an inn could attract unwanted attentions. This way, she could ensure both of them remained safe.

It had nothing to do with the need for a distraction.

It was a relief to have a plan. Reaching the country during pleasant weather and reasonable road conditions had been a boon to her bruised heart. But left to her own thoughts too long, and they drifted to imagining Perry in bed with the widow. Lady Slight arching and keening in passion in Emma's place. Perry licking the widow's nipples in Emma's place. Perry consummating the lovemaking with the ending they had never shared together … in Emma's place.

She sighed as Betty brushed out her hair to plait it for bed. It was not *her place,* and she needed to stop thinking of it so. Perry belonged to no woman, especially not herself. Emma chewed on her lip and wondered if she could ever look at another man and feel … something. Perry was the first to turn her head, and he was an extraordinary specimen of manhood. But more than that, he was intelligent and charming … and fun.

She knew she had a tendency to be too serious, to shy away from social interaction, to be overly confrontational with people instead of using polished manners to diffuse tensions. Perry had been good for her … until he wasn't.

Emma wondered what he was doing now. *Frigging the widow, most likely!*

Her lips curved at the mental curse, even as her heart twinged with pain. Growing up with boisterous brothers and their foul language, it was all she could do to not curse out loud.

When she finally climbed into bed, it was a genuine comfort to stretch her body out from a full day of being stuck in the carriage, but she held little hope of restful sleep with her thoughts to plague her.

There was an assembly coming up at the end of July in Rose Ash. Perhaps it would be well advised to give herself a chance. What could it hurt to meet some gentlemen in the area? Minimally, it would serve as a distraction, and eventually she might meet someone reliable who could debate with her and make her forget the rogue who had stolen her heart like a thief in the night.

She might even have children of her own one day, and while they might not look like little Ethan as she had envisioned days ago, they might look like someone new who had become dear to her. Thankfully, she still possessed her maidenhood, so a match with a man who enjoyed the country, and estate management and simple pleasures, was not too farfetched. After all, she had learned much about interacting from her almost beau.

Emma sighed. It was nice to think such things would one day be possible, but it would take a while before she stopped comparing every man she met with the rogue from London.

CHAPTER 16

"Are you reading a book on mathematics, Balfour? Never say you are attempting to do something useful with your brain?"

July 1816, Lord Julius Trafford to Peregrine, on his twenty-first birthday.

* * *

Perry had eaten as much as he could to prolong the time until their next conversation. He hoped his brother might tire of waiting and head to bed. After all, Richard had likely not had much sleep with the ball ending in the early hours and then facilitating Emma's departure that morning. However, the earl showed no sign of tiring while he waited for Perry to eat.

"Halmesbury advised me it would be better to have an awkward discussion on a full stomach and a good night's sleep, but with your recent evasion, I can only ensure the food and not the sleep." Richard had finally interjected when the fact that Perry dawdled could no longer be ignored.

"Why do we have to talk about this?"

"Because I truly care about you, and I cannot allow this erratic behavior to linger. We settle what ails you tonight, little brother. I may have taken too long to provide my ear, but now we will see you through this."

"I did not ask for your ear!"

Richard shrugged. "You asked for it when you acted like a contemptuous blighter with a young woman we care about greatly. You shall confess your dark secrets tonight!"

"And if I do not?" Perry feared the reply. Would his brother threaten to sever their connection?

"Then I plague you again tomorrow. And every waking hour I am not needed elsewhere."

Perry's stomach unclenched at this announcement. He would never admit it out loud, but Richard's insistence ... it felt like brotherly love. Richard had consistently been there, his only immediate family since their father's death, but this level of attention was new. It was the kind of loving attention he provided to his wife and little Ethan. Perry had never been on the receiving end of it from anyone.

Except for Emma. He soughed heavily at the reminder of how she had waited for him in his room to offer her aid a few nights earlier, but he had known he intended to betray her with cruelty at the ball she had worked so hard to prepare for.

I truly am a horrible person. Now Richard would force him to confess and then he, too, would know what a horrible person Perry was. He no longer feared his brother's abandonment, but he expected his disparagement when Perry revealed the darkness of his soul.

Would you prefer it was Halmesbury? No, it should be Richard who heard his guilt.

"What should be Richard?"

Perry grimaced. "Did I say that out loud?"

"You did."

"I was thinking I prefer to have this conversation with you instead of Halmesbury."

"Halmesbury already insisted it must come from me. He said it was not his place to intercede because I am perfectly capable."

"He is right."

Richard stopped. They had been walking back to the study together, but now his brother turned to look at him, appearing mildly pleased. "Truly?"

Perry nodded, giving a halfhearted smile. "I know he likely advised you how to go about this, but you are doing an excellent job of taking me in hand."

"Huh! Well, that is good to hear. I will remind you of what you said if you balk later."

"I think I might be ready to unburden my conscience. I certainly need guidance on making any reparations for my behavior because I would have fixed this if I knew how."

Richard cocked his head. "You have something specific that troubles you, then? Not simply a host of upsetting events under our father's influence?"

"There are plenty of upsetting events to ponder from living with the Earl of Satan, brother. But, no, it is what transpired at my hand that haunts me, not his."

Frowning, Richard turned back down the hall to head into his study. They each took their customary seats, and Perry stared at the bottle-green wallpaper. He loved this room since Richard had had it redecorated, wiping away the vestiges of his father's presence at Balfour Terrace.

"Will you forgive me what I am about to tell you?"

Richard chuckled. "No matter what you have done, Perry, I assure you I have done worse. You are in no danger of receiving my judgment tonight."

Perry cleared his throat. "When I was fourteen, I met a

young woman in the village at Saunton Park. She was blonde, delicate, and she smelled of gardenias."

Richard frowned, before exclaiming, "She reminded you of our mother!"

"She did. Laura was kind and sweet to a young man who was troubled. I believed our grandfather had abandoned me. The Earl of Satan had taken a personal interest in my manhood. I was utterly miserable until I met her in the village. Soon it was the highlight of my week to sneak from the manor and go visit her. She was a sweet woman, perhaps ten years older than me, and she worked in the all-purpose shop. I would find any coin I could to go buy something just so I could wander through the shop and chat with her."

"She lifted your spirits?"

Perry gave a curt nod. "One afternoon the earl came looking for me. I did not notice his approach, so he found me leaning on the counter and talking with Laura. The look on his face … I knew he had something planned. So I stopped visiting. I wished to draw his attentions away from the young woman. After a few weeks passed, I thought I might have succeeded. I failed to account for my fifteenth birthday."

Richard groaned, leaning forward on his elbows to stare at the rug beneath his feet. "The earl had some notions about celebrating birthdays and manhood. Forgive me, I think I shall pour us a drink."

"You no longer drink."

"I can make an exception. And Sophia will admit that certain events call for assistance."

Richard walked over to the sideboard and poured out a finger of brandy. He raised the decanter in his hand in offering. Perry nodded. The earl poured a second glass and brought the drinks back, handing one to Perry before taking his seat.

"I apologize for the interruption. The horror of my twelfth birthday was recently revived when those doxies were planted in my bed on my wedding night."

Perry grimaced at the memory of the events that had transpired a couple of months earlier. He was fortunate to have been absent during the doxies' trespass.

"So, what did the Earl … of Satan … do?"

Perry smiled at his brother's encouragement. Richard had never employed the moniker that Perry had for their father, but he was making an allowance tonight, which was appreciated. Perry's chest physically ached with the stress of reliving the night he would give anything to erase. He lifted a hand to massage the pain away.

"He acquired Laura for me as a gift."

Richard frowned. "Acquired? Was she … to be acquired?"

"She was not. In fact, she was a maiden, but when I walked into my bedroom on the night of my birthday, there sat Laura, sobbing in a French night rail while Father sat across the room in my armchair."

Richard downed the drink in his hand and sprang to his feet to pace in agitation. "He did not!"

"He did … He threatened to ruin her, to have her fired and evicted—even arrested—and offered her coin to spend the night with me. By his own recount, the young woman stood no chance of refusing."

"What did you do?"

"I told him I did not want such a gift. I would return Laura home. He told me I was to make a choice—I bedded the girl or he would."

"Fuck!" Richard whirled to hurl his glass into the fireplace, where it shattered into a cloud of shards.

"You have been making a habit of that recently," Perry remarked.

"It is only the third time I have done it, and emotions have been running high this year!" His brother was petulant in his response.

"Do you mind if I do it?"

Richard shook his head, waving his hand in encouragement. Perry stood up, downed the brandy, and then brought his arm back as if winding up to throw a cricket ball. Using a straight arm over the shoulder motion, he threw the glass as hard as he could into the fireplace. There was a satisfying thud, then a shower of glass. "Huh! That actually felt rather satisfying."

"There is a time and place where it makes sense," Richard agreed.

"Richard, do you think if I complete my story … will I be unburdened?"

"My experiences this year allow me to assure you that there will be less burden once you have told your tale. What is needed beyond that—I need to hear the rest of it to provide my insight."

Perry retook his seat. Stretching his neck from side to side, he continued. "My mind was racing. Obviously, it needed to be me, not him. Or at least I could pretend, so I told him I would take her. I thought I could play along, and that once we were alone together, I would sneak her from the manor and out of the village with whatever coin I could find to put her on a post-chaise out of the area. But the earl had gone through multiple evaded birthday gifts, and he was having none of it that night. He cackled at my decision and then informed me I could have her in my rooms until I tired of her and then she would come to his rooms."

"Bloody hell! It was never you *or* him, it was you *and* him, or him."

"Just so. I agreed, as it would still allow me to rescue her from the manor. Once he left my room, I could get her out of there and take his wrath in her absence."

"But?"

"But he would not leave. He said he would remain where he was seated to ensure I did my manly duty. His sons had thwarted his teachings, but no more."

Richard stared at Perry in agape horror. "He became that terrible?"

"The last couple of years, he was a lunatic. Between the pox and the mercury treatments, he was utterly addled. Not to say he was not a licentious, depraved roué throughout our entire lives. Just that his worsening health made him much worse. More concentrated."

"Oh God, Perry!"

"I considered trying to overpower him, but it was before my growth spurt, and even with him being unwell, I was not confident I would succeed—which would leave Laura at his mercy."

"What did you do?"

"First, I told him if I was to put on a show that drinks were in order. I collected his brandy from his rooms and brought it to him. My only hope was to get him so soused that he would pass out. Then I began, with him shouting out instructions. I disrobed Laura as slowly as I could, reproving him that a man has stamina when he complained I was taking too long. I took my time nuzzling her while she sobbed and trembled in my arms. I kept playing for time, but she was fully naked by the time he finally passed out. It was fortunate I could stop when I did … but by then … I had taken this wonderful, sweet woman who reminded me of our mother … and stolen her light."

"Oh, Perry." When Perry looked up at his brother, he saw a sheen in his brother's emerald eyes. "I am so sorry. I did not know he would do that to you or—"

"Or you would have come home to be forced into inflicting the same horror on some innocent? A housemaid? A daughter of an upper servant? A maiden from the village? Someone's wife? A vulnerable widow? It was better that you were not there."

"Did you ... consummate?"

"No ... but the damage was done. The young woman was terrified. Her innocence lost, even if she was still virtuous. I calmed her down, snuck her into the attics to hide, and then gathered anything of value I had and anything you had in your rooms."

Comprehension crossed Richard's face. "Anything that you could sell without getting a servant in trouble for stealing?"

Perry bobbed his head. "It was something I had considered for myself—to run away—so I had a plan of sorts long before that night. I rode all the way to Saunton proper and peddled all of it. Along with my own coin, I gathered about twenty pounds together. When I reached home, our father was in a fine state, bellowing for the servants to find me. I snuck in to collect Laura, then snuck into her rooms in the village to gather her things. Finally, I put her on a post-chaise bound for Cornwall where she had a cousin she could visit. I made her promise to sever all ties to the village so that the earl could not find her."

"You suffered when he found you?"

"Not as much as that young woman. Whatever punishment I received, I had earned for putting her in harm's way."

Richard slumped back in his chair, and they both sat in silence for some time. Perry wondered what his brother thought. Despite his assurances to the contrary, he did not believe Richard had ever been involved in something quite so ... despicable.

Finally, Richard ran his fingers through his brown locks,

leaving them in spiky disarray before he spoke. "I do not see it that way. I think you saved the young lady's life."

Perry frowned.

"If you had not bought her time, and our father had raped her, she would indisputably have contracted the pox and possibly been left to even carry his bastard."

"The earl would not have selected her if not for me and my interest in her."

"Then he would have picked someone else. When he discovered your interest in her, it gave him an especially spiteful target, but the plan for that night—I think he would have come up with that plan irrespective of the character he chose for the role. He appreciated showmanship, and he reveled in hedonism, and he loved to twist his sons up into his warped concept of manliness. Laura just provided that extra bit of entertainment for him. He was evil, Perry. You cannot blame yourself."

Perry rubbed his hands over his face. "Truly?"

"I shall ask my man of business to find out what happened to the young woman, but Perry ... you did the best you could as a young lad confronted with the most dire of circumstances and choices. Not that there was much choice in the melodrama you just described ... I am proud of your ingenuity, given your lack of resources to address the matter."

Perry nearly wept in relief. "Truly?"

"Brother, you acted with honor. I am sure if we find this Laura, she will tell of how a young lad of fifteen rescued her from a lecherous blackguard."

Perry was overcome. He nodded, fighting back a well of emotion. Richard was right—he felt unburdened just by telling his darkest secret. "Thank you, Richard ... for listening."

Richard smiled in encouragement. "Now, what will you do about Emma?"

He looked down, studying his Hessians carefully. "I love her, you know?"

"I do. She is a unique and lovely young woman."

"I am unworthy of her."

"You are a better man than you give yourself credit for. And Sophia married me when she should have known better. Fortunately, women are gracious enough to take us in all our arrogant umbrage and lust. They teach us to be better than we are without them. They take us to task for our insensitive natures and teach us to be members of a family. And Emma is a saint as far as this family is concerned, so I am certain you can win her heart back with a good deed. Halmesbury mentioned she was open to such a thing when he spoke with her ... if you had not done the unforgivable."

"The unforgivable?"

"You did not bed the widow, did you?" Richard winced at the question, clearly afraid of the reply. Perry, in his turn, had all but forgotten the sultry siren.

"I was in her bed, but only because I passed out drunk. I still had my trousers on come this evening."

Richard's eyes flickered to his trousers. "Based on the state of those trousers, I believe you."

Perry looked down. Of his disheveled attire, the trousers were indisputably the worst. "Thank you, I suppose."

"There is one more thing which I have been attempting to tell you for several days. When Grandfather came to see me, he informed me that he had created a trust for Shepton Abbey."

"His home? What of it?"

"When I turned twenty-five, I acquired a half interest. When you turned twenty-five the other day, I did not have an opportunity to mention that you gained the other half interest. I attempted to inform you of the trust many times over the years, but every time I brought up our grandfather, you claimed to have a pressing engagement and bolted. I eventually decided it could wait until it was *fait accompli*."

"Oh. That is good news ... I suppose." Perry was lost. Why was Richard telling him this now?

"You misunderstand. I think you should manage it. It is near Rose Ash, and it requires sophisticated stewardship."

"I have no comprehension of what that means."

Richard sighed. "Grandfather's estate produces income, but my man of business—Johnson—reports it is perfectly poised to be modernized and to turn the tenants to sheep farming. The local textile industry is thriving, and wool is at a premium in the immediate area."

"You failed to modernize it? You upgraded all your other estates?"

"This one is unique. The locals and the tenants are resistive to modernization. They even had a riot in the area a few years back to protest mechanization. They believe it will cost them jobs, but not in this instance. It would bring great wealth to the estate, owners and tenants alike, but it will require leadership and persuasion to convince them of such."

"Richard, I am tired and I know nothing about sheep farming. What is your point?"

"There is a certain Miss Emma Davis of Rose Ash, who has made quite a study of sheep husbandry and possesses experience in farm management. And I am looking at a man who has made a hobby of seduction, which one might say is merely a form of persuasion. It sounds perfect for a couple with such talents to manage such a project."

Perry groaned. "This is Sophia's proposal! She is always talking about me acquiring a project to give me purpose!"

"I thought I was quite inspired when I thought of this

plan. And, yes, Sophia will be delighted when I inform her, which in turn means I will be delighted soon thereafter."

"I do not even know if I can persuade the young woman to have me, yet you plan our future!"

Richard shrugged. "I am an optimist. Think about it. Let me know. My apologies for failing to apprise you that you own half an abbey and its lands. To be fair, you were kind of an arse on the morning of your birthday—rejecting gifts and whatnot—so truthfully, it is your fault I failed to tell you. I actually had the documents ready to give you that very morning after breakfast, but …" Richard waved his hand vaguely.

"I was being an arse?"

"Exactly. The good news is that all the income from the abbey has accumulated in an account these past years and is available to finance the upgrading of the estate. And there is a competent, if unimaginative, steward to work with."

Perry attempted to quell the interest this remark engendered. A project of his own? Master of his own estate with capital to finance improvements? And a partner too busy with other holdings to interfere? Despite his lack of sleep, Perry suddenly found himself awake to possibilities. He had loved the sprawling old abbey the few times he had been allowed to visit his grandfather.

Damn it! Sophia might be right about him needing his own purpose. But if she turned out to be right, he vowed quietly to himself that he would never admit it to her.

Richard interrupted his musings. "The young lady will require a grand gesture of some sort to prove you are sincere in your apology. Something that proves that you are worthy in your unworthiness."

"Do you have to be so damned amused by this?"

"It is not every day Lord Arrogant's rogue of a little

brother is tamed by a feisty bluestocking from rural Somerset. How could I not find this amusing?"

Perry muttered under his breath.

"Now, now, Perry. Do not let your ladylove hear you use such foul language."

CHAPTER 17

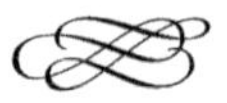

"Twins, Balfour? You disdain interest in a matching set of songbirds who step the boards of Drury Lane?"

July 1817, Lord Julius Trafford to Peregrine, on his twenty-second birthday.

* * *

Emma stared down at the page covered in ink blots, then at her hand smeared with errant ink, and frowned. If Perry were here, he would say—

"Look at you, making a mess."

Emma stared down at her work, perplexed. She must be losing her mind, because the memory of Perry's voice in her head was so vivid, it was as if he were in the room with her. Her head snapped up so suddenly it almost flew off from the force of it.

"Perry!" The exasperating desire of her heart loomed in the doorway, looking at her with guilt painted across his face.

"Indeed."

Emma stared at him, wordless. The duke had declared Perry would follow her, but she had not dared to hope it was true. She was too fragile to—

"Did he? Halmesbury always was an insufferable know-it-all."

Emma winced, realizing that she had voiced her thoughts. She really was losing her grip on reality. As it stood, she wanted to fly across the room and leap into his arms. Or fly across the room and slap his cocky face. Unable to reach a decision, she settled on polite sarcasm. "What can I do for you, Mr. Arrogant?"

Perry chuckled. "That is appropriate."

"I think so. You took your time?"

"I left the morning after you, but we were caught by rain and the carriages were bogged in the mud for three mind-numbing days. Not to mention, you had the best of the Balfour conveyances at your disposal."

"And what did you do the evening before you left?" Emma dreaded the answer. Images of Perry making love to that redheaded viper still plagued her thoughts.

"I had a *tête-à-tête* with the earl. We reminisced about my harrowing youth and my propensity for acting like an arse."

Emma closed her eyes in relief. "And the evening before that?"

"I drank myself into a stupor for inflicting such grief on you, then passed out with my trousers on."

She breathed deeply, lightheaded at this welcome news. "I am not … I … What …" Emma pursed her lips. She should have a coherent plan of what she wanted to say before she opened her mouth once more.

"I wish to be forthcoming, so I must admit that although my trousers were on, I was in the bed of Lady Slight. Trafford and Ridley carried me up from the drawing room after I passed out."

"Oh … Why were you unclothed?"

"I had spilt wine on my waistcoat and shirt."

"Sounds like a disastrous evening."

"That is the truth. Once I awoke, Lady Slight and I argued over you. I have been advised to never darken her doorstep again."

"That is … good." Which brought Emma to the most important question, aggravation at the time in the widow's company aside. "So, why are you here?"

Perry dropped his gaze to the floor. "I am here to apologize and provide an explanation for my erratic … and cruel … behavior."

Emma tensed. "I do not want to hear your excuses!"

"Not an excuse … merely an explanation. You deserve to know what has plagued me. Why I behaved so poorly."

Emma stood up. "Very well. We shall sit there by the fireplace so we will not be easily overheard. I cannot close the door."

Perry nodded, waiting for her to cross the room and lower herself onto the edge of a plump forest green armchair before he followed suit to take the opposite seat. "It is not a pretty story, I am afraid. But you deserve to hear it after how I treated you."

Emma gave a curt nod. "I understand."

Perry stared into the empty hearth for several moments while Emma waited, restraining her impatience lest he change his mind. This did not seem like the right time to rant or unleash her anguish and fury. She wished to express her disagreements over what he had done, but more than that, she needed to understand why he had done so. And why had he followed her to Rose Ash? If she interrupted him now, she might never learn the truth. He was finally going to admit what was at the root of his struggles, and she found herself intrigued he would entrust her with his secrets despite the difficulty it obviously presented.

Stretching his neck from side to side, Perry finally spoke. "My father ... was a cruel, maniacal man who enjoyed bedeviling his inferiors. He pursued pleasure at any cost, and after my mother died, one of his pleasures was to torment me."

Emma clenched her hands in her skirts. The disquiet on his face, she recognized it as the same that he had displayed on all those occasions just before he said something to push her away. She bit her lip to prevent any words from spilling out, any words that might prevent the explanation she needed to hear—to understand his motivation for the cruel confrontation at the ball.

If there was any possibility of reconciling, it was imperative that he finally reveal what had been tormenting him, so Emma forced herself to sit still and wait. Despite the hurt he had caused, it meant a great deal that he had come all this way to see her.

Perry exhaled, and then he elaborated on his youth and how, to dissuade the late earl's interest in him, he had developed a cool manner and glib attitude. As she listened, Emma's heart went out to the boy he had been. Jane had been right. Perry had been hiding great pain. If only it had been a matter purely of neglect, as they had hypothesized. It would appear Perry had been afflicted with far too much attention and what troubled him was much worse than the possibilities she and her sister had discussed.

After revealing the truth of his father's eventual decline and death, Perry stopped talking and glanced her way. She took several moments to notice, too bemused by the revelation of the earl's discreditable illness. As a learned woman, she was well aware of the pox, but she, fortunately, had never had the misfortune of dealing with the afflicted directly.

Emma drew a deep breath, realizing he now needed her to respond.

"Your father was a terrible parent." It did not seem an adequate acknowledgment to what he had revealed, but it did not seem the right time to break into a tirade over his parent's invasive tutelage, so Emma left it at that.

Perry gave a strained laugh. "Indeed. It is my great regret that I unleashed my confusions on you. There is more I could tell you, but it is of a more intimate nature, and I think it should wait for another time. I wanted to offer an explanation and to admit that meeting you disrupted the glib manners I have used to protect myself. I was ill-prepared for the connection we formed and reacted poorly to insulate not only myself, but you, although that might be hard to comprehend."

Emma inclined her head. "It was very unexpected … our relationship."

Perry gazed at her, his expression nervous, and he appeared to be gathering his nerve. "I deeply regret everything I said that night. It was intended to protect you by driving you away, but my thoughts were addled with an excess of dark emotion. It only took a matter of hours for me to realize that my logic was thoroughly compromised. I offer my most sincere apologies and hope you can find your way to forgiving me?"

* * *

MR. DAVIS WAS a stocky man of medium height, who had the black hair and eyes of his oldest daughter. He also shared Emma's sharp intellect and fierce family loyalty.

Her father was not aware of the specifics of what had happened in London, for which Perry could only thank the heavens. All Mr. Davis knew for certain was that his oldest child had returned from Town in a state of melancholy, and he did not appreciate that Perry was the one who had escorted her from his estate with promises that his daughters would be well cared for. It had taken some convincing to persuade the man to allow Perry's evening visit with the family, and he had only allowed for it if Emma proved to be amenable.

Which was why Perry was relieved when Emma did not immediately throw him out when he went to find her after his tense meeting with her father. It appeared she was amenable to discussion, as Richard had reported she would be. They had talked in the library, and he had made his apologies for his behavior, which she had failed to comment on, so he was uncertain of where he stood with her. He forcefully resisted the dark thoughts that threatened despair over the very real possibility of losing her. Their conversation had been stilted, but the first steps of their new dance had been taken, and Emma had listened with patience to his explanation. She had responded with quiet horror regarding his father's influence on his life, but she did not appear to be repelled by his woes.

Emma was talking to him, which was the important point. It meant the second part of his strategy was to be employed.

Emma had invited him to join her family for dinner, and he had departed for his room at the inn. When he stepped inside the taproom on the lower level, Trafford and Ridley beckoned him to the scarred wooden table where they sat. Perry installed himself and ordered an ale and a meal to accompany it. He had not eaten since breakfast, and dinner was some time away.

"Did the bluestocking receive you?" Trafford's query was drawled. Apparently, he had imbibed a couple of ales before Perry had returned.

"She did. And that is Miss Davis to you, Lord Insolent Oaf."

Ridley snickered into his drink. "I wish I had been there when the two of you argued, Trafford!"

"You were there, dunderhead. You were just too soused to hold yourself up. Or hear the quarrel. Perry, I am still confused why we—I—am here in Sleep Ash?"

"Rose Ash."

"Whatever. Why am I here?"

"You are to assist me in my grand gesture. I cannot do this unaccompanied."

"I still do not understand, no matter how many times you explain it in that supercilious tone you have been using with me for the past five days. I am sick of ale, and dripping rain, and mud, and trees, and inns, and … well … you! Once the young lady witnesses your grand gesture, she will be as sick of hearing from you as I am."

"One day, even Lord Oaf might be privileged to meet a woman capable of winning his heart, and then he will be glad that he has friends to assist him when he inevitably louses it up," Perry rebuked.

Trafford pulled a face at him. "Speaking in the third person? I think I know better than to flaunt a luscious baggage on my arm while giving my ladylove the cut direct, when that time comes."

Ridley snorted a laugh. "It really was not well-done of you, Balfour. I did not witness the cutting because I was occupied with a lovely widow in the far corner, but from what I hear …" He shook his head. "A young lady should be treated with respect. It is only fitting that you humble yourself, and I, for one, am more than willing to assist to restore the esteem of the young woman so unfairly treated."

"Not to mention, you wish to entertain yourself at my expense."

"That is an appealing benefit, but no, I dislike seeing young women mistreated, so I am here to ensure you succeed at repairing your ill-advised attack."

"I, for one, cannot wait for this evening," Trafford interjected. "It will be quite a lark to watch the Davis family fully comprehend what an inane fool you are."

Butterflies fluttered in the region of his stomach. Despite the hours of practice, Perry still dreaded embarrassing himself so wholly, but he would do whatever it took to put a smile on Emma's face and restore the confidence she had developed these past weeks under his tutelage before his disgraceful and public derision.

* * *

EMMA GLANCED out her bedroom windows and caught sight of the Saunton carriage pulling into the drive. Turning to Betty, her young maid with thick brown hair and a face covered in freckles, she urged the servant to hurry with setting her hair. The hair tonic created bouncy, luscious curls, but Emma was impatient with how long it took. She should be downstairs to greet Perry when he arrived for supper, but at this rate she would be the last to arrive.

Hurriedly both of them inspected her gown, Emma angling back and forth in the mirror, while Betty walked carefully around her, tugging at folds and tucking in errant bits. They had dressed her in a hurry, but now Emma was inexplicably shy to leave her room to greet their guest.

Why exactly Perry was here was not clear. He had made his apologies and then angled for an invitation to dinner with her family.

Did he intend to court her? Should she allow it? It was all so awkward. Not at all like their time alone at Balfour Terrace, with only her sister to witness their interactions.

Not all of our interactions!

Emma sighed and straightened. No, Jane had been absent for some, and asleep for most of the … encounter … in the music room.

Peering at herself in the mirror, she decided it was time to leave her room and display her mettle. She had put on a simple gown of deep blue velvet that brought out the stark contrast of her hair, which looked a deep black in the low light. She had chosen the garment to be fitting for an evening meal at a small country estate, but she would still be better dressed than her family, who were still attired in the clothing they had worn as tenant farmers.

After the humiliation at the ball, Emma was self-conscious about the difference in their statures in society. Perry would no doubt arrive looking effortlessly elegant, with a perfect cravat, snowy linen, a tailcoat meticulously prepared by his valet. Because they were in the country, he would probably wear his buckskins to dress down. His manners were impeccable, after all. *Impeccable with everyone but me.*

Emma exhaled a deep sigh at the memory of the stinging humiliation that the Duke of Halmesbury had graciously interrupted with his offer to waltz and their frank discussion. She had promised the duke she would consider an effort from Perry to make amends if he had not ruined it all. He said he had not shared a tryst with the widow, and Emma believed him because she had learned to read him—his explanation was sincere. She supposed that all that remained was to discover the reason for his visit and find out where it would lead.

Zounds, I cannot deny I would like it to lead back into his arms.

After the intimate—and embarrassing—secrets Perry had shared earlier that day, Emma had come to understand that the gentleman was beginning a journey on the road to self-respect.

He had traveled six days through the mud to deliver his apology and then bared his past to her, and she appreciated how difficult it must be for such a private man to reveal himself in the manner that he had.

She supposed she could summon some angry bluster, but her annoyances were usually short-lived and she did not bear grudges. In the large Davis family, bearing grudges would be a poor stratagem. Her twin brothers were incurable rascals, and one could not be caught in a war of retribution—one said one's piece and moved past it. Even if it involved frogs in the chamber pot.

And the *man* arriving downstairs for dinner had been raised as a boy with little guidance, she surmised from the confession regarding his parentage. It made her heart twist in her chest to think what might have happened to Ethan if they had not taken him in and treated him like one of their own clan. Perry had been Ethan's current age when his mother had died, and his tale from earlier proved that his father had been no parent worth mentioning.

Standing in her room contemplating the evening ahead would not shed any light on Perry's visit. She squared her shoulders, thanked Betty for her help, and left her room.

Hastily, she descended the stairs, slowing as she turned the corner that would reveal her to the guest in the entry hall. When the lower floor came into sight over the banister, Emma's breath caught at the tableau revealed below. Hesitantly, she continued down to stand in consternation at the foot of the stairs.

To her right, her family was gathered. Her father appeared polite but tense, while her mother smiled amiably. Her twin brothers, Oliver and Max, glowed from a fresh bathing, their damp blond hair glistening in the low light from the windows and the candle sconces in the vestibule. And her youngest brother, Thaddeus, was neat and soulful with his black hair slicked back from his forehead. He solemnly held hands with little Maddie, who stared at their ... guests?

For some inexplicable reason, Perry stood flanked on one side by Mr. Ridley and the other by Lord Oaf, whose wheat-colored thatch brushed over his eyes. Emma's eyes skittered around, unsure where to rest now that she found not one, but three pinks of the *beau monde* gracing their humble home in sartorial elegance. She clenched her fists while her stomach twisted in knots.

"Em—Miss Davis," Perry greeted effusively, remembering himself in time. Or not. Her father clenched his jaw at the failed attempt to disguise his familiar use of her name. Emma stood dumbstruck, offering a tentative but fleeting smile in acknowledgment.

Perry cleared his throat, coughing into his fist, before drawing a deep breath. Then all three men straightened, turning in her direction. A handsome trio of tall, elegant young men from the city, it was enough to turn the head of any young country miss. They hummed in unison before bursting into song.

Let Bucks and let bloods to praise London agree
Oh the joys of the country my Jewel for me
Where sweet is the flow'r that the May bush adorns
And how charming to gather it but for the thorns

Emma barely dared to breathe. They were serenading her? The popular Dibdin aria that they sang was unexpected —*The Joys of the Country*. She attempted to ascertain if they were singing in jest; the song being an ode to rural life while secretly poking fun at the nuisances of such. Yet they did not seem to be making sport as they sang the lively lyrics. Was this intended to be a reverent gesture?

Where we walk o'er the mountains
with health our cheeks glowing
As warm as a toast honey when it en't snowing
Where nature to smile when the joyful inclines
And the sun charms us all the year round when it
shines

Despite her best efforts to ignore them, the twins were attempting to hold back their mirth, hands clapped over their mouths while their eyes watered with the strain. Thaddeus had dropped little Maddie's hand in order to plug his ears with his index fingers, while their youngest sister's mouth hung open, her eyes wide in amazed horror at the spectacle unfolding.

Oh the mountains & vallies and bushes
The pigs & the screech owls & thrushes
Let Bucks & let bloods to praise London agree
Oh the joys of the country my Jewel for me
The joys of the country my Jewel for me

There twelve hours on a stretch we in angling
delight
As patient as Job tho' we ne'er get a bite
There we pop at the wild ducks & frighten the crows
While so lovely the icicles hang to our Cloathes

From the corner of her eye, she could see that her father stared at the ceiling, his lips quivering with a threatening gale of laughter while her mother gazed at the front door as if she contemplated running off into the early evening. All that protected Emma herself from guffawing like a jackass was the sheer surreal shock of it.

There wid Aunts & wid Cousins and Grandmothers talking
We are caught in the rain as we're all out a walking
While the Muslins and gauzes cling round each fair She
That they look all like Venuses sprung from the Sea

Emma flushed at the bawdy lyrics. She and her family had heard the aria many times, but being singled out and serenaded by three gentlemen from the city highlighted the naughty meaning of the lyrics. She squirmed with the awareness that her parents stood right beside her, restraining laughter at these theatrics. Emma bit her lip to prevent any reaction from crossing her face, but tears of mirth threatened when the trio of … tenors … began the chorus once more.

Oh the mountains & vallies and bushes
The pigs & the screech owls & thrushes
Let Bucks & let bloods to praise London agree
Oh the joys of the country my Jewel for me

Then how sweet in the dog days to take the fresh Air
Where to save us expence, the dust powders your hair
There pleasures like snowballs encrease as they roll
And tire you to death, not forgetting the Bowl

Where in mirth and good fellowship always delighting

We agree, that is, when we're not squabbling &
fighting
Den wid toasts & pint bumpers we bodder the head
Just to see who most gracefully staggers to bed

Oh the mountains & vallies and bushes
The pigs & the screech owls & thrushes
Let Bucks & let bloods to praise London agree
Oh the joys of the country my Jewel for me

As the song drew to a close, Perry fell to one knee at Emma's feet, his head almost at bosom level as he gazed up at her in adoration. She frowned down at him, nonplussed, doing her best to bite back the giggle that threatened to spill from her lips as he threw his arms wide and belted out the last line at the top of his lungs: *The joys of the country my Jewel for me!*

CHAPTER 18

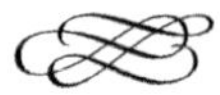

"Please, I beg of you, please never sing again! Hum, if you must, but never, never sing again."

July 1818, Richard Balfour to his brother, Peregrine, on his twenty-third birthday.

* * *

At the final, enthusiastic rendering of the song, shoulders shook and faces reddened as her family did their best not to break into belly-aching laughter. Max lost the struggle and howled like a braying ass, which meant his twin followed. Both boys doubled up, a forearm clutched to their bellies while they leaned over bent knees and the mirth overcame them.

Her father gasped for breath as he turned to rest a hand above his head on the wall, his shoulders shuddering with repressed humor while her mother had her lips firmly pursed and looked like she had stopped breathing altogether in the effort to keep a straight face. The room vibrated with good cheer while the occupants attempted to assemble their wits.

Emma peered down at the rogue at her feet in wonderment. "Uh … thank you?"

"You are welcome!" Perry smiled up at her, flushed with exuberance.

Emma sought for words while ignoring her family, who were attempting to collect themselves. "Mr. Ridley and Lord Trafford—"

"That is Lord Oaf to you, Miss Bluestocking," drawled the incorrigible Trafford.

Her father straightened at the slight, but Emma ignored Trafford to complete her comments. "—you are musically gifted, and it was an honor to hear such marvelous tenors in our home."

Mr. Ridley smiled in acknowledgment, revealing a warm character that in her previous encounter had been unapparent in his state of inebriation. From his affectionate expression, Emma grew more confident that this farce was not an elaborate lark at her expense. The two men bowed.

"They are excellent tenors," agreed Perry from her feet, his hands resting on his bent knee while he still panted from his exertions. He showed no signs of rising from his position on the floor.

Emma hesitated while her lips tried to find the words to address him. "Mr. Balfour, I am not sure how to break this news to you … but you are … not … musically competent, that is."

"True." He did not seem offended as a fresh rustle of chuckling broke out from her family and his friends.

"You are aware … that you are musically untalented?"

"I am."

Emma nodded in relief. She hated to offend such an

enthusiastic effort. "Why, then, have you regaled us with this ... unusual rendition of Dibdin's aria?"

"It seemed only fitting that I reveal, in the most humiliating and public manner, my most secret and deplorable flaw." His green eyes flickered to her family, showing his unwillingness to mention their awful interaction on the evening of the ball. Comprehension slowly awakened. She considered the brutal insults in front of Lady Slight. Then she contemplated the days leading up to the confrontation when Perry had avoided her and made her heart ache. With clarity, she recalled his confession and sincere apology earlier that day. Then she replayed the last few minutes in her mind, especially the violation of her ears by the musically ungifted gentleman.

"You are correct. Tonight, you have revealed your most distressing defect. We may never recover from what we just heard."

"Hear, hear!" Trafford's facetious remark prompted a fresh round of snickering.

Perry nodded, his face ebullient. "A most regrettable and, unfortunately, memorable performance."

Emma could no longer help it. She cracked into a smile, shaking her head at his ridiculous antics, letting go of any vestiges of hurt at the endearing overture.

"It is not my fault, to be clear. My father did not believe music was a worthy pursuit for a gentleman. My brother attempted a few years ago to rectify the matter, but after a few moments in the music room, he ran off complaining that his ears were bleeding from my incurable singing."

Trafford and Ridley bobbed their heads in agreement. "It has been an excruciating week, practicing with Balfour on the journey here," Ridley's warm tones interposed.

"Your father had much to answer for," Emma responded.

"That he did, but this night is about you." Perry reached

out a gloved hand to clasp one of hers. She saw her father stiffen in response, but her mother placed a soothing hand on his forearm and Papa eased back.

"Miss Davis, there are no words to describe how a country jewel slipped into my very soul to steal the heart from my chest"—Perry's fingers tapped over his left breast—"nor could I possibly ever compensate for being an irreparable idiot—"

"I can attest that Balfour *is* an irreparable idiot," muttered Trafford.

Perry ignored the interruption. "—You are wit, and beauty, and joy. Despite my many shortcomings, I hope you may consider my offer thoughtfully. It has recently come to light that I have a substantial estate to manage not far from Rose Ash, and I would be eternally grateful if you would accept the position of mistress of Shepton Abbey?"

Her parents gasped. As freshly arrived as they were to Somerset, even the Davises had heard of the large estate to the east of their own.

"You are moving to the country? A city buck like you?"

"I am. The city holds no luster without my country bluestocking. Alas, she harbors no love for the city, so I will come to her and attempt to make something meaningful of myself." Perry continued his unfaltering gaze of Emma as her heart slowly expanded with joy. The possibilities! Her romantic rogue at her side with a grand estate to manage!

"Like Edward Ferrars in *Sense and Sensibility*!" Thaddeus exclaimed, having finally unstopped his ears. Her little brother was following in Emma's studious footsteps.

"You wish to marry me?" Best to be clear.

"I do." Perry dropped his gaze, leaning in to whisper to her below his breath, "I hope I have adequately humbled myself for you to forgive me for imprudent deportment?"

Emma leaned down to whisper her reply. "You have.

Given that you brought Lord Oaf, word will spread of your lack of proficiency throughout the clubs of London. I foresee your humiliation will live on far longer in the memories of our acquaintances than my own."

Perry huffed a laugh as Emma straightened back up. In a loud, clear voice, she responded, "I accept, Mr. Balfour."

Applause broke out as her family rushed forward to embrace her in congratulatory hugs.

* * *

PERRY REFLECTED that his grand gesture had been a grand success. Emma's good spirits had been restored, and dinner had been lively. She had glowed with sparkling confidence, and Perry was gratified that the damage he had done to her esteem was now mitigated.

Even Trafford had relinquished his sardonic demeanor to enjoy hearty country fare, relaxed etiquette, and entertainment in the drawing room afterward. Mr. Davis did not withdraw from the women and children after the meal, preferring to stay in their company, and Perry had enjoyed the familial nature of their evening spent around the pianoforte and playing games with the various members of the family who admonished him not to sing along when song broke out.

Thaddeus earnestly remarked to Perry that his dancing skills were excellent despite his lack of musical gifts, which he took to be high praise from the solemn young lad.

Come morning, Perry visited with Emma and her parents. As agreed with the earl, arrangements were made for the family to attend Saunton Park for a wedding. Thankfully, they were amenable to nuptials in the Saunton Park chapel in just a few days when the Balfour family would descend to prepare for their impending house party. Now that Perry had confessed his regard, he and Emma had no desire to delay their union.

Perry discussed marriage terms with Mr. Davis, who was considerably friendlier since Perry's shameful display of musical incompetence. Apparently, any gentleman willing to recognize that Emma was a treasure, and humble himself for the hand of one of his beloved daughters, was all right by him.

It was unexpectedly uplifting to have such a loving father accept him into his kin. Perry understood they were taking the first steps of a long and lasting relationship and that this man would one day be a kind grandfather to the children he and Emma would bear. The contemplation of which brought a lump to his throat as he realized how his family would grow with this marriage. Perry finally understood what had overtaken his older brother three months earlier when Richard had embarked on a similar path to unite with Sophia, not to mention the Davis family who had cared for Ethan as if he were one of their own children.

Perry would gain five younger brothers and sisters, as well as new parental figures in close proximity, with the stating of his vows in the coming days—an astounding change of circumstances to consider after living such a dissolute life these many years. And it was reassuring to have Mr. Davis to provide valuable insight into understanding the minds of the tenants at the abbey when Perry embarked on the modernization of the estate.

After two days at Rose Ash, Perry was heartily tired of living in coaching inns, so it was with anticipation that he assisted the Davis family to board their well-packed carriages before joining Trafford and Ridley in the Saunton carriage. With a deep sigh, he sank back into the leather squabs and imagined being married to Emma within days. And then bedding his delightful wildflower. It had been all he could do to keep his eyes averted from the inappropriate parts of her body that tantalized his dreams at night.

"I must admit that Miss Bluestocking is quite comely. I see the attraction after spending time in the bosom of her delightful family, Balfour." Trafford's admission was high praise, coming from the bored heir who did little but flaunt his honorary title, drink, and chase skirts.

"Keep your eyes off my jewel, Trafford." Despite the rebuke, Perry wondered if the young lord could one day settle down with a love of his own. The man's willingness to traipse into Somerset to act as a third in their impromptu singing group had surprised him. Even Ridley had forsaken a delectable widow to join their mission to Rose Ash.

Perhaps, like him, his friends were reaching the end of their current rudderless paths. He appreciated their contribution to his grand gesture and would enjoy assisting them to find something more from their own lives.

"I did not know you intended to move to Shepton. Will you be spending time in London?" Ridley cocked his head, curiosity in his brandy eyes.

"As little as possible."

Trafford straightened up. "I thought that was a line for the country mouse?"

Perry let the sobriquet pass without comment. He could not expect the spoiled lord to change overnight. "I will be steadily engaged at the abbey, and I think it wise to avoid the entertainments of London while I adjust to married life. There really is no need to put Emma through the trials of encountering my recent paramours. Richard and Sophia have had to contend with many indecencies these past months since they married, and I do not have the same responsibilities to Westminster that he does."

Trafford scowled in horror. "You are becoming domesticated?"

Perry thought of spending his evenings with the scent of chamomile and wildflowers, while his fair bluestocking spoke with him about matters of sheep farming and estate management. He grinned at the sheer joy to be had with a lively woman who held him in true esteem. "Aye, I welcome my domestication with open arms."

Trafford shook his head in rejection. "One thing to settle down with one woman, old chap. 'Tis another to rusticate. We shall not be spending time together in the coming days, I predict."

"You are welcome to visit us at the abbey if you ever need respite."

"Or need to hide from one of your unhappy paramours," chuckled Ridley. "No one would think to look for you in Somerset."

Trafford thumped back onto his bench. "It would need to be a black day for me to come knocking on Balfour's door in such a remote location. I have never drunk so much ale as I have this past week. I need a superb wine forthwith."

"The wine will flow at Saunton Park to mark the celebrations."

"Thank God," groaned Trafford.

Their party arrived at Saunton Park later that afternoon. The earl had sent a missive on the same morning that Perry had left London, so a guest wing had been opened for the Davis family to settle into, while Trafford and Ridley were shown to the bachelor hall.

Perry coordinated with the senior staff to ensure the preparations for the chapel and the wedding breakfast met with his approval. The next afternoon he stood on the stone steps, watching the line of carriages arriving from Town with the servants standing at attention to greet the earl and his new countess, who was arriving at Saunton Park for the first time. The Saunton coat of arms was gilded on the first few, but Perry noted the Halmesbury ducal coach halfway down the line followed by two more of the duke's conveyances.

"My sister must be here!" exclaimed Brendan Ridley, who stood behind him.

His cousin and the duchess had elected to attend his wedding? A swell of emotion rose at the familial support of his decision to wed his country lass. Perry swallowed hard, then moved forward to greet his brother, who had just disembarked from the lead carriage.

"Richard, what is this?"

"Halmesbury insisted he accompany me when I told him the news."

"How did you know I would succeed?"

Richard shrugged. "I assured him you were quite persuasive when you intend to be."

"The duke did not have plans?"

"Philip changed them. He and Annabel are to attend our house party that begins in a few days, so he canceled the remainder of his meetings to witness your nuptials."

Perry pondered this for a moment. He had more familial connections than he had previously acknowledged to himself.

Richard walked back to converse with the butler when Sophia and Ethan disembarked to meet the servants, followed by Jane Davis. Introductions were made, the duke striding over while his duchess held the ducal heir, Jasper, up to see the Palladian manor as she whispered in the infant's ear.

Halmesbury walked up to thump Perry's shoulder with a large hand. "Congratulations, Peregrine."

Perry scowled. "Can you finally relent and call me Perry, Halmesbury?"

The duke cocked his head, his gray eyes bemused as he considered Perry's request. "Congratulations … Perry."

Perry smiled before calling out to his brother, "Richard, do we have the license?"

Halmesbury tapped his pocket. "The archbishop sends his regards."

"You arranged the license? Directly with the archbishop?"

"His Grace owes me several favors, and I like to provide him opportunities to offset them. I wanted to show my support of your momentous decision and ensure there were no issues getting it approved at the ecclesiastical court."

"I thank you, then. I would have been quite disappointed if it had not been processed."

They all headed inside as servants carried trunks in. The various families converged in the family drawing room, a raucous meeting with so many members crammed into the cozy space. Especially once Oliver and Max mimicked Perry's off-key singing for the entertainment of his brother and the duke.

Ridley did nothing to quieten the gathering, bouncing and cooing at his nephew, Jasper. One would think that Ridley had not just visited his younger sister and the duke for dinner the week before.

Perry wished that the morning could arrive. He dared not step foot into the wing that housed the Davis family to find Emma's room, but he was itching to take his little wildflower in his arms. Even now she glanced at him across the room with a yearning in her black eyes while she conversed with her sister.

Not under the watchful eye of her father. He grimaced. Another long, sleepless night battling his impatient lust was a prediction he would lay money on.

* * *

Emma contemplated Jane, worried over the news she had just imparted. "You are still not sleeping? Did you see the physician whom Sophia mentioned?"

Jane shrugged. "There is no need. It is just excitement."

Tilting her head, Emma narrowed her eyes at her younger sister. "I wish you would see a physician or an apothecary. It is most unlike you to struggle with sleep. Even when we moved from Derby and the entire family was awake all hours from the anticipation, you slept without trouble. I recall my envy at the time."

Jane pulled a face and changed the subject. "Now that you are to wed—as I predicted, mind you—it is my turn to find a beau. The countess mentioned there are several eligible landowners arriving on Friday for the house party, so I am sure to find a gentleman who captures my heart like Perry has caught your own."

"Is that important to you? That he be a landowner?"

Jane considered the question. "I do not know. It is just the epitome of success, I suppose, for a young lady to marry a landowner. Honestly, I do not know what type of gentleman would make a suitable match for me. Perhaps someone young and fun?"

"Perhaps, but it would be good sense to consider what you would like your future to hold. The man you marry will heavily influence the course of your life. I wanted to be with Perry, but while we sparred in London, I was uncertain if we could ever work out our differences—considering I would have had to commit to living in London. His decision to take the reins at Shepton Abbey played an important role in my decision to accept his proposal. It will shape my entire life, and there is no question I was destined to be involved in estate management in some capacity."

Jane's forehead puckered. "I do not know what my

destiny is. I am afraid I never thought past finding a gentleman to love and a future family to nurture."

"Perhaps you should consider your course before the guests descend on Saunton Park, Jane. Consider what your personal dreams might be so you may judge whether a young man is an appropriate partner."

Her sister huffed. "Good Lord, Emma. You are such a pragmatic bluestocking. Are you actually claiming you would have turned Perry down if he had not had a satisfactory plan for the future?"

Emma nibbled her lip, turning her head to smile at her betrothed across the room. His green eyes found hers, his lips curving affectionately in acknowledgment. "Perhaps I would have risked it regardless, but I am relieved he reached the decision he did. This is an excellent opportunity for him —for us. We shall be very happy at the abbey."

* * *

The earl broke away from the lively group in the corner and approached Perry, who was taking air at the open window. He was eternally grateful to discover he had so many relations who wanted to spend time in his company, but it took getting used to being surrounded by so much kin after years of loneliness.

"How was your journey here, Richard?"

"Uneventful. We left after the rain had stopped, but you must have been caught?"

Perry grimaced. "We barely moved for three days."

"Hmm … how long did it take to reach Rose Ash?"

"Six days. With Trafford whining the entire journey."

Richard chuckled. "Trafford likes his creature comforts."

"I appreciated his help, but there were times I wished to push him under the carriage wheels."

They both looked over to the spoiled lord who was conversing with the studious young Thaddeus, an expression of perplexment on the lord's face. It was an unlikely pairing.

"I have news, Perry. I am hoping you will delay your departure for the abbey until the end of the week because there is someone you need to meet."

Perry raised an eyebrow. "It would need to be someone remarkable for me to agree to stay under your roof with this many guests assembled."

"A brother?"

"What?"

"You recall our discussion earlier this year? When we hypothesized that our father might have sired by-blows we are unaware of?"

Perry swallowed, stretching his neck to ease the tension the remark had caused. "Back in May. I was not aware you pursued the question."

Richard nodded. "Johnson found one. I met with him before we left Town and convinced him to join us for the house party."

Perry's stomach knotted at the news. On the one hand, he would gain a new brother, on the other he considered how difficult the boy's life as a bastard must be. What Ethan would contend with in the future. Perry had struggled with his own issues because he was a mere spare, but his unknown brother would have had a much worse time of it.

"Was it difficult—when you moved Ethan into your home?"

Richard sighed. "A couple of servants quit. Some acquaintances disdained me—us—but I would make the same decision a second time. I cannot abide disloyalty to those who are owed our commitment."

Perry nodded. His recent act of disloyalty to Emma had consequences to his self-respect. He was thankful he had come to his senses so swiftly and been able to make up for what he had done before it festered. And that Emma had been so gracious in forgiving him.

"Why did … our brother … need convincing? Surely, given his circumstances, he would desire a connection to an earl and the assistance that would provide him in the future?"

"Barclay Thompson is successful in his own right and has no need of funds. It took my most persuasive powers to convince him to acknowledge the connection."

"Barclay Thompson? Why does that name sound familiar?"

"His grandfather is Tsar Thompson."

Perry's jaw dropped. "Tsar and Barclay Thompson? The architects?"

Richard nodded. "Just so. Our new brother is older than us. He would have been the earl, not myself, if our father had done right by his mother. It required Tsar's full support, and a persuasive argument regarding the advantages our family could offer Barclay's young daughter, to obtain Barclay's reluctant cooperation. I would be grateful if you could be here to welcome him when he arrives, so I might demonstrate those advantages."

Perry shook his head in disbelief. "I suppose we can depart the following morning. I was foolish, indeed, to believe I was almost alone in this world."

"I regret that you were led to believe that in your youth. You are taking aggressive steps to reject our father's influence"—Richard gestured over to where Emma and Jane were sipping tea—"and I am proud of you, brother."

Perry gazed at his bride-to-be, who smiled affectionately in response. Emma would become his wife come morning, and Perry was elated at the prospect. "I am so pleased she agreed to be my wife."

CHAPTER 19

"I understand your trepidation, but it is imperative that I wed to protect the people who rely on me."

July 1819, Richard Balfour to his brother, Peregrine, on his twenty-fourth birthday.

* * *

Emma shut the door to the hall and turned to Perry. "Well, husband, we are finally alone and wed."

"With our entire family cognizant of what we are doing in our room now that we are finally alone."

Emma chuckled at his gruff tone. "I think we might forget their presence if we go about this correctly."

Perry huffed a laugh. "I shall take that as a personal challenge."

He stepped forward, circled an arm around her waist, and pulled her against his hard body, lowering his head to capture her lips. Emma moaned, her lips parting to accept him. She had dreamed of him each night, but since his arrival in Somerset, they were—thankfully—lustful dreams of Perry making love to her, rather than the ginger strumpet, Lady Slight.

Long, blunt fingers reached behind her bodice to fiddle with her tapes, but she pulled back to remonstrate her groom. "I think I should have an opportunity to undress you this time!"

Perry shook his head as if to clear it of passion, his glazed green eyes slowly regaining focus as he stared down at her. "Very well, but leave the buckskins on or this will not last as long as you might hope."

With that, he let Emma go and stepped back to wait patiently. She blushed. Although she had asked for what she wanted, and he had granted it, she was ill-prepared to take the next step. She bit her lower lip in contemplation before closing the distance between them. Perry watched her closely as she raised trembling hands to loosen his cravat. Fortunately, it was easy to pick apart the knot with her slender fingers and she made quick work of it. Taking hold of one end, she slowly dragged it from his neck, his eyes blazing in response when she laid a hand on his broad chest and slowly ran her fingers down the contour of his muscles.

She held his gaze while unbuttoning his tailcoat, before grabbing both wool lapels of his coat firmly in her hands. She yanked them apart aggressively, an unsubtle mirroring of the night he had ripped her night rail, before pushing the coat down and off his powerful arms. His sculpted lips quirked in amusement even as his breathing sawed with restrained desire.

Emma brought her hands back up to the linen of his shirt to explore the solid wall of his male chest through the fabric, while he slowly closed his eyes to groan in pleasure at her touch. He emanated heat, even with the linen between them, and Emma licked her lips in anticipation of feeling his hard body over hers when they reached the bed. Taking the hem of the shirt in hand, she lifted it up to throw it off, eager to reveal his body. Then fumbled as she realized their disparity in height would only allow her to lift the shirt so high, and no more. Perry swallowed a smile, raising his arms to remove the shirt. Emma watched in fascination as the shirt rose and then dropped to reveal his bulging biceps, the powerful muscles of his chest, and the crisp curls of hair that arrowed down to his buckskins that she had been cautioned not to touch.

She grazed fingertips over the expanse of his muscles, traced around the flat disks of his nipples, before running her hand down the fine hair to the waist of his breeches where she dipped into his navel for a second. Perry captured her hands.

"My turn."

Turning Emma around so she faced the door, he reached down to grab her by the palms and raised her arms. Understanding his intent, she leaned against the door while he unlaced her bodice. As he loosened the lowest tape, she felt his hands drift lower to slide over her buttocks, which he kneaded and caressed, leaning in to nuzzle her neck.

Her head fell back in invitation as his hot mouth stroked and tickled along sensitive regions she had been unaware of, causing her to moan as tingling sensation shot across the surface of her skin and found its way to the pulsing, pooling heat between her thighs.

Perry snaked an arm around her waist and pulled her back against his body, where she felt his excitement straining against her back. His large hands came up to push the loosened bodice, and the gown she had wed him in slowly dropped, a little squirming assisting it to drop farther and pool at her feet.

With relief, she felt him reach to remove her petticoat.

His hands rose once more to cup her breasts through her stays and chemise. Emma growled in protest that the thick cotton padding prevented her from feeling his touch directly. Perry must have felt the same. His fingers moved to tear at the tapes of the stays, ridding her of the chemise underneath impatiently before his hands rose once more to cup her bared breasts and pull her closer. She was finally free of her clothing except for her stockings and the garters holding them up.

The feel of his hot, naked skin against her back made her arch back in delight, rubbing her smooth back against his hair-roughened chest in a manner so feline she felt beastly in her lascivious desire for him. He drew his thumbs over her puckered nipples, causing her to buck against him as he rhythmically rubbed his straining erection against her. Emma exhaled loudly—between her legs, her folds swelled and her core pulsed in anticipation of finally consummating their lovemaking tonight.

Kicking off her slippers, she turned in his arms. Perry groaned loudly as her breasts plumped against him, his eyes drawn to the rounded fullness. He looked undone in his reverent fascination, before he dipped down to lift her in his arms, careful to extricate her from the pile of clothing accumulated at her feet.

He turned toward the bed, which he approached with a determined stride. Once he reached it, he appeared to be nonplussed. Emma realized the counterpane was firmly in place, and his arms were occupied with holding her. She reached an arm down and, grabbing hold of the counterpane, she threw it firmly aside so he might lower her down onto the sheets.

Stepping back, he pulled off his boots before raising his fingers to the buttons of his falls. His gaze found hers in the low light as she panted and swallowed. With great deliberation, he undid the falls, kicking off his buckskins and small clothes to reveal the hardened appendage between his legs. Emma's gaze fell to look upon his proud erection, gasping at the unexpected size of it.

"Oh."

Perry looked down. "It will fit, I swear it."

Emma cocked her head in thought, then parted her stockinged legs in invitation, drawing Perry's gaze to the aperture of her thighs. His breathing hitched as he made quick work of his own stockings and quickly approached to lower himself over her on the bed. She gasped at the delightful sensation of his skin against hers once more, her toes curling into the mattress in delight when his erection pressed against her cleft in a silky slide of hot, hard flesh.

"Emma, do you know what to expect? That the first time is uncomfortable—perhaps even painful?"

"I had a notion, but Mama explained it to me fully last night."

Perry was leaning over her, a thick forearm stretched to hold himself above her so he might see her face, but he reached his free hand up to swipe it over his reddening cheeks. "I will need to grow accustomed to being a member of such a large and involved family."

"One learns to treat it like background noise," Emma commiserated. "Expect them to visit us at the abbey frequently."

"So many relatives!" Perry groaned in dismay before he lowered his head to suckle on her earlobe. Emma keened and bucked at the unleashed pleasure of the simple gesture.

"Emma, I am so ..." Perry continued his suckling while his hands strayed over her bountiful breasts and quivering belly. "... so damn grateful you accepted me as your husband. The man to school you in ..." Perry dragged his mouth down to draw a turgid nipple into his heated mouth. "… the art of …"

Emma trembled and pushed up against his questing tongue. "Art?"

"Bed sport." She huffed at his callow humor, but quickly grew distracted when his fingers reached her center to gently explore the folds of her slick core. As before, it was indescribably wonderful, making her shiver and shake with passion as her feet dug into the mattress so she might lift her hips to be closer to him.

"Patience, wildflower," Perry whispered against her flushed skin as she chased the pleasure of his exploring fingers that ran lightly across the spot she yearned to feel him. He knew what she wanted as he firmly stroked over and over, lifting her to heights of desire until she crested in amazed fulfillment, white-hot pleasure exploding out in every direction.

For a moment, Emma stopped breathing altogether in sheer delight, before slowly settling back into the sheets in sated passion.

She opened her eyes to find Perry watching her closely. "That was … highly gratifying to observe," he whispered before pressing his hardened male staff to her dripping center.

"Your turn?" Emma joked.

"Our turn," Perry replied, then he took her mouth in a deep, intoxicating kiss that reawakened the pulsing heat between Emma's thighs. She moaned as she felt the blunt tip of his appendage insinuate against her opening, spreading her legs to accept him. But Perry did not press the advantage, rather teasing his tip against her core, which clenched in yearning to feel his invasion. Slowly, deliberately, he pushed into her. Emma winced from momentary pain, Perry pausing before he gently slid in to seat himself to the very hilt, and her muscles stretched as she grew accustomed to his length. Her head fell to the side in rapture at the feel of his fullness inside her body. Indescribable.

"Does it always feel this good?"

"Only with me," he warned.

And then there were no more words. He slowly rocked his hips, dragging in and out of her clenching channel, both of them breathing hard as he gradually quickened the pace. Once again, he reached between their joined bodies to stroke the pearl at the apex of her thighs, and Emma cried out as a second wave of pleasure intensified and spread to thrust her into paradise. As she lost all sense of her bearings, Perry increased the speed of his motion until he groaned loudly, frozen in ecstasy. Emma felt wet heat being released inside her in satisfying contractions. Finally, his eyes reopened, and he looked down at her with an expression of wonder. Dipping his head, he pressed a firm kiss to her lips before carefully rolling off to her side.

Emma felt boneless as Perry left their bed to gather a towel that he dampened at the washbasin. Approaching her, he gently wiped her between her legs before wiping himself and returning the cloth to the basin.

Then he returned to lay in bed and pulled her against him in a close hug.

As her breathing settled and she slowly drifted off, Emma mumbled into his hard chest, "I love you, Perry."

The hand stroking her back stilled for a moment. Then Perry pressed a kiss to her dampened temple. "I love you, Mouse."

Emma humphed in fading aggravation, halfheartedly jabbing her elbow into his midriff before curling closer. Perry chuckled and she sighed in happiness, causing the crisp hair on his chest to rustle. Then she knew no more, as sleep took her.

EPILOGUE

"Happy birthday, my love."

July 1821, Emma Balfour to her husband, Peregrine, on his twenty-sixth birthday.

* * *

July 1821, Shepton Abbey

PERRY WOKE at the low knock on the bedroom door. Opening one eye, he saw Emma cross the room to open it. Murmuring ensued before she accepted a tray from Betty, bumping the door closed with her hip. Placing the tray on a table, she approached the bed and climbed back in.

Reaching to her side table, she picked something up and turned to him as he remained wrapped in the bed's warm embrace, reluctant to begin the day yet.

Squirming up behind him, Emma planted a teasing kiss behind his ear.

"Happy birthday, my love," she whispered. Perry smiled. It was. A happy birthday, that was. Stretching, he turned to take her in his arms, but Emma scooted back to evade him. She grinned at him before placing a wrapped gift on his chest. Perry squinted down in surprise. He had not received many birthday gifts in his life. Perry grimaced at the memory of his father's so-called gifts. Most of those gifts, he had felt the need to return.

But he and Emma had been married nearly a year now, and he knew her well enough to know that whatever the gift was, he would assuredly appreciate it. Pushing himself up against the headboard, he took hold of the small box tied in a ribbon. He felt like a small lad as he untied the ribbon with a frisson of anticipation.

His mouth fell open in amazement when he revealed the contents of the package. His fingers trembled as he took hold of the delicate silver rattle inside and lifted the toy to stare in wonderment at the engraved floral design glinting in the morning light.

"Truly?"

"I confirmed it last week, but I withheld the news for your birthday." Emma reached for a hug, her eyes suspiciously moist. "In six to seven months, we shall welcome a new Balfour to the abbey."

"Oh, Emma! How did you hide this for a week? You must have been overcome!"

"I was overjoyed at the news—it was excruciating to not inform you immediately," Emma mumbled against his cheek.

"Of course it was, my love. You have yearned for this for so long." Perry reached a finger up to gently wipe away the tears gathered on her sooty lashes.

"I will write to my family this very morning to inform them of the news."

Perry reached an arm around his wife to embrace her firmly. His eyes prickled in the most threatening manner as he pressed his face into her hair. His life had grown to be so utterly perfect these past twelve months. Now they would have a son or daughter to share their blessings with.

"And so our family begins," he responded hoarsely. Then he blinked at the realization that the Davises would practically live at the abbey once their first grandchild made an appearance.

"Shall we share a cup of tea to celebrate before we venture downstairs? I am sure the earl would like to hear the news."

Perry blinked. "Richard is here?"

"Betty just informed me. I had planned to breakfast with you here this morning, but it would appear that the servants have prepared breakfast downstairs because of the earl's arrival."

"Then we shall drink our tea before I go to my rooms. I am sure my valet is waiting for me by now."

"It is later than we usually rise, but we spent more time awake than usual."

Perry's lips curved into a lecherous smile as he leered at her bosom. "It is not my fault the new night rail was so alluring."

"I purchased it with your birthday in mind," Emma replied pertly. "I wanted to make this year special for you."

"No matter what you did, this would be special for me. Come here, wife!" Perry leaned in to give Emma a resounding kiss on her lips.

Less than an hour later, he descended the stairs and searched for the earl, whom he eventually found enjoying a cup of coffee in the breakfast room. Perry gathered his breakfast plate together from the offerings to be found on the sideboard before taking a seat across from Richard.

"Good morning, brother."

Richard leaned back in his spindly chair and smiled at Perry. "Happy birthday, Perry."

"Is that why you are here?"

Richard nodded, his sable locks gleaming in the morning light. "It occurred to me that I have been so busy this past year, I have barely visited you. After hearing me lament my oversight for several days, Sophia pointed out that your birthday was the perfect time to check on you and shooed me out at dawn to drive over for a visit. We leave for the King's coronation in a couple of days, so this was my final opportunity to visit before I spend yet another July in London. I hope I am not interrupting anything you had planned?"

Emma entered the breakfast room at that moment. "Just Perry's birthday breakfast with his wife."

Richard rose to bow. Emma laughed in rejection, waving a hand at him for his foolishness. "No ceremony, Richard. We are family!"

Perry beamed. "With more family on the way."

Richard stopped, turning to his younger brother. "You do not mean that—?"

"Your nephew or niece should be happy to receive you long before my next birthday."

Richard's eyes glowed with appreciation. "Well, this is good news!"

The three of them celebrated over breakfast before Emma left to write to her family. Perry knew to brace himself for a visit as soon as they learned about Emma's condition.

He turned to his brother once she had left them to each other's company. "Why are you really here?"

"I am sure I do not know what you mean."

"You have been tirelessly working this past year, so you did not drive here on a whim."

Richard grinned. "I had one or two reasons for ensuring I made it to your birthday breakfast this year."

"What is the first?"

"I received a report last month on your young woman from the village—Laura."

The very air in his lungs froze as Perry swallowed hard. "What of her?"

"It took some time to locate her. She severed ties with the village as you warned her to do. My man finally found her living three towns over from where you sent her on the post-chaise that night."

Perry exhaled, wondering if he wanted to hear the rest. "And?"

"She married a few months after reaching Cornwall. To a baker. They have three healthy children, and my man said Laura is in good spirits. Happy."

That was excellent news.

"And as predicted, you are the hero of the tale. They named their oldest child Peregrine."

Perry stretched his neck from side to side to ease the tension that had formed. He could not have ruined the woman's life if she wanted a reminder of him. "They have a son named Peregrine?"

Richard swallowed a laugh, raising Perry's suspicions. "Not precisely. It is their oldest daughter they named for you." Unable to contain himself, his brother burst out laughing, while Perry huffed in disbelief. Picking up a piece of toast, he threw it at his gleeful brother, who caught it deftly in his right hand to place it on his plate.

"What is the second reason for your visit?" Perry asked once his brother's mirth subsided.

Richard shrugged. "The abbey has been in your hands for

nearly a year now. I hoped you might show me the improvements you have made."

"That I can do. I am quite happy with our progress, but you should know that from the reports I send to you?"

"I thought I would like to see the progress firsthand."

Perry nodded. As part owner, Richard had the right, and Perry had no qualms about touring his brother through the estate. It had been doing well when he had arrived with Emma to take the reins, but now it bustled and prospered with the improvements.

He and the earl rode out across the rolling green lawns directly after breakfast, heading down to where the tenant farms began. Perry talked Richard through what had been there when they arrived and what had changed.

Then they discussed the several breeds of sheep that had been introduced over the past year, inspecting a flock of young tan-faced Portlands which grazed and ruminated on cud while fleecy red lambs frolicked among the ewes. Richard asked detailed questions about the wool yields that could be expected over the coming years.

"I have not encountered Portlands before. What was your reason for obtaining this breed?"

"Emma was eager to work with them when she learned they are hardy and require little assistance with lambing. These particular fields are currently rough grazing, but Portlands thrive in these conditions, which allows us to put this area to use until we can evaluate further."

Richard's face split into a grin. "I never thought I would witness the day when you discussed the tolerance of sheep, brother."

Perry chuckled wryly in response. "I confess that my understanding of what precisely any of it entails is rudimentary at best, but Emma tells me that their fleece is beautiful and dyes easily. Personally, I am focused on managing the relationships." He could not deny his swelling of pride when he told his older brother of the new connections he had formed with local mills, along with the cooperative measures they engaged in with their tenants. The abbey was progressing well to a new diversification of income sources, with Emma's and Mr. Davis's insights to guide their path.

Finally, the brothers returned to the sprawling stone buildings of the abbey and settled down to enjoy coffee in the library, Perry's preferred place to work.

"I am impressed, little brother. You have done a competent job of moving the estate forward into the future. Grandfather Landry would be most satisfied with your leadership here."

Perry smiled. "I suppose I will finally admit that Sophia was correct about my need for a project. Running the estate is unexpectedly invigorating. I am no longer an indolent spare wasting his annuity."

"Indeed, you are not. In that spirit, I would like to reveal the true reason for my visit." Richard reached into a pocket and withdrew folded papers. Leaning forward, he laid them open on Perry's desk. "Happy birthday."

Picking up the documents, Perry skimmed the contents. "What is this? Contracts? You are signing over your portion of the abbey?"

"I confess I did not tell you about the entirety of Grandfather Landry's visit to Oxford. He always intended for the abbey to be yours one day. He included me in the trust as a precaution. During our conversation, he made me promise that when the time was right, I would sign over my portion of the estate."

Perry fell back in his chair. "He did what?"

Richard smiled. "The old man had a soft spot for you, Perry. He told me about what a sweet boy you had been. Apparently, you would bring him gifts when he visited.

Apples you had picked in the orchards, flowers that our mother was fond of, chestnuts you had gathered. He said you were our mother's son, and he wanted to leave you a legacy that would outweigh any damage that being our father's spare had done."

A lump formed in his throat. Perry lifted a hand to ease it away. "This is unexpected."

"You think so? I always knew he favored you. Grandfather Landry saw potential in you."

"As Emma did."

Richard smiled in agreement. "As your Emma did."

"I … thank you, Richard. You need not have done this. You could have simply kept the conversation to yourself."

His brother shook his head. "Never. My inheritance was certainly large enough that I see no reason why I should have even been included in Grandfather's legacy. Frankly, I had a difficult time keeping it from you this long. But the time is right, and you earned your place as master of your own domain."

"Thank you, Richard. I appreciate this more than you know."

Richard cleared his throat. "It is not all good news, alas."

Perry raised an eyebrow in query.

The earl pasted an earnest expression on his face, drawing his eyebrows together, but it was obviously feigned as he sternly made his announcement. "Now that you are a landowner in your own right, I shall discontinue your annuity. You are now a man of independent wealth."

Perry burst out laughing. "Fair enough. We shall economize, then. Drink three cups of coffee a day instead of four."

"As if there is a world in which you would drink less coffee. Shall we find Emma to inform her of the good news?"

They rose from their seats. "Emma will be ecstatic to learn we now own the abbey outright. We are starting our family, after all. There will be new mouths to feed and inheritances to think of."

Perry followed his brother from the room, reflecting on how different this birthday was from the last one. Or the birthday ten years before that.

They found Emma in the garden in her hideous straw bonnet, now trimmed with colorful feathers, and Perry forgot everything in that moment as the earl announced his news and Perry gazed upon his wildflower's delighted face, her coal-black eyes shining in the sunlit afternoon.

How fortunate he was to have been dispatched to the country the year before to fetch his fair bluestocking. The journey had unveiled the wonders of family and freedom, and he was eternally thankful he had agreed to it. Taking his wife's hand to help her rise, and bending his head, Perry breathed in the scent of chamomile, wildflowers ... and love.

AFTERWORD

The included version of the lyrics for *The Joys of the Country* were copied onto music sheets in Jane Austen's own hand. I have not edited the lyrics but left them precisely as she wrote them. It is worth noting that in her time it was fashionable to capitalize important words which are liberally sprinkled throughout the verses.

The description of the two flower girls is based on an account from the Victorian journalist, Henry Mayhew, in his work, *London Labor and the London Poor,* published in a series of articles in 1851. His article gives a detailed account of two young sisters: their physical descriptions, details of their lifestyle and earnings, and their landlady, who helped them out when the weather took a turn for the worst and impacted their earnings. I took the liberty of assuming there would have been flower girls in similar circumstances thirty years earlier.

Portland sheep were introduced to Calke Abbey in 1835, but not widely bred during the Regency itself. Earlier than that, King George III noted the delicacy of its mutton and demanded it be served whenever he visited the region.

Emma's proximity to the Isle of Portland, off the coast of Dorset, would account for her knowledge of the breed, and Perry's skills in negotiation got her what she wanted.

In regard to Perry and his dark past, it is unfortunate that some children do not receive the kind of parenting which every child deserves. Something I learned firsthand working in drug rehabilitation. It became clear when working with troubled youth that some had never had access to the mentorship that good parenting should provide.

Drug abuse and poor decision-making skills can be learned behavior—parents drinking too much, popping too many pills, arguing, and failing to realize that little eyes and little ears are observing their every move.

Fortunately, having mentioned such dark topics, I can attest that it is never too late for a young man or woman to learn a new method of approaching their lives. It usually requires some kind of mentor, guide, or access to people of good conduct so young people may witness firsthand that there is a different way of doing things.

Setting a good example can influence others much more than most people realize.

Perry is raised as one of the unfortunate children who need to learn a different way, and Emma, the Davis family, and even Richard become the loving guides that he never had.

With an initial envy of the love and care that Ethan receives, Perry comes to realize that when he is with Emma he feels better, he makes better choices, and that a life of purpose is more interesting than his former idleness. Something that Jane Austen had the insight to write about more than two hundred years ago in her seminal novel, *Sense and Sensibility,* in which Edward Ferrars eventually finds his own path in life with the assistance of Colonel Brandon.

I hope you enjoyed *My Fair Bluestocking* and the

confrontational bond between Perry and Emma. In the next book of the series, *Sleepless in Saunton,* will Jane Davis be the next Inconvenient Bride when she meets a man who loved deeply and lost?

Only time will tell when we meet Barclay Thompson, a by-blow who married for love and now pines for his late wife. It will take a very special woman to heal his heart and assist him and his young daughter, Tatiana, to move into a brighter future.

DOWNLOAD TWO FREE BOOKS!

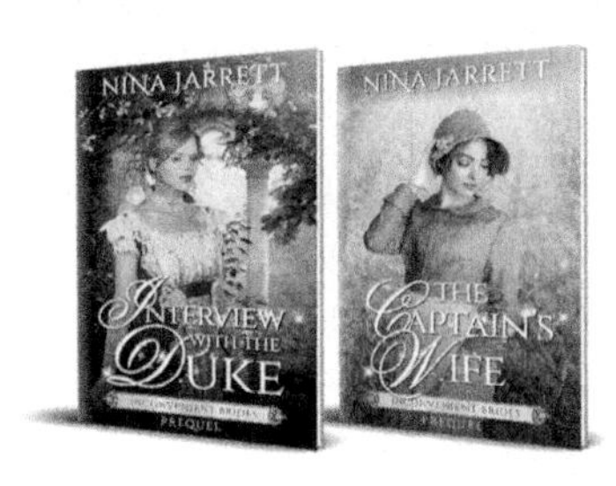

A wealthy merchant's daughter and a struggling writer.
A missing bride and her estranged husband.
Can these gentlemen woo the ladies they desire?

Interview With the Duke and *The Captain's Wife* are the delightful prequels to the Inconvenient Brides Regency romance series.

If you like worthy heroes, fast-paced plots, and enduring connections, then you'll adore Nina Jarrett's charming collection.

Subscribe for instant access to these twin tales of passion:
NinaJarrett.com/free

ABOUT THE AUTHOR

Nina started writing her own stories in elementary school but got distracted when she finished school and moved on to non-profit work with recovering drug addicts. There she worked with people from every walk of life from privileged neighborhoods to the shanty towns of urban and rural South Africa.

One day she met a real life romantic hero. She instantly married her fellow bibliophile and moved to the USA where she enjoyed a career as a sales coaching executive at an Inc 500 company. She lives with her husband on the Florida Gulf Coast.

Nina believes in kindness and the indomitable power of the human spirit. She is fascinated by the amazing, funny people she has met across the world who dared to change their lives. She likes to tell mischievous tales of life-changing decisions and character transformations while drinking excellent coffee and avoiding cookies.

ALSO BY NINA JARRETT

INCONVENIENT BRIDES

Prequel Novella: Interview With the Duke

Prequel Novella: The Captain's Wife

Book 1: The Duke Wins a Bride

Book 2: To Redeem an Earl

Book 3: My Fair Bluestocking

Book 4: Sleepless in Saunton

Book 5: Caroline Saves the Blacksmith

INCONVENIENT SCANDALS

The Duke of Halmesbury will return, along with the Balfour family, in a new suspense romance series.

Book 1: Long Live the Baron

BOOK 1: THE DUKE WINS A BRIDE

Her betrothed cheated on her. The duke offers to save her. Can a marriage of convenience turn into true love?

In this spicy historical romance, a sheltered baron's daughter and a celebrated duke agree on a marriage of convenience, but he has a secret that may ruin it all.

She is desperate to escape...

When Miss Annabel Ridley learns her betrothed has been

unfaithful, she knows she must cancel the wedding. The problem is no one else seems to agree with her, least of all her father. With her wedding day approaching, she must find a way to escape her doomed marriage. She seeks out the Duke of Halmesbury to request he intercede with her rakish betrothed to break it off before the wedding day.

He is ready to try again...

Widower Philip Markham has decided it is time to search for a new wife. He hopes to find a bold bride to avoid the mistakes of his past. Fate seems to be favoring him when he finds a captivating young woman in his study begging for his help to disengage from a despised figure from his past. He astonishes her with a proposal of his own—a marriage of convenience to suit them both. If she accepts, he resolves to never reveal the truth of his past lest it ruin their chances of possibly finding love.

Can be read as a standalone book or as part of the Inconvenient Brides series of Regency romance books.

* * *

BOOK 2: TO REDEEM AN EARL

A cynical debutante and a scandalous earl find themselves entangled in an undeniable attraction. Will they open their hearts to love or will his past destroy their future together?

She has vowed she will never marry...

Miss Sophia Hayward knows all about men and their immoral behavior. She has watched her father and older brother behave like reckless fools her entire life. All she wants is to avoid marriage to a lord until she reaches her majority because she has plans which do not include a husband. Until she meets the one peer who will not take a hint.

He must have her...

Lord Richard Balfour has engaged in many disgraceful activities with the women of his past. He had no regrets until he encounters a cheeky debutante who makes him want to be a better man. Only problem is, he has a lot of bad behavior to make amends for if he is ever going to persuade Sophia to take him seriously. Will he learn to be a better man before his mistakes catch up with him and ruin their chance at true love?

Can be read as a standalone book or as part of the Inconvenient Brides series of Regency romance books.

* * *

BOOK 4: SLEEPLESS IN SAUNTON

An insomniac debutante and a widowed architect befriend each other. Will little Tatiana finally get the new mother she longs for before this country house party ends?

In this steamy historical romance, a sleepless young woman yearns for love while a successful widower pines for his beloved wife. Hot summer nights at a lavish country house might be the perfect environment for new love to bloom.

She cannot sleep ...

Jane Davis went to London with her sister for a Season full of hope and excitement. Now her sister is married and Jane wanders the halls alone in the middle of the night. Disappointed with the gentlemen she has met, she misses her family and is desperate for a full night's sleep. Until she meets a sweet young girl who asks if Jane will be her new mother.

He misses his wife ...

It has been two years since Barclay Thompson's beloved wife passed away. Now the Earl of Saunton has claimed him as a brother and, for the sake of his young daughter, Barclay has acknowledged their relationship. But loneliness keeps him up at night until he encounters a young woman who might make his dead heart beat again. Honor demands he walk away rather than ruin the young lady's reputation. Associating with a by-blow like him will bar her from good society, no matter how badly his little girl wants him to make a match.

Can these three lonely souls take a chance on love and reconnect with the world together?

Can be read as a standalone book or as part of the Inconvenient Brides series of Regency romance books.

* * *

BOOK 5: CAROLINE SAVES THE BLACKSMITH

A fallen woman. A tortured blacksmith. When the holidays force them together, can they mend their broken hearts?

She has a dark past that she must keep a secret. He has a dark past he wishes to forget. The magic of the festive season might be the key to unlocking a fiery new passion.

She will not repeat her past mistakes ...

Caroline Brown once made an unforgivable mistake with a handsome earl, betraying a beloved friend in the process. Now she is rebuilding her life as the new owner of a dressmaker's shop in the busy town of Chatternwell. She is determined to guard her heart from all men, including the darkly handsome blacksmith, until the local doctor requests her help on the night before Christmas.

He can't stop thinking about her ...

William Jackson has avoided relationships since his battle wounds healed, but the new proprietress on his street is increasingly in his thoughts, which is why he is avoiding her at all costs. But an unexpected injury while his mother is away lays him up on Christmas Eve and now the chit is mothering him in the most irritating and delightful manner.

Can the magic of the holiday season help two broken souls overcome their dark pasts to form a blissful union?

Can be read as a standalone book or as part of the Inconvenient Brides series of Regency romance books.

Printed in Great Britain
by Amazon

40266866R00158